W9-CDK-561

"I can take anything you English throw at me."

Dewhurst's hand flexed on her waist, the threadbare bombazine hiding nothing of the sweet curve of her back and the swell of her hip. She was warm—as hot as the fire in her hair. "So this is to be war between us?" he asked, his voice little more than a whisper.

"What else? Neither of us can forget what the other is," she retorted, but her rich voice was even lower now. Ragged and husky and full of sweltering days and sweaty nights.

"I'll make you forget. I'll make you surrender." He bent his head close, brushing his lips against hers with just a hint of pressure. She inhaled sharply and tried unsuccessfully to pull away.

"Only if you surrender first."

"Never." He took her mouth with his in a relentless kiss. She gasped, and her body went rigid with shock, but he gave no quarter . . .

Other **AVON ROMANCES**

The Bride Hunt *by Margo Maguire*
A Forbidden Love *by Alexandra Benedict*
Gypsy Lover *by Edith Layton*
Keeping Kate *by Sarah Gabriel*
A Kiss Before Dawn *by Kimberly Logan*
Kiss From a Rogue *by Shirley Karr*
Scandalous Miranda *by Susan Sizemore*

Coming Soon

The Bewitching Twin *by Donna Fletcher*
A Study in Scandal *by Robyn DeHart*

And Don't Miss These
ROMANTIC TREASURES
from Avon Books

The Lord Next Door *by Gayle Callen*
Scandal of the Black Rose *by Debra Mullins*
An Unlikely Governess *by Karen Ranney*

ATTENTION: ORGANIZATIONS AND CORPORATIONS
Most Avon Books paperbacks are available at special quantity discounts for bulk purchases for sales promotions, premiums, or fund-raising. For information, please call or write:

Special Markets Department, HarperCollins Publishers, Inc., 10 East 53rd Street, New York, N.Y. 10022-5299. Telephone: (212) 207-7528. Fax: (212) 207-7222.

SHANA GALEN

Pride and
Petticoats

AVON BOOKS
An Imprint of HarperCollinsPublishers

This is a work of fiction. Names, characters, places, and incidents are products of the author's imagination or are used fictitiously and are not to be construed as real. Any resemblance to actual events, locales, organizations, or persons, living or dead, is entirely coincidental.

AVON BOOKS
An Imprint of HarperCollins*Publishers*
10 East 53rd Street
New York, New York 10022-5299

Copyright © 2006 by Shane Bolks
ISBN-13: 978-0-06-077316-8
ISBN-10: 0-06-077316-2
www.avonromance.com

All rights reserved. No part of this book may be used or reproduced in any manner whatsoever without written permission, except in the case of brief quotations embodied in critical articles and reviews. For information address Avon Books, an Imprint of HarperCollins Publishers.

First Avon Books paperback printing: February 2006

Avon Trademark Reg. U.S. Pat. Off. and in Other Countries, Marca Registrada, Hecho en U.S.A.
HarperCollins® is a registered trademark of HarperCollins Publishers Inc.

Printed in the U.S.A.

10 9 8 7 6 5 4 3 2 1

If you purchased this book without a cover, you should be aware that this book is stolen property. It was reported as "unsold and destroyed" to the publisher, and neither the author nor the publisher has received any payment for this "stripped book."

For Mom,
who in every crisis
tells me that I only have to do
the best I can.

For Dad,
who reminds me that it's the journey,
not the destination.

Acknowledgments

Eternal gratitude, love, and thanks to my longtime critique partners and best friends, Christina Hergenrader and Courtney Burkholder.

The ladies who drop everything and critique when I ask—Linda Andrus and Tera Lynn Childs.

Robin Popp, for being my partner in the trenches. Why do we do this, again?

May Chen, for your insight and suggestions. You really *get* me.

Evan Fogelman, who calls me princess when I feel down.

Chapter 1

London, 1813

"It ain't proper. It just *ain't* proper. You acting no better than a brazen hussy," the dark-skinned woman beside Charlotte grumbled. "You hear me, Miss Charlotte?"

Charlotte stopped in front of a dilapidated gray building on Thames Street near London's Custom House. "Yes, Addy." She'd heard her maid loud and clear all the way across the Atlantic Ocean. Six weeks of Addy's huffing and harrumphing, and Charlotte was ready to use the braided cords of her reticule to strangle the woman. Looking down at the small shabby pouch she held in one gloved hand, Charlotte mused that the frayed braiding would probably snap if she so much as yanked it closed too quickly. The slim strings had no hope of holding up against Addy's solid neck. Gingerly pulling the black reticule open, Charlotte glanced a last time at the smeared address on a crumpled yellow paper, then stuffed it back inside.

"Look around you, girl. This ain't no place for a lady," Addy said.

Charlotte took a quick survey of their surroundings and didn't argue. They'd been in London all of three hours and she'd yet to escape the smell of rotting fish, unwashed bodies, and stale liquor. She and Addy had departed their ship at the London docks, trailing their scant luggage behind them as they made their way past the Tower of London and into the city.

As they'd walked, the terrain and the inhabitants had become steadily rougher. Charlotte couldn't imagine this city at night. It was dangerous in the sunlight—or at least what passed for sunlight in England's fog-shrouded capital.

Thank George Washington that they had finally arrived. She tried not to wonder why the building before them looked more like a dockside tavern than a residence. "Well, we're here now," Charlotte said.

"We here? You ain't really going to knock on that door?" Addy asked. "Head hard as a cast-iron pot," she mumbled.

Charlotte frowned at her. "Oh, hush. You're the stubborn one. I keep telling you I'm trying to make things better."

"We can make do without no charity from

Cade Pettigru. Troublesome rascal." She muttered the last.

"Addy, Cade is a good man, and he's been a good friend to our family for years. We can trust him, and we need his help." She didn't add that he was very likely their last hope.

Addy straightened to her full height, which was almost six feet. "Chicken spit. I satisfied with a roof a new shawl. Oh, and I could do with a heap of some simple home-cooked food."

Charlotte winced at the reference to the repulsive fare they'd endured on the long sea voyage. The main staple had been cabbage soup, and Charlotte, who'd never cared for cabbage, had been forced to abandon it for bread and water after one particularly noxious bowl made her violently ill. She, too, longed for the delights of home—cornbread, sweet potatoes, fried chicken. Most especially she longed for the warmth and friendliness of Charleston. She hated these English with their harsh accents and arrogant manners.

But she would endure them. One glance at Addy reminded Charlotte of her reasons. The expensive shawl Addy had received as a gift from Charlotte's father and had always treasured was now little more than a rag, and Addy's dress was wrinkled and dusty. But worse than Addy's scuffed shoes and tattered shawl was her face. It was heavily lined with weariness, giving her cheeks the appearance of the hull of a shipwreck—a once-proud vessel left to wither in the sun.

Charlotte turned back to the gray ramshackle building and took a deep breath. If only Addy knew how much Charlotte hated surprising Cade like this, how low and common she felt asking him for money, Addy wouldn't be so hard on her. What if Charlotte asked him to be her new business partner, and he turned her down? It would be beyond humiliating. But Charlotte could see no other way. She was responsible for Addy, and she would not allow the older woman to suffer any more than she already had.

Charlotte pinched her cheeks to heighten their color and righted her bonnet, tucking up the loose red tendrils of her hair. "We're here now, Addy, and I know you've missed Cade as much as I have."

Addy gave her a look that said she'd missed the rambunctious young man about as much as she missed changing Charlotte's diapers when she'd been a babe.

Charlotte held up a hand before Addy could expound on the subject. "This is the direction Mr. Porcher gave me." She looked up and down the street, noting the trash and offal littering the ground under the windows of the dilapidated houses. "I hope this is correct." It certainly didn't look like where she'd imagined Cade living.

Addy huffed. "We been over land, over water, in

carriages, on foot, and even on those godforsaken beasts." She pointed at a horse and rider clopping toward them through the crowds of dirty people. "We's here, and if you dead set against turning around, best get it done with. The sooner you go in that there door, the sooner we can go home."

"Not much home to go back to," Charlotte murmured, and the feeling of loss pierced her gut like the sharp point of a dagger. "But if we can convince Cade to invest, everything will be like it used to."

"Your heart is too soft, Miss Charlotte. Those people ain't your friends. When you done lost all that money, they disappeared fast as a pitcher of lemon water on a hot day."

Shame and humiliation heated Charlotte's cheeks, and she looked down at her worn boots, the toes of which poked from beneath the skirt of her dress.

With a sigh, she straightened her shoulders and took a step forward, then paused as behind them the hoofbeats from the approaching horse slowed. Charlotte and Addy glanced 'round as the rider reined in his mount and swept his beaver hat from his dark curls. "Do my eyes deceive me, or is that Miss Charlotte Katherine Burton from Charleston, South Carolina, standing on my walk?"

The nervousness in Charlotte's belly flitted away, and the sun pierced the skies above them.

"The one and only. But you, Mr. Cade Pettigru, are a knight on a white horse." She fluttered her eyelashes, mocking the flirtatious Southern belles back home, and heard Addy grumble, "It ain't proper."

Charlotte ignored her. She needed a knight right now, and Cade was as close as they came. His horse was indeed so pale a gray as to appear white, and sitting astride the beast, Cade looked magnificent in leather breeches, knee-high leather boots, and a fine blue riding coat.

He threw his leg over his horse and jumped down. When he stepped closer, even Addy had to crane her neck to peer up at the tan, dark-eyed Southern gentleman. Looking at him was a biting reminder of her brother, and Charlotte's resolve not to cry faltered. She could only pray that Cade was the balm she needed for her tear-swollen eyes.

He opened his arms to her, and Charlotte went willingly, laughing as he tightened the embrace into a bear hug, then swung her around until her feet left the ground and her dress belled around her. Charlotte squealed, and Addy said, "Lawd Almighty! Mr. Pettigru, you let Miss Charlotte go." But Charlotte cried out with pleasure. It had been more than five years since he'd swung her around like this. She'd been eighteen and without a worry in the world. For a moment, she was transported back to that carefree time.

Finally Cade released her and made a bow to

Addy. Before Addy could chastise him further, however, he gathered her up and repeated his welcome. Thankfully, his treatment of Addy was somewhat more reserved. When he'd set Addy down and taken Charlotte's gloved hands in his again, she squeezed his fingers and said, "I can't believe it's really you, Cade. I can't believe how good you look."

He winked at her. "And you've grown into a fine woman. What are you doing here, and why didn't you write? I would have arranged for us to meet somewhere more suitable."

"I'm glad you didn't. I have something of a delicate nature to discuss with you."

Cade raised a brow. "I see. Business or pleasure, Lottie?"

Charlotte smiled. How long had it been since someone had called her by that childhood endearment?

"Lawd Almighty," Addy wailed when Charlotte's smile wobbled. "Now don't you start crying again, Miss Charlotte." Addy pulled out her ever-present handkerchief. "Don't you dare start, sugar." Through the tears she was desperately attempting to hold back, Charlotte saw Addy give Cade a look that would have wilted cotton. "Now look what you done, Mr. Cade."

Cade opened his mouth, closed it, then seemed to take careful note of Charlotte. She tried to look cheerful, but she knew that nothing could turn the somber bonnet and the black bombazine day dress into a pretty cap and gay ball gown or make her red, puffy eyes sparkle as they used to. He put his hand on her elbow. "Come inside. I don't have much time, but I'll do what I can."

After a quick perusal of the street, he hurried them and the luggage inside the building, shutting the door and locking it behind her. Charlotte had the distinct sense that he didn't want her there, and once inside she saw why. The place was indeed a tavern. It was still too early in the day to boast any customers, but the signs of their presence the night before flourished. Chairs and tables were overturned and those that stood upright were caked with thick, sticky residue. Broken glass littered the floor, and a large gray thing—Charlotte prayed it was a cat—scurried through a crack in the wall.

Cade navigated the public room with ease and showed Charlotte and Addy to an office in the back that held a desk and a large divan, pushed against a dingy window.

Charlotte stood in the doorway, finding it difficult to conceive of Cade working here. It was so different from the ornate Pettigru house in Charleston. Cade followed Charlotte inside, then hollered for a woman called Bess. No one appeared. Cade called again, and Charlotte took advantage of his distraction to give Addy a meaningful look, which she, of course, ignored.

Charlotte knew her maid was intent on playing the chaperone, but now that she'd finally found Cade, Charlotte did not want to wait to speak to him. Not to mention, sending Addy after the errant Bess was a good way to ensure she had Cade to herself. Charlotte reached over and pinched Addy's arm. Addy scooted away.

"Where could she be?" Cade said, walking toward the office door. Charlotte reached out and pinched Addy again. Hard.

"Ow!"

Cade turned, looking at Addy with a puzzled frown, while Charlotte tried to stare Addy into compliance. Finally she capitulated. "Mr. Cade, you and Miss Charlotte set there and talk. Lawd knows I can find my way round a kitchen to make two cups of tea. I's be a minute." She looked at Charlotte. "A very short minute."

"Thank you, Addy," Charlotte said sweetly, settling herself on the long divan. It creaked in distress, and Charlotte prayed it would not collapse. When Addy was gone, Cade crossed the room and leaned against the desk so that he faced her. His eyes flicked to the window, and a shadow passed over his features, but then he smiled at her and the darkness was gone. She returned the smile, and he shook his head. "She hasn't changed a bit. Makes me miss my own mammy back home. She'd whip me faster than a fish on a June bug."

"Lot of good it did," Charlotte said. "You and

Thomas were the scourge of Charleston with all your pranks." As soon as she'd spoken her brother's name, Charlotte's chest tightened, and she put a hand to her lips to quell their trembling.

Cade knelt beside her. "Lottie, what's happened? Tell me."

She shook her head, her voice failing her. She felt as though her throat were in the clutches of a ruthless taskmaster, intent upon squeezing every last ounce of grief from her. Finally she managed to whisper, "Oh, Cade."

He gathered her in his arms, holding her while she wept. She'd cried enough tears to float a ship, and the ocean of salty rivulets running down her cheeks hadn't changed anything. All the tears in the sea wouldn't bring her father and Thomas back, wouldn't restore her to the carefree days of the past. Cade patted her shoulder and shushed her, and Charlotte hiccupped. This was what she'd wanted, what she'd needed from Cade.

"Was it the British?" Cade asked finally, leaning back to look in her face. She nodded, and he swore. "I told your father he was a fool and a half. Leaving you home and risking his ships and skinny neck for a pile of lace, silk, and French wine."

Charlotte nodded. She, too, had pleaded with her father and brother to cease the illegal smuggling runs, but with the British blockade strangling all trade, the value of European goods was too high to resist. "We needed the money," she murmured. "Prices in Charleston—" She waved a hand as though to indicate exorbitance too excessive to put into words. She left out mention of her father's gambling debt entirely, for that remembrance was a price too high for even her shattered pride.

"And you've come to me for help." Cade's look was grim, and Charlotte knew it would turn grimmer still when she told him the true state of affairs. Cade remembered her as the spoiled Southern belle. He had no knowledge of how she'd begged and scraped and lowered herself to keep the family together. And in the end her efforts weren't enough. The house on Legare Street, the family's savings, the last vestiges of social respect—gone. Snatched away with the bang of the cannon and the slow sinking of *The Glory*. Had it really been only a year ago she'd received word? It felt like yesterday. The pain in her belly, fresh and raw, hit home like a dagger plunged to the hilt.

"I didn't know where else to turn," she began, but Cade shushed her.

"You did right to come to me. But as you can see, I—" He looked away, listening intently.

"What is it?" Charlotte began. Suddenly there was a crash from the public room, and the sound of Addy screeching. Charlotte would have sprung to her feet, but she was grasped from behind in a viselike grip that all but stripped her of breath. In the shock of the moment, it took several heart-beats before she realized that her attacker was be-hind the divan and had probably been hiding there. Looking to Cade, she made a strangled cry of need, but he did not hear. He had a pistol in his hand and was staring at the office door. She watched as Cade rounded the desk, pulled out a drawer, grasped a sheaf of papers, and stuffed them into his waistcoat, never taking his eyes from the door.

The door flew open and two men burst in with pistols pointing at Cade. One's face was dis-guised by a high collar and an old-fashioned Eliz-abethan hat pulled low over his eyes. The other's collar was still turned up, but he must have lost his hat because Charlotte could see he had blond hair and an angry expression. The blond one or-dered Cade to drop his weapon. Cade shook his head.

"Dewhurst. I should have known." He turned to Charlotte, and his eyes widened as he noted the arm about her neck. Then he raised and pointed his pistol at her. Her heart stopped, causing a sharp pain to lance her chest. Then he fired, and the window behind her exploded in a shower of glass. Her assailant cried out as glass shards pierced his skin, and his hold on her loosened. Cade leaped forward, knocked the man's hand away from her throat, and grasped her wrist.

"Lottie, listen to me." He tried to force her to rise, but, paralyzed with fear, she couldn't move.

Charlotte wanted to scream, but the authority in Cade's voice was too compelling to resist. She stared at him.

"I must go, but know this. I will come for you. I will come!" He kissed her hard, then released her just as the man behind the divan reached forward and caught her skirt again. Then she was tumbling down, her fall broken with the thud of her head against the floor.

The world fell down around her. She heard glass crunching beneath boots, muffled voices, shouts, and gunfire. Cade was beside her, struggling with the man behind the divan, and Charlotte took the opportunity to roll away. There was another gunshot, and just when she was certain the next bullet would be for her, she was grabbed by another man, hauled to her knees, and dragged across the room. She fought to rise to her feet, and when she finally succeeded, he was yelling at her.

She gaped at him. It was the blond man Cade had recognized, and this close he resembled a golden angel.

"I say, stop flailing about," the angel said again. "You're ruining my tailcoat." He pulled her to her feet. "Can you stand, or shall I be forced to prop you up all afternoon?"

"I—I can stand."

The angel nodded and released his hold. She stepped back, surveying the destruction with amazement. Cade was gone, and she couldn't imagine how he'd escaped, unless—had he gone through the shattered window? Not only had the window been smashed, the divan was overturned, books and papers lay scattered on the floor, and there was a man with a pool of blood around his head lying not a foot from where she'd fallen. With a jolt, Charlotte clutched the thin fabric of her dress. Cade had deserted her.

I will come for you. Trembling and petrified, Charlotte held on to Cade's words like a lifeboat in stormy seas.

"You're not going to faint, are you?" the angel said. Charlotte was in no danger of fainting, but she had to shove her fist up against her lips because she was in serious danger of screaming. The man gave her a stern look. "And don't cry." He turned to his companion. "How is he?"

The other man knelt on the floor beside the bloodied man and shook his head. "Pettigru, that bastard, shot him before he went out the window. He's dead."

Charlotte turned away, inadvertently landing in the angel's arms. She tried to step away, but he took her elbow and held fast.

"This is a mare's nest," the angel said to his companion. "Pettigru's escaped, the neighbors have probably called the watch, and where the devil did this bird come from?" He shook her arm, and Charlotte realized she must be the *bird*.

"Damned if I know," the other man said, standing and wiping the blood from his hands on a rag. He removed his hat and lowered his collar then, and Charlotte was amazed at how much he resembled the angel. His eyes, a startling blue, met hers, and his angry expression changed to an engaging smile. " 'What lady's that, which doth enrich the hand of yonder knight?' "

Charlotte blinked in confusion. Beside her, the angel muttered, "Oh, dash it. Not now."

The angel's companion came closer. He was dressed in Venetian breeches, a white shirt with pleated ruffles, and—Charlotte narrowed her eyes—a doublet? " 'O, she doth teach the torches to burn bright! It seems she hangs upon the cheek of night as a rich jewel—' "

"Stubble it, Romeo. We don't have time for poetry at present."

His companion ignored him and took her free hand, kissed it, and said, "Sir Sebastian Middleton. Charmed to make your acquaintance."

Charlotte blinked again. A moment before, bullets had been flying and she'd been choking. Now this man was acting as though they were performing in a Shakespearean production. Had the lack of air caused her to hallucinate?

No, she was still in Cade's office, and there was still a dead man on the floor. Charlotte glanced at the angel beside her. "Is he mad?" She pointed to the man called Middleton.

"Mad? Absolutely. No cure. We call the illness Fits of Shakespeare."

Charlotte wasn't sure if she should laugh or express sympathy, but then there was another crash, and Charlotte turned to see Addy kick the office door open. Charlotte was thankful for the angel's hand on her arm, especially when three huffing men burst in after Addy. Once inside, they pounced on Addy, and one of them, red-faced though younger and stronger than Addy, said, "Caught her, my lord." He nodded to the angel. "She put up a fight."

"Wot's going on in there?" Someone outside banged on the door.

"Ah, that would be the neighbors and the welcome party I predicted," the angel said.

"What do we do with her?" one of the men holding Addy asked.

"To the ship!" Middleton cried, extracting a sword from the belt around his waist and brandishing it like a pirate.

"No!" Charlotte screamed at the same time the angel said, "Ship?"

"We'll never make it through the crowds with these two." Middleton waved the sword at Charlotte and Addy. "The river's the only way. We'll sail for Westminster."

"No ships," the angel said. Charlotte nodded. She had no intention of going anywhere with these lunatics.

"Buck up, man," Middleton said. "It's only a little water." And then he jumped through the window and motioned for the rest to follow.

The angel's grip tightened. "I suppose there's nothing for it. Come on."

"No!" Charlotte protested. Who knew where this fallen angel and his demon followers might take her or what he might do to her and Addy? Apparently unaffected by her struggles, the angel pushed her forward. "Stop! Unhand me, sir." She managed to wriggle one hand free and grabbed the desk, holding on until the angel wrested her away. She retaliated by biting his hand.

He jumped back, shaking his hand incredulously. "Ow! Little hellion bit me!"

But he'd released her, and she made for the divan, scrambling toward the door in a desperate bid to free herself. The angel caught her ankle and dragged her back, ruching her skirt to her knees. "Stop fighting."

She ignored him and fought harder. And then she felt him run a finger over the back of one knee, and she froze. "Stop fighting. There are worse things than leaving with us. Cease or I might begin to wonder if you're this much of a hellcat in bed." His breath tickled her neck, and the effect was complete paralysis. The angel took advantage of the truce and heaved her through the window, into Middleton's waiting arms.

And then, while Charlotte stood on the other side of the window, she saw the angel inside bow to Addy, and she could swear that the man who'd threatened her with violence a moment before said to Addy in a most charming voice, "After you, madam."

Addy looked confused but she obeyed, and soon the whole party was dashing toward the wharf a few yards away. There was a trim yacht tied there, and before Charlotte could even think of escape, much less plan one, she was belowdecks, thrust onto a berth, and the angel was standing above her with a length of rope.

"I didn't want to have to do this, but I can't be seen about Town with teeth marks on my person. Not a'tall fashionable." He made a move to take her arms and she glared, at which point his face turned hard and his voice harder. "I can see I shall have to be blunt with you. Bite me again, little hellion, and I'll pull out your teeth."

Charlotte blinked, but she didn't struggle this time when he took her arms and then proceeded to bind her wrists behind her back.

"If you attempt another escape, I'll be forced to bind your feet as well."

Charlotte took a shaky breath, pushing herself deeper into the berth and as far away from the devil's angel as possible. Tears of exhaustion and fear threatened to spill forth, and she concentrated on keeping them at bay. With her hands tied, she felt vulnerable and defenseless, and she wished she could shrink until she was invisible.

But who were these men anyway, and what had they wanted with Cade? Why had Cade run and left her and Addy to fend for themselves? The angel was binding Addy now, but he was being far more civil to her servant. "You must forgive me for this," he was saying. And then he asked, "Are those too tight?"

Charlotte scowled. He hadn't asked her if her bindings were too tight. Insolent Brit. She wanted to kick him, tear his eyes out. As though he could read her mind, the angel turned from Addy and fixed jade green eyes on her. And for the first time, Charlotte saw him clearly.

George Washington, he was no mere angel. Archangel was a more apt description of this man with golden locks. Perhaps fallen angel might do, as his hair was in disarray and long enough that it curled about his neck. But his nose was straight and patrician, cheekbones high and pronounced, eyes accented by slashing brows, a shade darker than his hair color. His eyes on her were intent, his mouth tight. "What is your name?" he asked. The low tenor of his voice was marred by the clipped British accent she so hated.

She sat straighter. Showing her fear was the

surest way to defeat. Men, whether creditors in Charleston or thieves in London, were the same. They thrived on fear and intimidation. And this man was the sort she hated most. At first she'd thought him a fool—a macaroni, as her fellow Charlestonians would say—but now she understood that was only a façade. This man was a warrior, and he would view compassion and emotion as little more than weakness and surrender.

"I said, what is your name." It was no longer a question.

Charlotte made a fist under the table, digging her nails into her palm to fortify her resolve not to relent.

"Is that any way to treat this heavenly creature—this sun?" Middleton elbowed the angel out of his way. " 'Arise fair sun. It is my lady. O, it is my love!' " Middleton knelt before her. "What is thy name, fair maid?"

Charlotte exchanged a look with Addy. Addy's expression said it was clear the man was madder than a loon. Charlotte looked back, and Middleton was watching her expectantly. She hadn't wanted to give her name, but it was difficult to feel threatened by this Sebastian Middleton. He was no warrior. And she supposed that, given the choice, she'd rather deal with him than the fallen angel.

"Charlotte Burton."

"Where are you from, Miss Burton?" the

archangel asked, stepping in once again where he'd not been invited. "You don't sound English."

Charlotte twisted her bound hands. Should she tell the truth? Lie? Too late, she regretted giving anything away.

The angel bent closer, pushing Middleton aside, and notched her chin up with one long, aristocratic finger. Charlotte's pulse quickened with fear, and she looked past him at the cabin door. But even if she'd been willing to desert Addy, there were two men between it and her; not to mention, her wrists were still bound. Oh, how she wished she had even the meager freedom to put a hand between the fallen angel and herself.

"Miss Burton. I don't think you realize the gravity of your situation," the archangel said, his breath warm on her cheek. "I heard what Pettigru said to you before he ran through that shattered window. Now I want to know who you are, what you mean to Pettigru, and what you know about his activities in London and Paris. Either talk or I will be forced—much to my regret, but I assure you I will do it—to employ stronger methods of persuasion."

Charlotte stared at him. She believed him. His warrior's eyes were hard as emeralds. He looked . . . ruthless. She took a shaky breath. What information did she have that these men could use against her? Against Cade? Whatever he had done, she had to protect him. Addy, too.

"Very well," she said with a last gulp of breath. "Do what you will to me, but you mustn't hurt my maid."

Middleton laughed. "We couldn't if we tried. That woman is strong as an ox."

The archangel's gaze did not waver from Charlotte's. "You have my word that no harm will come to your"—he paused—"servant. Now who are you, and what is your relationship with Mr. Pettigru?"

Charlotte shook her head. "I'm no one. Cade and I are old friends from Charleston. I came to . . . visit."

"Where is this Charles Town? In the colonies?"

Charlotte felt her fear subside and the heat rise to her face. "Colonies? It is in the state of South Carolina, sir. *State*. We are no longer your colonies." The archangel looked unrepentant, despite her chastisement. "Furthermore, the name is not Charles Town." She made an effort to pronounce it in the harsh, clipped way he did. "It's Charleston."

"And the dark-skinned woman is your slave?"

Charlotte opened her mouth to answer, then paused, considering her answer. "Not in the way you mean."

The archangel raised a brow. "Does she work for you?"

Charlotte nodded.

"Does she receive wages?"

"No, but—"

"Then she is a slave. Despicable." He waved a hand, dismissing her protest. "What exactly is your business with Mr. Pettigru?"

Charlotte shook away the hair that had fallen in her eyes. Somewhere she had lost her bonnet, and her bound hands itched to brush the loose tendrils from her face. "That, sir, is none of your concern."

"I see. How long have you been Mr. Pettigru's . . . companion? Who else do you service?"

Charlotte stared. "Are you suggesting I am a—I am Cade's—" She swallowed, unable to find the words. Cade was a friend, her brother's friend—nothing more. Hot, heavy shame coiled in her belly at the insinuation. The angel arched his brows, his expression arrogant and knowing. Charlotte seethed. He knew *nothing*. Instead of ignoring the comment, she spluttered, "How dare you, sir!"

Middleton held up a hand. "Miss Burton, if you do not wish us to make assumptions, kindly explain for yourself."

Charlotte continued to glare at the archangel. "Cade is—was my brother's best friend in Charleston. We never—he was never . . ." She looked down.

The archangel stepped forward, once again crowding her into the berth. "If you are not Pettigru's mistress, then what is your business with him? He said he would come for you. What are you to him?"

"I told you. We're friends. This was just a friendly visit," she lied. She would never tell these bastard English why she was really here, how much pain and anguish their kind had caused her. Tears pricked at her eyelids, and she willed them away. Emotion would not sway this man. Like all warriors, he feared it.

"And you came all this way to visit Pettigru?" Middleton asked. "How long has he been a family friend?"

"Who are his contacts? His sources?" the archangel inquired. "How will he find you?"

Charlotte shook her head. The questions were becoming a rapid barrage, and she couldn't concentrate as the men's voices melded into each other's. Who, why, when?

"Dash it all!" the archangel finally exploded. "Miss Burton, are you or are you not spying for the French?"

"What?" Charlotte stared at him, then at Middleton. "Are you both mad—"

"Cade Pettigru is a spy," the archangel growled. "An enemy working with the French government and the Americans against England. My friend, a loyal Englishman, died today at Pettigru's hand. I will not allow another of my countrymen to die at the hands of a spy or"—he gave her a hard look—"the soiled hands of a slave owner."

Charlotte narrowed her eyes. "Who are you?" She glanced at the other men. "Who do you work for?" She was afraid she knew, but she had to ask anyway.

The archangel bowed low, sweeping his hand across his chest. "Lord Alfred Dewhurst, baron and agent for the British Foreign Office."

Charlotte's knees gave way, and she was glad to have the berth beneath her. Oh, George, but she was doomed now. British spies! How had she managed to stumble into the very men she most wished to avoid? "Please," Charlotte murmured, "I am not a spy, and neither is Cade. This is all a terrible mistake—"

"No, Miss Burton. There is no misunderstanding," the archangel said. "Cade Pettigru is a spy, and by association, you are as tainted with guilt as he. Now I suggest you either tell us what you know or you'll be tried for treason and"—he lifted a strand of her copper hair—"burned for the witch you are."

Chapter 2

Freddie groaned as the first wave of nausea hit. The men had released his cousin Sebastian's yacht from its moorings, and it was now drifting steadily down the Thames. London Bridge swayed before Freddie's eyes.

"Lord Dewhurst," one of the crew said. "We're under way."

Freddie nodded.

"Are you well, my lord?"

"Course. Splendid. Capital."

The man gave him a dubious look before retreating. Freddie leaned over the rail and retched.

Sometime later—he couldn't begin to say how much later, as he'd spent a good portion of his time with his head over the ship's rail—they reached Westminster. Despite the melee, they had not left their fallen comrade behind, and Sebastian went ashore to make arrangements for the body and to fetch Edwards. When he arrived, the cousins sat with their superior in a cabin adjacent to that of the American woman.

"I think you were a bit hard on the poor chit," Sebastian said, spearing his mutton with a fork. "Her face went white as a specter when you said she'd be tried for treason."

Freddie looked at his wine—a rather good merlot. He would have liked to sip it, but his stomach was still queasy. He'd ejected the whole of his insides, including several vital organs, over the rail of the ship, and he felt relatively sure nothing but his stomach itself could come up now, and at this point he wouldn't mind losing that dashed organ, too. Bloody ships. They would be the end of him.

Freddie swallowed his nausea and pushed the wine aside. "Good. If she's frightened, she might talk." And the sooner he could return to his town house. The little hellion had torn the cuff of his Spanish blue tailcoat of superfine.

Edwards finished his wine and leaned back. "I think she's told you what she knows," he said, "but it matters not. She'll protect Pettigru whether she believes him innocent or guilty. Her family was killed by our warships. She has no love for the English."

Sebastian shrugged. "So what now? She's loyal

to Pettigru, and we can't exactly lock the girl up for the duration of the war."

"No," Freddie agreed, though that would have been the easiest thing. She had the temper of a hell-cat and could plant a facer to rival Gentleman Jackson. This was no pink and powdered Society miss.

Still, all in all, not a bad bit. Her mourning dress was not fitted properly, so he couldn't form a good impression of her figure, but she appeared unremarkable in stature and build. If he'd looked no further, if she hadn't spoken, he'd have dismissed her from his mind by now.

But she had spoken, and her voice was slow and lush. No one could mistake that drawl, so typical of the Southern colonies. The words rolled from her tongue leisurely, her mouth rounding on each vowel and softening every consonant. As she spoke, he could not tear his eyes away from those full lips, almost too full for her face. The black bombazine didn't suit her coloring, but neither did it tarnish her roses-and-cream complexion or dull the sherry-colored eyes, edged by thick lashes against her ivory skin.

And still he might have dismissed her as a mere inconvenience. He'd known beautiful women. It might even be fair to say that his acquaintanceship was largely restricted to women one might classify as not only beautiful but witty and stylish in addition. But his downfall—the reason he was still thinking of the colonist—was her hair.

It was the most glorious shade of auburn he'd ever seen, swept back in a simple style without all the waved curls ladies were currently wearing about their faces. Cinnamon with a dash of gold, it was a rich, warm color he found difficult to believe was natural.

He had a weakness for ginger-pated chits. A weakness he fought valiantly to override, considering the color was dreadfully unfashionable. But all the milk-and-honey blonds and peaches-and-porcelain brunettes failed to hold his attention like a woman with fiery tresses and a temper to match.

Freddie lifted his merlot, remembered himself, and set it down again. The last thing he needed was another woman on his mind. He'd been raised in a household of women: his mother and four sisters. Growing up, Freddie could not remember a time when emotions had not run high. His sisters were always overreacting to some perceived problem or other. From an early age, Freddie had learned to control his own sentiments. He would not tolerate another emotional female weighing him down.

Edwards pulled out his pipe, lit it, and said, "Am I the only one among us who thinks Miss Burton might be useful?"

"Yes," Freddie said slowly, afraid he knew the direction of his superior's thoughts.

"How would she prove useful?" Sebastian asked.

Edwards puffed on his pipe, then held it aloft between thumb and forefinger. "Pettigru himself gave us the answer. He said he would come for her. We've watched him for months, but now he'll be harder to find than a hare in a bramble. We could chase him all over the country, or we could let him come to us."

"And Miss Burton is the bait?" Sebastian asked. "I like it."

"But in the meantime, Pettigru has lists of British troops and supplies," Freddie said. "Our national security may be compromised."

Edwards shook his head. "The information is undecipherable using the old codes. What good are the lists if the French generals can't understand them?"

Freddie considered this. Pettigru was a loyal American aiding the French under the assumption that a British defeat by the French on land would mean an American victory at sea. To that end, Pettigru filched the codes the British commanders used to cipher their missives to one another. He then sold them to the French army for a profit. But now the codes Wellington used had been changed and Pettigru's information was useless.

"Pettigru will have to stay in London in order to lay his hands on the real codes," Edwards continued. "And when he does, we'll lure him out with Miss Burton. We'll make her irresistible. He'll come after her not only because she's his friend, but because she has access to his enemy—to one of our best agents."

Freddie stood. "Very well. How do we make Pettigru believe all that?"

Edwards smiled. "Couldn't be simpler. In fact, all I require from you are two tiny words."

Freddie rubbed his temple where a headache still drummed. Better and better. He wanted the whole business with Pettigru and the hellion behind him. The Season was over, but there still were many choice engagements he was missing. "Two words, eh? Good-bye?" Freddie said hopefully.

"No. Try, I do."

She was going to die. They'd taken Addy, George knew where, and now Charlotte was going to die alone, in the dark, and no one would ever know or care. She'd been trapped in the cabin for days—at least it seemed like days. She was hungry, cold, and scared, terrified she'd never see Addy or Charleston again. She didn't want to die in this dank hole. She sat on the berth, resting her head on her knees, which she'd pulled close to her body for warmth. At least Dewhurst had untied her wrists. Perhaps he was not made of stone after all.

There was a distant sound of footsteps, but she did not look up. She'd heard them many times over the hours and screamed for someone to let her out, but no one had come.

Now the footsteps were louder, closer, and Charlotte lifted her head to peer into the darkness. Nothing. The men had taken the lanterns with them, and the darkness often preyed on her imagination. But as Charlotte peered into the gloom, a sliver of light and the creak of hinges made her heart race. She jumped up, tripping over her skirts as Dewhurst and Middleton entered, both carrying lanterns and followed by a servant with a tray of food.

Charlotte's mouth watered, but she vowed not to touch the tempting fare. Five minutes before she might have sold her soul for the chance at freedom. Now, faced with that prospect—however slight—she wanted no charity from these men. Death was preferable. The smell of warm bread and cheese assaulted her nostrils, and she clenched her fists in her skirts to quell the desire to snatch the tray and wolf down the food.

The servant set the fare on the table, then quickly retreated, closing the heavy cellar door behind him. Dewhurst stood beside the table, watching her. Middleton spoke, "Miss Burton, you must be hungry. Please eat."

Charlotte shook her head. "I want nothing from you, except my freedom."

"That might be arranged," Middleton said. Charlotte glanced at Dewhurst. He looked bored and disgusted by her.

"If this arrangement involves me lifting my skirts for one or both of you"—Dewhurst gave her a derisive glance before turning away—"you might as well kill me now, for I'd rather die than allow one of you to touch me."

"Miss Burton," Middleton said in a soothing tone that didn't fool her for a moment, "you wound us. We are not going to hurt you. In point of fact, we need your help."

Charlotte scowled. George, but she wished they would take the bread out of her sight. The smell was making her dizzy. "I already told you. I am not a spy. Mr. Pettigru is not a spy. I don't know anything, and if I did, I wouldn't reveal it to you lying British bastards!"

"Lovely," Dewhurst said, pulling out a chair from the desk and settling in it with a bored air. "We're wasting our time here, Middleton."

"Give it a chance, coz."

Charlotte watched the exchange closely. Cousins. Yes, that would account for the similarities in their appearance, evident even though their mode of dress was centuries apart.

"Miss Burton," Middleton said, "if you don't wish to aid us, are you willing to cooperate to help Pettigru? You might be able to clear his name."

Charlotte pushed a heavy lock of her hair behind her ear. The red tangle was free of its pins and streaming down her back. She licked her dry lips, eyeing the flagon of wine. "What would I have to do?"

Middleton waved his hand. "Merely act out a part in a small play. Have you ever been on the stage, Miss Burton?"

"No."

"Ah, well, then this will be something new. We have reason to believe Pettigru will turn up again in London. If you were there as well, you might arrange to meet him, talk to him, help him clear his name."

"Lure him out so you can hang him, you mean," Charlotte shot back. Did they take her for a fool? She did not care if Cade was another Benedict Arnold. She would never betray her friend and countryman.

Middleton held up a hand. "I will not lie to you, Miss Burton. If Pettigru is guilty, then he will be tried, but with or without your assistance, we will catch him. That is inevitable. What is not inevitable is the matter of his guilt or innocence."

Charlotte licked her lips again, and Middleton must have noted the gesture. He poured her a glass of wine and brought it to her. "I give you my word as a knight and an Englishman—" Charlotte snorted. "Very well, I give you my word as a man of honor that we will treat Mr. Pettigru fairly and take into account any evidence you find of his innocence." He handed the glass to Charlotte. She took it, allowing herself a small sip. George, but the liquid felt good on her parched throat.

"What do I have to do, Mr. Middleton? You mentioned acting."

"Ah, yes, but not in the theater. You will play your part on a different stage—that of the *haute ton*. What we propose"—he motioned to Dewhurst, who was sitting tight-lipped at the desk—"is for you to act as Lord Dewhurst's wife—"

Charlotte's jaw dropped. "What? *His* wife? Never."

"No, no. It would be a counterfeit marriage, though you would have to give every appearance of it being genuine."

Charlotte glanced at Dewhurst. His expression was dark. He didn't want this any more than she. So why was he going along? "What exactly would I have to do?" Charlotte asked.

Middleton shrugged. "Live in Dewhurst's town house, attend the social functions with him, play the dutiful wife. Pettigru knows my cousin's identity now. He will be watching us, and when he sees you with Dewhurst, we do not think he can resist the dual temptation."

"It seems too easy," Charlotte said. Dewhurst gave a short laugh.

"It is anything but easy, Miss Burton." He turned his full gaze on her, his green eyes hard and catlike in the dimness. "No one who knows me would ever believe I would marry a woman like you. You're plain, uncouth, and completely without style. You'll be tossed out of the first ballroom you step into and shipped back to the colonies."

"The United States," she corrected, venom rising in her blood. "And if you are so certain I will fail, then why are you going along with this asinine plan?"

He leaned back, silent for a long moment. "Are you a patriot, Miss Burton?"

She frowned. The answer seemed obvious. "Yes."

"Then you understand what it means to love your country. I love my country, and I'll fight for my country. Your friend killed my countryman today, and his actions will kill many more if he's allowed to continue. Right now, you're our best hope of catching him."

Middleton spoke again, "Miss Burton, Dewhurst supports this proposal. He was merely trying to impress upon you the significance of what you will be attempting. To lure Pettigru out, you must be visible, which means you will have to go into Society with Dewhurst. You must be convincing as his wife and not draw undue attention with social blunders. Therefore, Dewhurst will teach you all you need to know to be a success."

Charlotte frowned and sipped her wine again. It still seemed too easy. What would Dewhurst have to teach her? Perhaps something about titles, but surely she knew the rest. She had been to her share of society gatherings in Charleston before her family's business faltered. But what would she get out of this? She was not so gullible as to believe these men would really give Cade a fair chance. But what good would she do Cade locked in this dungeon? If she went along with their plan, she might be able to save Cade.

And then what? What if Cade had no money to

loan her? She had intended to ask him to become a partner with her, loaning her money to buy back Burton & Son Shipping. But after seeing where he lived and now the troubles he was having with the British government, she wondered. Would he be able to afford to help her? She would help him no matter what, but perhaps she might find a way to repay the British bastards for the deaths of her father and brother.

Charlotte looked at Dewhurst. "Pray, what do I get out of this? If I play the part of your wife, if I lead you to Cade, what then?"

Dewhurst spoke without looking at her. "We fake your death and you go back to the col— the Americas. I go on as a widower, and life goes back to normal."

Not for me, Charlotte thought. "But what do *I* get out of this?" she repeated, and Dewhurst narrowed his eyes at her.

"What do you want?"

Charlotte pretended to consider. First and foremost, she wanted to know where Addy was and if she was safe. Secondly . . . she studied Dewhurst. This man obviously had money if he was part of the highest social circles in London. She had a responsibility to the memory of her father and brother to rebuild Burton & Son, not to mention Addy needed her. She'd sacrificed as much as Charlotte—possibly more than Charlotte—to buy them fare to London and a chance at rebuilding their lives. She couldn't fail Addy. But how much should she ask for? How much did she need? Four hundred dollars? Could she persuade him to give her five hundred? "Money," she said, stalling for time in which to calculate.

The gentlemen glanced at each other. Dewhurst's look was that of a man used to money grabbers and toadies. But this had been his idea, not hers. She had every right to expect compensation. Cade's safety came first, but money was a close second. Dewhurst rose and strode to where she was standing, stopping mere inches from her.

He wore the same clothes, and his hair was still too long, but now she saw something of the aristocrat in him. The condescension in his eyes, the derisive curl of his lip, his haughty manner. And yet she did not step away or back down. His body was warm beside hers, his closeness making her pulse race. She wanted to pretend her reaction to him came from anger or fear, but she knew it was not true. He was an attractive man, for all that he was the enemy.

"If I am to marry you, madam, I expect your performance as my wife to be spectacular. Furthermore, I am in charge. You do what I say, when I say, how I say, and I'll brook no argument."

"And if I agree?" Charlotte said, tilting her chin up to look him in the eye.

"Then I pay you one thousand pounds and never have to see you again."

Chapter 3

Freddie put a hand over his eyes and tried to imagine he were somewhere else—anywhere but traveling in Middleton's yacht with a colonist who was to be—to play, he amended—his bride. Middleton had left them to inform Edwards she'd agreed to the scheme and to give the captain orders to sail into one of the docks.

Separating his fingers, Freddie peered across the room at his "bride." Charlotte's jaw was clenched, her expression stony, and she looked as though, were he to turn his back, she'd be eager to play Brutus to his Caesar.

What was he about? Had he gone completely daft? This scheme was mad—no one would ever believe he'd marry a colonist. A Yankee with no name, no family, no eye for fashion. Not to mention, there was a sense of desperation, a hunger hanging about her. She was a fighter; he could see it in her eyes. But he did not want to probe too deeply into the nature of the skirmishes she'd won and lost.

Over the years, Freddie had painstakingly constructed the persona of a dandy to deflect suspicion from his activities in the Foreign Office. He didn't mind his role. After all, he had an eye for a well-tied cravat and a fine tailcoat. But there were times when he found the part constraining. This was one of them. How was he to play a pink of the *ton*, a tulip of the goes, a fashionable of the highest order with a dowd in tow?

Freddie lowered his hand and glared at the dowd in question. He supposed she wasn't hopeless. With a bit of Town bronze she might look well enough. But that accent, her style of speaking, her common manners. Freddie Dewhurst, exquisite and choice spirit of the *ton*, married to a ginger-pated, bran-faced colonist? It was enough to make a cat laugh.

But his mother wouldn't be laughing. Lady Dewhurst would be furious and full of questions, and he'd have to appease her while pretending to be in love with an American. Neither would Josephine find any amusement in this new state of affairs. His mistress was somewhat proprietary—a quality he'd found amusing. Until now.

Dash it. He hadn't considered that he'd have

to give up Josephine to ensure this preposterous sham was believed. Freddie ground his teeth. How had Edwards talked him into this? The answer was simple: he hadn't. Edwards had *ordered* him to marry the girl, and Freddie wanted the bastard Pettigru enough at this point to agree to just about anything. The girl would be useful; that he did not dispute. But making her his wife? During his tenure with the Foreign Office, Freddie had been shot, stabbed, and beaten within an inch of his life, he'd slept in hovels, in the open, and in stables; he'd traveled by horse, by coach, and even by dashed ship when he was forced to. And he had never—well, almost never—complained. But this marriage was pushing his loyalty to its limits.

At least the woman did not appear as overly emotional as some females, and she was certainly unlikely to threaten the security of his own controlled emotions. Freddie patted his breast pocket and felt the sheaf of papers: a false marriage license and doctored papers.

"Mr. Dewhurst," the colonist said, her honeyed voice making him forget the direction of his thoughts. "Is there something keeping you here? If so, pray, state your purpose. I prefer to keep our exchanges quick and painless."

"If only that were possible, Miss Burton. But, you see, you've already drawn blood." She gave him a puzzled look, a delicate crease forming between her sherry-colored eyes, and he explained, "It's Lord Dewhurst."

She waved a hand. "Of course."

"No, not 'of course.'" Freddie stood and was dismayed to realize his legs were still somewhat unsteady. "The order of precedence is a matter of great significance among members of the upper ten thousand, and you would do well to learn it and learn it perfectly. But first I want some information from you. How long has it been since you last saw Pettigru?" He leaned against the wall and rested a booted foot on her berth.

"It's been five years since I've seen him," she said, giving his boot a pointed look.

"And in that time, you never thought to come to London and visit before?"

She shrugged, and he tried not to notice how large her brown eyes were in the dim light or how her hair reminded him of a river of molten lava streaming across her back. Bloody hell, but she was aggravating. He clenched his fist. "I want to know what motivated your visit. Was it money? Your father and brother were killed, but what about your mother?"

A look of pain flashed across her face, and she seemed to sink into the berth. "She died when I was very little."

"So you have nothing." She did not answer, but her dark eyes never left his face. "And if Pettigru loaned you, say, a thousand pounds, how were you going to pay him back?"

"I told you, he's my friend."

"Did you expect he'd marry you? Take you as a mistress? Is that what you wanted?"

"Mr. Dewhurst—"

He held up a hand. "It's Lord Dewhurst."

She gave an exaggerated roll of her eyes, and he clamped his lips shut to keep from shouting at her. Irritating little chit. He would *not* lose control of his temper because of her. He knew all he needed to for now. One: she was alone in the world. Two: she needed money. Three: she'd gone to Cade Pettigru for help.

Now God help him, because he had a monumental task ahead of him. He pushed away from the berth and strolled across the small cabin. "It might be best if we start at the beginning, Miss Burton."

"The beginning?" She pushed a strand of hair from her face and raised a brow. "I am not a fool, sir."

Freddie leaned a hip against the large desk bolted to the floor of the cabin. "Don't put words in my mouth, Miss Burton."

"Not necessary, sir, when you have an overabundance as it is."

Freddie frowned. Had the chit just insulted him? He narrowed his eyes, and she watched him warily from her seat. The contrast of her white face and flame-colored hair beside the dark counterpane and somber black gown made her look small and harmless.

Freddie decided he'd misunderstood her. "Miss Burton, as I understand it, you are from Charles Town and you—"

"Charleston," she interrupted.

"What?"

"I told you. I'm from Charleston."

Freddie raised a brow. Hadn't he said that? Her version sounded like his except she ran Charles Town all together. He tried another tactic. "You are from South Carolina." He paused in case she felt the need to correct him. Apparently she did not. "And as such, there may be some customs and expectations involved in the London Season with which you are unfamiliar. As my wife and an outsider, your every move, every action will be scrutinized. It falls to me to ensure your introduction is done to a cow's thumb. I do not mean to crow, but I have a reputation as a pink of the *ton*, and in order to—"

"What language *are* you speaking?" she asked.

"English," he retorted, frowning.

"It does not sound like any English I have ever heard."

"Now you go too far. *You* are disparaging *my* English?"

She snorted. "You're not one for originality, are you, Mr. Dewhurst?"

"It's *Lord* Dewhurst," he erupted losing his patience. "I am a *lord*, not a mister."

She raised an eyebrow, and he scowled, thinking how he must have sounded. Dash it if this chit wasn't getting the better of him.

"Please accept my humblest apologies," she said, her face contrite, but Freddie could have sworn there was a very healthy measure of sarcasm in her voice.

"You hoaxing me, madam?"

"I declare, I would never hoax you, Mr.—Lord Dewhurst." Her eyes sparkled with restrained laughter.

Freddie eyed her suspiciously. "Do you even know what 'hoaxing' means?"

"No. But I am sure I would never do it." She blinked innocently, and then he knew she was making fun of him.

He ground his teeth. Not only was the chit distracting him from his lesson, she'd annoyed the hell out of him, too. Freddie tapped his fingers on the desk in a halfhearted attempt to relax and refocus on the task at hand. It might have been easier if her cheeks hadn't warmed with color and her eyes hadn't brightened with mischief at her game.

Without thinking, he reached for the bottle of wine standing upright on the desk. Uncorking it, he looked around for a glass, found none, so drank a healthy dose from the bottle. The American looked unperturbed. Probably used to men with manners no better than an ape's. He frowned, thinking the comparison didn't reflect too well on him at the moment. "Miss Burton, I am trying to establish where to begin our lesson. I see we need to work on titles, but I think—"

"Lesson?" she said, all traces of mischief gone. "I hardly think I need a lesson in etiquette from you, sir."

"Oh? You are familiar with the intricacies of life among the *ton*?"

"I have no idea what you just said, but I am familiar with the social graces to which you are probably referring. After all, we *do* have a Season in Charleston."

"Stuff and nonsense," he said, dismissing the idea out of hand.

"Not at all. Before I began working at my father's business, I attended many social engagements. I am sure, given a little practice, the graces to which you are referring will all come back to me. I can be quite charming when the occasion calls for it."

Freddie took another swallow of the wine and said, "A charming American. An oxymoron to be sure."

"Pray, sir, keep insulting me, and you'll see the barrel of my pistol."

Before he realized what he was about, he'd crossed the tiny cabin, grasped her arm, and wrenched her to her knees. "Don't threaten me, little Yankee hellion."

"I am a Southerner, sir. Not a Yankee."

"You're a pain in the—neck. And my good humor and noblesse oblige only extend so far."

She made a fist with the hand he held. "You speak of nobility, sir? You don't know the meaning of the word. I've seen what you bastards do in the name of nobility, and it sickens me. *You* sicken me."

He pulled her forward, hard against him, until he could see the smattering of freckles on her nose. "Best you inure yourself to the taste, Miss Burton, for you will have a hale and hearty dose as long as we are together." And then to his surprise, he cupped the back of her neck, bent, and kissed her. Hard.

Her body went rigid with shock, but it was a temporary paralysis. Her free hand came up and made a feeble attempt to push him away, but Freddie was determined to show her who was master. He'd told her he was in charge, and now he intended to prove it. Hardheaded Americans. Always fighting battles they were sure to lose.

And this colonist was losing. He could feel her softening. Feel her lips opening to him, feel her body—which was far more lush than the ill-fitting gown would have one believe—pressing against him, feel her breathing become more rapid, feel—

Freddie broke the kiss and stepped back. His stomach was churning, and the room had started spinning. Too late, he realized he should never have drunk the wine. These dashed yachts would be the end of him. He took a deep breath, but it was no use. Even Charlotte was spinning now. Spinning round and round and—"Dash it," he swore, and snatched open the door.

Charlotte put a hand to her beating heart, alarmed at how hard it was pounding. He had kissed her! The arrogant, overbearing despot had actually kissed her. The last thing she had expected him to do was assault her.

He'd been standing there, so presumptuous, so autocratic, so full of pride. And he'd actually tried to lecture her! As if he could teach her anything. Oh, George Washington, how was she ever going to survive this charade when they reached his home? She'd spent all of a half hour in the man's presence, and already she hated him. And he hated her, too. He'd looked positively green when he'd broken their kiss. He'd rushed from the room as though his life depended on it. Thank God. Who would have saved her if the Brit got it in his mind to rape her?

She rose and walked slowly around the cabin, moving with the gentle swells from the river beneath them. She'd been on ships since she was a baby and had her sea legs firmly under her. It would have taken a violent storm indeed to unsettle a seasoned sailor such as she.

Then why had this Dewhurst unsettled her so

easily? She hated him, as she hated all things British. And just like a warrior to try and play on her softer emotions for leverage. George help him if he ever tried to kiss her again. Then she'd show him . . . what?

Why hadn't she showed him earlier? Why had she just stood there and allowed him to kiss her? The pit of her stomach knotted but not from nausea. She wished she could go on deck to clear her head. Her conflicted response to him was most unnerving. She, who hadn't the time or inclination to look at a man in years, had been—however momentarily—swept away by an . . . *Englishman.*

Of all the men in the world, the English had to be the least appealing. This man was the enemy of her country, her father, her grandfather, dear George Washington himself. Dewhurst was from that stock of people who had forced unfair restrictions and provisions on her country, invaded her home without provocation, killed and enslaved her countrymen by the thousands. He was her enemy, and from now on she'd treat him as badly as his kind had treated her countrymen.

An hour or so later, Charlotte, Addy, and Dewhurst disembarked at another dock. It was early morning, but one would not have known it here. A pervasive haze hung over the ships and passengers, making the sky look dark. And the place was a veritable beehive of activity. Groups of passengers and seamen streamed by, carrying trunks and valises, or were followed by servants carrying the luggage for them. Carts and carriages popped up like weeds at every turn.

Dewhurst steered her and Addy through the throngs, chatting amiably to Addy but admonishing Charlotte more than once to keep her head down and the hood of the mantle close around her face. Charlotte did not mind the mantle—it was cold and damp outside—but she did mind missing all the goings-on about her. Dewhurst stopped to allow a group of boisterous seamen to pass, and Charlotte turned, surveying the tangle of masts rising like spires in the channel behind her and the barrels of rum being hoisted off a ship and onto a platform. Officials ticked off each barrel on their logs while uniformed guards eyed anyone passing by too slowly with menace. Finally her gaze rested on Addy, who stood directly behind her, clutching her meager shawl and frowning something monstrous.

She gave her maid a weak smile, but she could understand how Addy felt. Would they ever be home again?

"Dash it, girl. Keep your head down." Dewhurst chastised her again.

Immediately she lowered her head, but only because she did not want to attract attention any more than he wanted her to be seen. She'd meet all his high-brow friends and supercilious acquaintances soon enough.

She wondered fleetingly if her mother had ever been to these docks—if Katherine Abernathy had walked on this same ground before her fateful trip to the colonies, where she'd met and fallen in love with George Burton. Charlotte did not have many memories of her English mother, but she could not imagine the gracious, demure woman she did remember in a noisy, dirty place like this. Perhaps by the time Charlotte had been born, the last festering pus of her mother's British origins had been extracted.

"Here we are," Freddie said, indicating an old carriage for hire. He pulled open the door and held out a hand to Addy. "Madam, if you will allow me." He handed Addy inside, then looked at Charlotte. No frilly words for her. He jerked his head toward the coach, and when she took his hand, he practically shoved her inside before climbing in himself. The driver opened the hatch above them and said something Charlotte could never hope to decipher. Dewhurst must have understood because he replied, "Take us to"—he glanced at Charlotte, considering—"Bruton Street. Number sixty-four."

"Difficulty remembering where you live, Mr. Dewhurst?"

He frowned at her from across the carriage. "Not any more than you have remembering my title, Miss Burton." He opened the curtains a bit. "Ah, good. The sun is up. You'll be able to see the city."

"I declare, your city holds no interest for me." She crossed her arms and looked at Addy for confirmation, but Addy was staring openmouthed out the window. Charlotte frowned, then shivered. Now that she was out of the hustle and bustle, she was even more conscious of the damp cold seeping into her bones and pulled her mantle tightly around her. It was late June, and when she'd left Charleston in May, the weather had been balmy. Here it was cold and dreary, the sun Dewhurst had touted invisible behind the sooty clouds.

The weather reflected the city. The coach drove past dingy buildings, dirty streets, and rancid smells. The London sky was darkened by a thick fog, and she had the feeling that it wouldn't dissipate with the morning. The few shops that were open were lit as if it were perpetually evening.

The hordes of city dwellers off on their morning errands seemed not to notice their bleak surroundings. In all the racket, how could they? Charlotte pressed her palm to her forehead, finding it difficult to take in the press of carriages and horses, the swarms of humanity, and the hollow, haggard faces of the beggars on almost every corner. Then there was the added strain of redcoats. The city appeared under siege from the sheer numbers of enlisted men milling about, waiting to go to war or hoping to avoid it.

"Oh, Lawd," Addy murmured at the sight of the soldiers.

"Not to worry, Miss Addy," Dewhurst said. "You are quite safe here."

Charlotte snorted, and Dewhurst looked at her. "Old friends, Miss Burton?"

She grimaced. "Hardly friends, Dewhurst, but we are acquainted."

"If you'd like to renew your friendships, I could take you to the daily parade of the Horse Guard from their barracks to Hyde Park."

"Only if you promise to meet our American boys in uniform. I'd be happy to introduce you," Charlotte answered with a smile. Dewhurst looked as though he knew the kind of introduction she'd give him—one guaranteed to see him hanging from the nearest tree branch. She allowed her gaze to rest on him briefly—this man who would play her husband—noting that he looked tired and pale. Was he dreading this ordeal as much as she?

A few moments later, the crowds thinned and the streets were quieter and less congested. She caught a glimpse of green up ahead and leaned forward to better see the trees and grass. "Berkeley Square," he said. "I have friends there." Charlotte blinked. There were some very fine houses in Charleston but few rivaled these. "Would you like to see Grosvenor Square, Miss Addy? I'll tell the jarvey to drive us."

"No." Charlotte answered for her. She wanted neither Addy nor herself to be impressed by these English. The coach slowed then and the coachman—what had Dewhurst called him, a jarvey?—announced their direction. Or so she assumed for she still did not understand the man.

Dewhurst swung out, first handing Addy down and then taking Charlotte's hand. She stepped onto the walk and looked up. The house was white and pretty, three or four stories. It was not huge, but neither could it be called modest. She started forward, and Dewhurst grasped her elbow. "Are you ready to begin our charade, Charlotte?"

She gave him an icy glare. "I have not given you leave, sir."

"I'm your husband. Our marriage tends to imply a certain familiarity. The servants will expect it."

He was right. She took a breath. "Very well. What shall I call you?"

"My given name is Alfred, but my friends call me Dewhurst."

"Alfred, then." She turned back to the house, but he swung her 'round again.

"My close friends, my family, and my mistress call me Freddie."

Charlotte's eyes widened. "Mistress?" she hissed. "You said nothing of mistresses!" She glanced at the house. "I don't know what you were thinking, but I am not entering a house of prostitution."

He chuckled. Actually chuckled! "Josephine has her own house, and I assure you I will give her a public congé. I suppose I have to if this marriage is to be believed," he muttered.

"Pray, don't appear so eager, Alfred. I might not believe you've really ended it."

"It's Freddie, and I assure you I will end things with Josephine. Just as I know you will bring Cade Pettigru to me."

She inclined her head. "A fair trade."

He laughed. "Hardly, Charlotte. Hardly." Then he bent down and swept her up and into his arms.

"What are you doing?" she cried, squirming to be free.

"Old English custom, Lady Dewhurst. I'm carrying you over the threshold." He reached forward, undid the gate, and started up the walk. Charlotte could hear Addy grumbling behind them.

"I do not need to be carried," she said, but the words came out feebly. He had called her Lady Dewhurst. Oh, George. She had not realized how strange it would be to think of herself as an Englishman's wife. To be a titled Lady, with a lord for a husband. What had he said his title was? Baron? Was that like a prince? And then they reached the landing and the polished black door with its brass knocker opened and a small man with a pale face and dark hair, meticulously combed back, stood frowning at them.

"My lord!" he crowed, sounding like a bird who'd just had a tail feather plucked.

"Wilkins," Dewhurst said, nodding. Charlotte noticed that though he had just carried her up the walk, he did not sound winded in the least. His color was back now, and if his smile was to be believed, he was enjoying himself indeed. He carried her through the door and set her down with a flourish in a large foyer. He bowed deeply and theatrically, and said, "Your humble abode, my lady."

Charlotte wanted to swat at him. He was finding far too much amusement in the situation.

"My lord, what happened to your coat?" the man Dewhurst had called Wilkins screeched. He reached out a trembling hand, brushing Dewhurst's coat with one finger. He shuddered visibly. Charlotte frowned. The coat looked fine to her.

"The wrinkled look is all the go in the city these days," Dewhurst said jauntily. "Haven't you heard?"

"No," the man said, looking horrified. "You cannot possibly be serious, my lord. That coat is *ruined.*"

Dewhurst shrugged. "Even so."

Charlotte couldn't suppress a smile. Poor man. Dewhurst was—what had he called it on board ship? hoaxing?—Dewhurst was hoaxing the man, and the gullible servant believed it.

"Lady Dewhurst, meet Wilkins, my valet. He keeps me in top form."

Charlotte held her hand out to the servant, but the man simply gaped at her. "*Lady* Dewhurst, my lord? Whatever can you mean?"

Dewhurst smiled, that lazy smile that gave him so much charm. "Congratulations are in order, Wilkins. I've taken a bride."

Wilkins gasped, gave her a look rife with disapproval and disbelief, then took a full two steps back. Charlotte glanced down at her dress. She didn't look that unkempt. Did she? She searched for something to say. It was important to have the support and loyalty of the servants if her time here was to be tolerable. She settled on complimenting the house.

"You have a lovely home, Dewhurst," she said, glancing at the black and white marble stairs and the gleaming chestnut banister. The chandelier itself sparkled as though covered with a million diamonds. How much was it worth? How much were the paintings on the walls worth? And what of the rest of the house? There were doors on either side of her, stark white, but closed so that she couldn't glimpse their treasures. She had best not become too used to living amid such elegance. It would not last. "You are to be commended, Mr. Wilkins," she finished.

Wilkins stared at her, then turned to Dewhurst. "My lord?"

"No, Wilkins, she's not British." He grinned at her, taking her hand in his. Charlotte was suddenly glad of the solidarity between them.

Though it was nothing more than a sham, it was all she had.

"Scottish, my lord?" the valet continued, as if she weren't standing there.

"American," Dewhurst said, and the valet put a hand to his throat. If possible, his pale face turned paler. "Now might be a good time for you to pay the hack's driver, Wilkins."

"Of course, my lord," he said, voice sounding thin and reedy. He turned to the door, still standing open, and promptly screamed like a little girl.

"Lawd Almighty. What the matter with that man?" Addy asked, stepping into the foyer. "That noise's hurting my ears."

"Wilkins," Dewhurst said, raising his voice to be heard over the din. "Stop that infernal noise. This is Miss Addy, Lady Dewhurst's maid."

"That"—Wilkins pointed to Addy—"that *giant* will be living here, my lord?"

"And she's to be treated with all due respect," Dewhurst said. Wilkins swallowed, took a step forward as though to greet Addy, then fell on the floor in a heap.

"Oh, good God. This is intolerable." Freddie turned to Charlotte, expression looking weary and frustrated "You—you've felled my valet." He gestured to the fallen man in accusation. "What now, madam? Midnight rides? Yankee Doodle? Tea parties on the Thames? Dashed upstart colonists." And he strode away.

Chapter 4

Charlotte watched her "husband" retreat. Even though he must be as exhausted as she, he held himself with undeniable aristocratic bearing. Arrogant, imperialistic, condescending: her "spouse" was everything she'd always hated about the British. And more. She let out a small, inelegant, decidedly unaristocratic snort. British nobles and their misguided sense of honor. She'd been in England all of one day and his house not twenty minutes, and the so-called nobleman was already abandoning her. So much for honor.

Well, she wasn't going to stand for it. Lord Dewhurst was about to have a minor American rebellion right here under his roof. She lifted her skirts, prepared to follow him, when a small but redoubtable-looking woman stepped into the foyer. The petite, iron-haired lady looked Charlotte up and down and up again, then said, "I am Mrs. Pots, milord's housekeeper."

"Hello," Charlotte said and tried to scoot around the woman, but the housekeeper blocked her path. Charlotte tried again, but when she went right, the woman followed, and when Charlotte went left, the woman bounced in front of her again.

"And who are you?" the woman asked. She gave Charlotte a dubious look that reminded her of the look Addy gave stray cats begging for scraps at the back door of the house in Charleston.

Charlotte tried one last time to skirt around her, but Mrs. Pots was having none of it, so Charlotte mustered a smile and introduced herself. "Charlotte Burton." She held her hand out, trying to look friendly and sweet and pathetic all at the same time, as those were the traits that had generally won the cats' favor. Mrs. Pots, however, did not appear swayed, so Charlotte went on, "I am Lady Dewhurst now."

"Ridiculous," Mrs. Pots replied, shaking her head so that her gray bun bounced.

"Rid—" Charlotte blinked. No wonder her father's generation had seen the need to forcibly expel these British from American soil. Even their servants were insufferable. "Now look here, Mrs. Pots—"

"No, you look here, young lady," the housekeeper interrupted. "I don't know who you are, or why His Lordship has brought you here." Her gaze scoured Charlotte from head to toe again. "Though I can probably guess."

Charlotte's jaw dropped, and she tried to speak, but only a sputter came out. If one more of these people accused her of being a loose woman . . .

"I draw the line at dishonesty," the housekeeper warned.

With effort, Charlotte shut her mouth. Thank George Washington, she was not a stray cat. This woman probably scalded the poor creatures with boiling water rather than give a puss the smallest morsel of chicken. Ha! Charlotte thought. She wouldn't rate even a chicken bone if this continued.

But the formidable Mrs. Pots was not finished with her scalding. "The dowager is the only Lady Dewhurst I know, and you, miss, have a long way to go before aspiring to her class."

"Be that as it may," Charlotte said, straightening her spine. "I am your new mistress, and as such—"

Mrs. Pots turned her back. "Now what have you done to poor Wilkins?" she asked, peering at the man still sprawled on the floor. Charlotte exchanged incredulous looks with Addy, while the housekeeper motioned for a girl hovering near the stairs with a basin and linen to come forward. "Hester, dab his face with that water. Lazy girl. Be quick about it. That is sure to revive him."

Hester followed the order, kneeling beside the

poor valet. A moment later, the man spluttered awake, snapping, "Not the cravat! Don't dampen the cravat!" He sat up, hands protectively clutching the stiff linen at his throat.

"Ah, back to his old self," Mrs. Pots said. "Now, what other havoc have you wreaked?" Mrs. Pots said, glancing about.

Addy stepped forward, obviously unwilling to tolerate any further insult to her mistress. "Don't you talk to Miss Charlotte like that. I won't tolerate no disrespect."

Charlotte put a hand on Addy's forearm. "Addy, let me—"

"Don't interrupt, Miss Charlotte. I is talking to this woman, and she mighty confused." Charlotte threw up her hands. Now even Addy was shushing her. "I think you owes Miss Charlotte an apology."

On the floor, Wilkins whimpered, but Mrs. Pots frowned, puffed her chest out, and rose to her full height, which was at least a foot shorter than Addy. "Addy, is it? Addy, you are mistaken. It is *you*, not I, who are in error."

Addy crossed her arms. "Fancy talk isn't worth chicken spit."

"Oh, dear Lord!" Wilkins cried, shrinking back.

"I ain't going to hurt you, little man," Addy growled, then added under her breath, "Unless you give me reason."

Wilkins made a small sound of distress and

swooned yet again, and Charlotte, worried she might be trapped in the foyer all day if she didn't take action soon, pushed forward. "Mrs. Pots, I know all of this must come as quite a shock, and I am certain Dewhurst will answer any questions in his own good time, but for now, would you please take me to him?"

Mrs. Pots frowned. "I don't think—"

"Oh, never mind," Charlotte said. "I'll find him myself." And she started down the hallway in the direction Dewhurst had taken.

"Where are you going?" Mrs. Pots called after her. "Come back here!" Charlotte kept walking, past door after door after door. She paused to stare at the mammoth, polished wood edifices spaced evenly before her. Dewhurst could be behind any of them. She turned in a full circle, noting the fine rosewood ornamental tables and the treasures they displayed. Three of those fine porcelain vases, two gold candlesticks, or one of the antique clocks would absolve her of money worries for a half year or more. As she stared, a blue and gold liveried footman emerged from a hidden door in the wall behind her and, when he saw her, bowed.

Charlotte nodded, and the man began to walk away, but Charlotte called after him. "Wait! Sir!"

He turned back, seeming surprised.

"Can you tell me where—ah, His Lordliness—Lord Dewhurst is?"

"Yes, madam. I believe he retired to his room."

Charlotte nodded and turned back to the row of doors. "And which door might that be?"

"His Lordship's room is two floors up, madam." Charlotte frowned back at the foyer. She had been standing there a moment before, looking up at the high chandelier and the glossy black and white marble steps. The footman seemed to note her confusion. "I believe he took the servants' stairs to avoid the"—he followed her gaze down the corridor, where they could hear Addy chastising Mrs. Pots and the housekeeper giving as good as she got—"commotion. Through there, madam," the man said, indicating the wall panel.

"Thank you, sir," Charlotte said, grasping his hand.

He smiled. "Andrews, madam."

"Andrews." She squeezed his hand, then slipped through the panel and started up the stairs. When she emerged on the third floor, she was staring down another corridor lined with towering doors. George Washington, but this place needed street signs! Well, there was nothing for it but to try each door and hope she didn't intrude on anyone. She took a deep breath and started walking, pausing at each door to try the handle. The first three were locked, but the fourth turned.

"Success!" she whispered and pushed the door open.

"Do you always sneak about other's houses, opening doors without knocking?"

Charlotte jumped, slammed the door shut again, and spun around. Dewhurst was standing across the hall, leaning on a doorjamb, his expression a cross between amusement and exasperation. Her first impulse was to apologize, but she didn't give in. She'd done nothing wrong. Instead she said, "I was not sneaking around. I was looking for you."

He inclined his head. "You've found me." And she had. Her heart was only now slowing to a pace that allowed her to take him in. George Washington, but he was magnificent. He wore a dark blue double-breasted coat, buff pantaloons, and polished Hessian boots. His shirt was fine white linen with a frill at the neck and collar. The points of his stand collar almost grazed his ears, and his cravat was stiff and intricately tied. Even his golden hair had been tamed and pulled back into an artfully careless queue, and his jaw was clean-shaven. How in heaven had he had time to wash, shave, and dress?

Her heart thumped heavily in her chest. How was it possible that a man—an Englishman—could be so sinfully handsome? He really did appear every inch the archangel. It was so unfair—beside him, all her faults felt so keenly apparent. She'd never been a beauty, and even with the most exquisite coiffure and the finest clothes, she would never measure up.

"In the future," he said, interrupting her examination, "I'd appreciate it if you confined your snooping to your room or the drawing room. The rest of the house is mine."

Already on the defensive, Charlotte bridled. "Need I remind you that in the eyes of the rest of the household, this is my house as well as yours? I have every right to any and all rooms."

He gave her a long, hard stare, then stepped back. "Very well, then, come in. But I warn you not to become too comfortable. You're not staying."

"You couldn't pay me to stay," she retorted, stomping in after him.

"No? Then I shall pay you a thousand pounds to go."

Charlotte knew she had walked right into that one, but she might have thought of a biting rejoinder anyway, except that she lost all vestige of cogent thought as soon as she saw the room.

His room.

Her first impression was that she had taken a wrong turn and stumbled into the royal palace. The room was that sumptuous. All crimson and gold, Dewhurst's suite dripped dignity and majesty. In the center of the room, large but by no means overpowering the capacious suite, was a tester bed, which looked to be antique. The headboard was paneled walnut, intricately carved, and the foot posts were supported by pedestals, which in turn supported the heavy velvet weight of scarlet bed hangings. Charlotte supposed that had she been more familiar with the English design periods, she could have placed the furnishing as from the era of Henry VIII or Louis XIV—or was Louis from France?

On the far side of the bed, in a corner, were a cheval mirror and mahogany clothespress. The mirror was freestanding, decorated with ormolu, and had what appeared to be adjustable candle arms on the posts. Behind the clothespress were large windows overlooking the garden, the red and gold damask drapes tied back to allow the pale gray light into the room.

Charlotte took another step inside and peered 'round behind her. On this side of the room were the fireplace, a high-backed, rounded chair, and a small kingwood urn table on which stood a bottle stand with cabriole legs and paw feet. The stand was full, and there were two additional decanters beside it. Farther along the wall, Charlotte took note of a satinwood house desk and a Chippendale chair with claw feet. The room was not carpeted, instead there were various fine rugs interspersed throughout. But the last items in the room stood on the gleaming wood floors—a large mahogany washstand with a bowl and pitcher.

Charlotte looked back at Dewhurst in his perfectly tailored clothing and his carefully tousled hair. Here in this ornate, ostentatious room, she realized again that he was everything she detested about the British. He was the embodiment of her disgust for a nation that had tried to exploit and suppress her own for purely selfish reasons. Unfair, crippling taxes, restrictions on trade, unlawful seizing of ships and sailors. The British and their misguided sense of superiority!

Dewhurst gave her a lazy smile, and she was tempted to cross the room and smack it off his full, sensuous lips.

She gripped her skirts, forcing a grip on her thoughts as well. He was a handsome man. That could not be denied. Neither could she allow it to cloud her senses or make her forget her purpose here.

"Well?" he finally said, making a sweeping gesture to encompass the room. "Is it all you'd hoped when you were sneaking about, trying every door handle?"

She glared at him. "I was not sneaking about. I was looking for you, Mr. Dewhurst. A task that would not have been necessary had you not abandoned me downstairs with that ogre of a housekeeper."

"It's Lord Dewhurst," he said and arched a brow. Charlotte's gaze flitted to his eyes and was caught. His brows, just a shade darker than his golden hair, framed his eyes—amazing dark green eyes that had so captivated her even on their first meeting. Eyes half hidden under his heavy eyelids and framed by thick lashes, he watched her as a cat does its prey. His gaze was slow, unhurried, and distinctly predatory. He would not be rushed. This was a man who preferred to tease his quarry before giving the deathblow.

Charlotte blinked, unnerved at the train of her thoughts. He was a powerful man, indeed. She had seen past the puffed-up clothing and overdone suite to the warrior underneath. She would have to be careful. Charlotte cleared her throat. "Mr. Dewhurst," she began, averting her attention from his eyes. "I—"

"It's *Lord* Dewhurst," he said again.

"I know. I don't choose to use it." She waved her hand dismissively, and he shot to attention.

"My title is not a luxury to be used when the mood strikes. It is an absolute. As are all the titles of the aristocracy. If you wish to damn this venture before we even begin, then by all means, continue to disregard my rank."

Charlotte wrinkled her nose. "Very well, I shall make more of an effort to remember."

"No." He shook his head. "Not good enough."

"I beg your pardon?" Charlotte said indignantly.

"Unless you intend to insult half the people you meet and alienate me from my friends and acquaintances, you must learn the order of precedence inside and out. Backward and forward. If this ruse is to work, you must know it as well as your own name. As well as—"

"I take your point, Alfred."

"I believe I suggested beginning a lesson on titles aboard ship. Are you a bit more amenable to the idea now?"

"Not if you continue to behave as an arrogant jackass. Pride is one of the seven deadly sins."

"Ah, but if you were not already so prejudiced, you might realize that pride—where there is a true superiority of character or society—is not distasteful a'tall. So the question, then, is are you willing to put aside your ill-conceived judgments and see our society through neutral eyes?"

Charlotte bit her lip. She was not prejudiced, but neither was she as informed as she might be. She supposed she was going to have to make some concessions if she were to fit into his world. "Very well." She moved to the high-backed, rounded chair to her right, seated herself, and gave every appearance of rapt attention. She might not care for the lesson, but she'd show him that, like all Americans, she was a quick study.

For his part, he assumed the stance of a well-seasoned teacher. He stood across from her, struck an oratorical pose, and began what would likely be the longest, most tedious lecture she'd yet to bear. Even more tedious than old Miss Crudsworthy, the half-deaf, mostly blind teacher at her school in Charleston. Fortunately Miss Crudsworthy had retired after half a year and was replaced by Miss Joyce, who was young and pretty and vibrant.

Charlotte looked at Dewhurst. She would get no reprieve this time.

"Britain's *haute ton*, what we might call in English the fashionable set or high society," Dewhurst began, "adheres to a strict set of unwavering rules. You must not only learn the rules, but master the rules, if you wish to become a diamond of the first water."

"A what?"

"A diamond . . ." He paused, and the look that crossed his features was almost pained. "One of the most fashionable ladies. As my wife, nothing less is acceptable. At present we have ended the Season but . . ."

Charlotte stifled a yawn and allowed her attention to wander over to the bed again. Every time she looked at it, prickles of . . . excitement? fear? . . . cascaded down her back. She had never been in a man's room before, especially not alone and unchaperoned. Not that there was a need for a chaperone as the household and soon the entire city would think she and Dewhurst married. But she knew they were not husband and wife. He knew it as well, though her presence in his bedroom seemed not to faze him. It certainly didn't prevent him from going on and on about someplace called Almack's.

And perhaps that was a good thing. She did not want the kiss on the ship repeated, particularly not here in the presence of such a sinfully plush-looking bed. George, but it was huge. It was probably the largest bed she'd ever seen. Why did he need such an enormous bed, and did it ever swallow him up?

She turned to ask him about the furnishing, but he was still going on about the upper ten thousand or some such. She shook her head. He treated the rules of his *ton* as though they were a matter of life or death. He went on and on with his lesson, and the longer he talked, the more difficult Charlotte found it to school her face into the studious expression he seemed to expect.

Remember the thousand dollars, Charlotte chided herself when she had to squelch another yawn. She supposed it would be churlish to complain that he was boring her. He seemed to enjoy hearing himself speak, and she—well, she had to admit she enjoyed looking at him.

He was arrogant as the governor when she actually listened to his words, but if she tuned out his voice and focused on him, the experience was not altogether unpleasant. He was undeniably the most handsome man she'd ever met or probably would ever meet.

And his clothing, though a bit extravagant, was impeccable—not a crease, not a wrinkle. It fit him perfectly. Too perfectly. From her position on the chair, Charlotte couldn't help but notice how well the buff-colored pantaloons molded to his exquisitely muscled thighs and slim hips. Feeling the color rise in her cheeks, she quickly focused her attentions higher.

But that view was no better. As broad-shouldered and muscled as the boys she'd known in Charleston, Dewhurst destroyed her image of the fat, lazy English aristocrat. No, with his blond hair, green eyes, and boyish good looks, this man was more like a golden angel than a stuffy English lord.

Which was actually rather annoying. She wasn't used to dealing with men who were so much prettier than she. Not that his good looks daunted her. Charlotte had always judged others more on personality than looks. It was the way she preferred to be judged, as she prized equality. That, and she was no paragon of idyllic beauty—American or British.

Dewhurst adjusted his cravat, changing absolutely nothing as far as she could tell, and turned his emerald eyes on her.

"I believe we shall review the order of precedence," he was saying. Charlotte nodded enthusiastically, not remembering him discussing this order earlier but willing to listen if it was required.

"At the top of the order of precedence are the King and Queen, followed by their offspring," he said. "The male royal offspring are referred to as dukes, for example, the Duke of Cumberland. Now you would address the Duke of Cumberland as either 'Your Grace,' 'Duke,' or 'Your Royal Highness.' You will hear him spoken of as Cumberland, though.

"Below the royal dukes are the nonroyal dukes. They are addressed in the same fashion as the royal dukes without the addition of 'Your Royal Highness.' Do you follow?"

Charlotte nodded sagely, wondering how she would know a royal duke from a regular duke, but decided to just call all of them "Your Grace" so as not to have to distinguish.

She frowned. Addy would say the whole order sounded far too blasphemous. Didn't one pray for God's grace? Weren't you to refer to God as the Lord? And wasn't it a bit arrogant to expect everyone to go around calling you "Your Grace"? She missed the next part of Dewhurst's lecture—something about an earl.

Charlotte really did *try* to attend, but he was speaking so quickly and there was so much to take in that she found herself distracted—first by his eyes, then his mouth, his thigh muscles again . . .

She listened harder, but a moment later she was intrigued by his inflection on particular words. His tongue seemed to roll over some syllables and pause on others. He had the pronunciations all wrong, but oh, how she liked to watch his lips form those words.

Charlotte took a deep breath and sighed, then bit her cheek in frustration. She had almost forgotten that she hated British accents. They were *not* appealing. Not at all. Not even his . . .

With renewed determination to concentrate and learn, Charlotte caught Dewhurst's next words. "Now below an earl is a viscount. A viscount is not a viscount of anything. He is simply Viscount Brigham, for example. His wife is a viscountess. You refer to her as Lady Brigham. You refer to the viscount as Lord Brigham. I hope you are attending because you may meet Lord and Lady Brigham."

"Oh, yes," she lied. Then, because she could not help herself, "What are you?"

He gave her a frustrated look. "As I have told you before, I am a baron. However, no one speaks of barons by their title. I am always referred to as Lord Dewhurst."

"And your wife is Lady Dewhurst, correct?"

"Yes, as my wife, you are the Baroness Dewhurst, but you will be addressed as Lady Dewhurst." He was still talking, but Charlotte didn't hear. A sudden surge of warmth had infused her when he'd called her "wife." She couldn't say why, didn't want to speculate. The meanings were too horrendous to contemplate.

"Traitor!" she whispered.

"Eh?" he asked.

"Oh, I said, so then our children would be Lady Dewhurst and Lord Dewhurst as well."

He frowned. "We are not going to have children."

"Of course not! I wasn't implying—"

He held up a hand. "But were a baron and baroness to have progeny, they would not be titled. As I have explained to you, only the offspring of a duke or a marquis are given titles."

Charlotte pursed her lips. She did not remember him saying that. He narrowed his eyes. "What is the wife of a duke called?" he quizzed her.

That one was easy, and Charlotte smiled. "A duchess." Ha! Let Dewhurst *try* to get the better of her.

"And the wife of a marquis?"

She thought for a moment. "A marchioness?"

He nodded. "An earl?"

"An earless," she answered confidently.

Dewhurst blanched.

"No, no!" she hurriedly added, "I meant an earlette."

He clutched one of the bedposts, knuckles turning white. "A countess," he said so quietly she could hardly hear him.

"Oh, of course," she replied, hoping he was not about to collapse. His face was flushed and red, and he seemed to be having difficulty breathing. After a moment, his color returned, and she said, "But I thought a countess was the wife of a count."

Dewhurst pulled on his coat sleeves, jerking the

material fiercely. "There are no counts in England," he said, voice hitting each word.

"Well, that makes no sense. You have a duke and a duchess, a marquis and a marchioness, a baron and a baroness. But a countess and an earl? That doesn't seem quite right."

"You questioning my knowledge on the matter?" he demanded.

"No. There's no need to raise your voice. I was only wondering."

"Wondering? What about *listening?* You're driving me mad, woman." He glanced at the clock and swore under his breath. "Dash it. I'm going to be late."

"Late for what?" Charlotte asked.

He shook his head. "Do you realize I've been talking for over an hour, and you still haven't grasped the basics?"

Charlotte huffed. "Well, maybe if you had a mite more patience—"

"Patience! I'll have you know that I have the patience of a saint. I've sat for days—*days*, mind you—waiting out foreign operatives, I've endured over a dozen operas by a mediocre soprano who could barely carry a tune because proof of my devotion was required before I could bed her, and I once went two whole weeks without a suitably tied cravat because that dashed valet of mine got it in his head to go on strike. I have patience, madam!"

"I see. Well, cravats and opera singers aside, sir, you have as much to gain from this venture as those. If you could just begin again—"

"Begin again?" He stared at her as though she'd grown two noses. "Even if I were so inclined, I haven't the time. I have an appointment with Josephine in a quarter hour, and I will be late as it is."

"Josephine?" Charlotte gaped as indignation coiled in her belly, making her cold all the way to her toes. "Your *mistress*!"

"Good God." He jerked at the sleeves of his tailcoat again. "You sound like a wife already."

"And can you blame me? You're going to see your mistress? Dressed like that? And on our wedding day?" She jumped up and stomped over to him.

"What's wrong with my attire?" He angled so that he could see himself in the large cheval mirror. "These boots too drab? I should have Wilkins—"

"Oh, never mind. Your clothing is as puffed up and narrow as you!" She flicked his cravat and stiff collar for emphasis. "Go to your mistress, and I don't care if you ever come back!" She turned, crossed the room in three strides, opened the door, and slammed it with all the force she could muster. A maid dusting one of the portraits in the long corridor jumped, and a footman dropped the candle he was using to light one of the wall sconces.

Behind her, Dewhurst's door swung open again, and he barked, "You dare slam my door in my face? You ungrateful little wretch."

"You arrogant, preening flamingo!" she shot back. "I have nothing to say to you." She gripped the edge of the door, prepared to slam it again, but he put his hand over hers, stopping her.

"But I have something to say to you, my upstart colonist. And when I am ready to say it, you *will* listen." This time he shut the door so hard that the house rattled.

Chapter 5

Freddie strolled into Brooks's in full dandy mode—despite his former mistress's attempts to turn into a human catapult. He rubbed his cheek. Josephine had thrown a variety of objects, and her heavy hairbrush had struck home. Dashed woman was dicked in the nob. Perhaps this charade with the colonist would not be all bad. When a woman like Josephine became too attached, it was time to end the affair. Best to send her back to Alvanley. Perhaps having her back would smooth the baron's ruffled feathers.

Alvanley's potential reunion with Josephine was the topic of the evening during dinner at Brooks's. Romeo Coates wagered Alvanley's good humor would return in three weeks, Lord Yarmouth wagered seven, and Golden Ball

Hughes and George Hanger both put money on a fortnight. Freddie wagered a week; namely because when he had won Alvanley's favorite hunter the year before, Alvanley had been in high dudgeon for ten days, and Freddie couldn't imagine being more upset over a woman than a horse. Especially now that, after only three months, Josephine would be amenable to taking her former lover back.

Freddie had just begun perusing the wedding notices and wondering how he should word his—once-elegant dandy married to uncouth insignificant colonist?—when Alex Scarston, the Earl of Selbourne, thrust himself into the chair next to Freddie. Without so much as a word, Alex grabbed the gin and poured himself a large glass. Freddie frowned at the usurpation of the gin and then grimaced even more harshly when he got a better look at his friend. Alex's hair was in wild disarray, as though he'd been running his hands through it, his cravat hung sloppily down his linen shirt, and his boots were scuffed and lacking polish.

"Has Hodges deserted you, old boy?" Freddie asked, referring to Alex's valet.

"Unfortunately not."

Freddie opened his mouth to comment on the state of Alex's attire, but shut it quickly at a look from Alex. He'd known the earl since they'd been schoolmates at Eton, then Cambridge. Freddie was a few years younger than Selbourne and prided himself on being a good deal more charming. As a boy, he'd deliberately cultivated the good graces of the older and somewhat dangerous Selbourne, and the effort had saved him more than once from the abuse younger boys at Eton endured. But Freddie had repaid the favor more recently and therefore felt no compunction in needling his friend. "You're looking a bit Friday-faced, old boy. Dare I ask if something has happened to alter your exalted state of conjugal bliss?"

Alex threw Freddie a murderous look, drank his gin in one swallow, and motioned to the waiter to bring another bottle. Freddie raised an eyebrow.

"I don't care what you say, Dewhurst. Just don't say it in Italian," Alex grumbled.

Freddie threw back his head and laughed, causing several of the other gentlemen in the club to turn and stare. A few smiled. "I assume you've been to see Lady Brigham?" Freddie asked.

"I left Lucia with her parents. I couldn't take it another second. That house is Bedlam."

Lucia was Lady Selbourne, Alex's wife of seven years. Her mother, Viscountess Brigham, was well known for her obsession with all things Italian and her frequent use of her woefully scant Italian vocabulary.

Watching Selbourne pour another drink, Freddie decided it might be worse. He suspected that Alex's irritation with Lucia's mother had less to do with Italian and more to do with her hounding the couple about when they would have a child. After seven years, they had no offspring, and Freddie knew it was not for lack of trying.

And it was certainly not for lack of grandchildren that Lady Brigham complained. Lucia's sister, Francesca, and her husband, Ethan, the Marquis and Marchioness of Winterbourne, had four children, three boys and one girl. The undeniable fact was that Lady Brigham liked to meddle, and her daughters were fair game. Dash it if the viscountess hadn't had him in her sights at one time or another as well.

Alex nodded and took another drink, and Freddie said, "Dipping rather deep, aren't you, Selbourne? I don't relish the notion of delivering you home and watching you fall flat on your face at your wife's feet."

Alex glared at him and deliberately took another drink.

"Besides," Freddie continued, stepping lightly "My own wife is waiting at home for me."

Selbourne choked on the gin, and Freddie had to pound him on the back. When Alex could breathe again, he said, "Your *what*?"

Freddie was loath to say it again. *Wife* had come

out sounding unnaturally loud. It seemed to reverberate in the room like a death knell. He swallowed and forced himself to go on. He would have to convince the whole of the *ton* that, not only was he married to the American, he was besotted with her as well.

Freddie reached for the gin again. "Ah, I see the tittle-tattle hasn't reached you yet. I have finally followed you into the parson's mousetrap, Selbourne. I carried my bride over the threshold mere hours ago."

Alex's eyes narrowed. They were gray and piercing as a hawk's. Freddie allowed his gaze to wander about the room as though Selbourne wasn't mentally eviscerating his words and putting them back together in a fashion Freddie doubted would be to his taste. Before Selbourne sliced too deeply, Freddie said, "Don't look so surprised, old boy. It was going to happen sooner or later. What is it the poets say? 'Under love's heavy burden do I sink'?"

Selbourne slowly arched one brow. "I think it is more along the lines of 'oh, what tangled webs we weave.' "

Freddie smiled. "Be assured that I am quite willing to play the fly in Charlotte's lovely web."

Selbourne looked unimpressed. "Charlotte?" he said, voice bland. "Do I know the lady?"

Freddie took another sip of gin. "Doubtful. Unless you have been to America recently."

A flicker of interest lit Selbourne's eyes. "The lady is an American?"

Freddie tried to look pained—not a difficult proposition considering Charlotte's regrettable nationality. "Yes. Bit of jolt there, I know, but the power of love and all that."

Selbourne's other brow rose. "Love?"

Freddie swallowed more of the gin. This was going to be dashed harder than he thought. Selbourne gave no indication of being convinced. In fact, he looked as though he were waiting for the final jest.

"Yes, Selbourne, love. How we mighty have fallen, eh?" He lifted the glass to his lips again, belatedly noticing that he'd already drained the gin. He continued dry-mouthed. "Met her, fell instantly, madly in love, and married her by special license. Whirlwind romance and all of that fluff—uh . . . fortuitous circumstances."

Alex seemed to ponder this last for a moment, and Freddie dared hope his friend might finally be convinced. "A redhead?" Alex asked.

"The chit does happen to be ginger-pated. How did you know?"

"You can't resist redheads."

Freddie sat back dramatically. "Alas, I fear 'tis true. And the color is so dreadfully unfashionable!"

"Right. Keep it up and Brummell will revoke your membership in the Fops and Dandie's Club."

"There's a club?" Freddie asked in mock seriousness.

"What game are you playing?" Alex asked, leaning forward and speaking in a lowered voice. "You cannot possibly expect me to believe you met and married an American, brought her home to London, and are sitting here with me now while she settles into your town house. I fail to see the humor in this joke."

"Because it's not amusing," Freddie grumbled.

"Wait a moment. Is this woman why Pettigru slipped through your fingers?"

"Pettigru hasn't—" Freddie clenched his jaw, and Alex wordlessly reached for his glass and refilled it. "Thank you," Freddie managed before downing a healthy portion. "I don't need to tell you that this must remain in strictest confidence."

Alex waved a hand, indicating that was a given.

"Charlotte is Charlotte Burton. Her family in Charles Town was on intimate terms with Cade Pettigru."

Alex stilled. It wasn't an overt gesture, more of a sense of total calm and concentration that swept over his features. "And she has agreed to aid in that gentleman's apprehension?" Though it was highly unlikely they would be overheard, Alex was careful not to repeat Pettigru's name.

Freddie turned that question over in his mind. "She has not so much agreed as given in to pressure and greed." Alex shook his head, and Freddie said, "We've offered her one thousand pounds and the freedom to return to America if she plays the role of my wife and lures our friend from hiding."

"Dangerous proposition." Alex cocked a brow. "You'll have to bring her out in public if you want to set a trap. It could mean your social annihilation."

"I know," Freddie said, feeling a bead of sweat run down his back. "I know. If I'm to minimize the damage, she'll have to improve her manners. We continue our etiquette lessons tomorrow. Pray she's a fast learner."

"How does the role of tutor suit you?"

Freddie sat back. "Not a'tall, I'm afraid. Either the chit has a brick for a brain or I'm not a very gifted instructor."

"You?" Alex said with what looked suspiciously like a grin. "Say it isn't so."

"Ridiculous notion, I know, but the girl actually accused me of lacking patience."

"No." Alex shook his head.

"Exactly. Me lack patience? Was I not the picture of fortitude when Wilkins got it in his head to valet for Alvanley last year? Was I not the soul of tolerance when Lady Helmsley lured me to her bed and then insisted I not only—ah, entertain her but Lady Wrothgar as well?"

"Yes, that must have been terribly trying for you."

"And now to be called impatient by an upstart

colonist, too ignorant to know the most fundamental tenets of proper etiquette!"

"Not to be borne," Selbourne said and lifted his gin in a toast.

Freddie frowned. "Why do I have the feeling you are secretly enjoying my troubles?"

"Never," Selbourne said, not managing to hide a smile. "Though I will admit I prefer our roles reversed. It's been some time since I've seen you all sentimental over a woman."

"Sentimental? Ha!" Freddie barked. "Emotion has no part in this. It's business." He placed a hand over the breast pocket of his tailcoat and extracted a paper. "See this list? It proves I'm in complete control of the situation."

Alex creased his brow but held out a hand for the paper. He unfolded it, read it, then erupted into howls of laughter. Freddie gritted his teeth. "Something funny, old boy?"

"No, no," Alex said, snuffling the last of his chuckles. "This is priceless. Rules for dealing with your wife. Oh, I approve it wholeheartedly."

Freddie smiled. "Ah, then you think I shall succeed?"

"Oh, I didn't say that. You'll fail miserably, but I'll enjoy watching you stumble." Alex reached for the bottle of gin, but Freddie snatched it away.

"Not so fast, Selbourne. I'm not feeling inclined to share."

"Is it my fault you're smitten with the girl?"

"Smitten? I don't care in the least—"

Alex slipped the paper from Freddie's hand and pointed to a sentence. Freddie read it over, then blanched with horror. "Slip of the pen," he said, crossing the mistake out ruthlessly. "Doesn't mean a thing."

"Glad to hear it." Selbourne rose as though the matter were settled. "In that case, we're for home."

"Home?" Freddie said, appalled. "It's still early."

"Early for a bachelor." Alex grinned. "But we besotted husbands actually enjoy being home with our wives."

Freddie frowned. "I'll be bored out of my mind."

Alex slapped him on the shoulder. "Welcome to domesticity."

Not long after Dewhurst—*Lord* Dewhurst, Charlotte amended—left his bedroom for a visit to his mistress's boudoir, Mrs. Pots appeared and pointed Charlotte to her own room. It was the next door down from Dewhurst's room, a locale that equally thrilled and annoyed her. George, but she had never felt so low, so uncouth and common as she had these past hours in Freddie Dewhurst's house. Standing outside what was to be her room for God knew how long, Charlotte took a fortifying breath. She had to remember who she was and where she had come from.

Certainly her family had fallen from favor. Whereas once she'd never wanted for anything and her house had been, if not as grand as Dewhurst's, nothing to sneeze at, all she had now were her wits and the clothes on her back. She touched the emerald necklace she wore hidden beneath the high collar of the black gown. The mourning gown was the last memory of her father and brother, and the necklace a dim reminder of her long-dead mother. Everything else had been auctioned, sold, or abandoned.

But for a promise made by a man—a British man at that, and one she didn't know or trust—Charlotte and Addy had nothing.

Mrs. Pots seemed to relish keeping Charlotte in her place. She refused to call her anything but *miss*, scoffed when Charlotte asked if she could see the menu and the household accounts, and resolutely placed Charlotte and her needs at the bottom of a long list of other tasks, beneath even the feeding of Dewhurst's two large dogs. Finally the woman saw fit to show Charlotte to her room, which if Charlotte had known was not fifteen paces from where she'd been arguing with Dewhurst, she would have found herself.

"Here you are," Mrs. Pots said, opening the door. "Miss Dewhurst decorated the room, so you'll note the abundance of white."

Charlotte nodded, pretending she knew who Miss Dewhurst was and why the color white should be associated with her, then stepped into the room. Mrs. Pots closed the door behind her, and Addy turned from a small nightstand, which she'd been dusting with her handkerchief.

"Here you is," Addy said, putting her hands on her hips.

Charlotte nodded. "Yes, here I is." There seemed to be a fog as persistent as that hovering over London, and her senses were as gray and cloudy as the buildings of the city. The room was large—far larger than she'd been used to in recent years—and for a moment she wondered if she'd been shown to the wrong suite. She stared blankly at the bright walls and unfamiliar furnishings, feeling as though her life were a bad dream.

What finally woke her senses was the sight of the bed in the center of the room. It was not nearly as large as Dewhurst's but it would certainly be the largest bed she'd ever slept in. The most beautiful as well. Fluffy and white as a summer cloud, the counterpane was the color of milk, turned down to reveal a froth of vanilla silk sheets. From an open canopy, ivory drapes of the thinnest silk descended in a V past the abundant pillows and lightly dusted the floor. It reminded Charlotte of the mosquito nettings she was so used to at home, and she stepped forward to finger the fine material. How many dollars—rather, pounds—had this material cost?

She might not be married to His Baronship in truth, but she certainly felt like a princess. The room was a suite fit for royalty—luxurious but tasteful and decorated in the Greek style. There were not many furnishings, as it appeared the room was rarely occupied, but what was there was of the best quality. Overall, the effect was rich without being ostentatious, understated without being too austere.

Whoever this Miss Dewhurst was, Charlotte had a feeling she'd like the girl immensely. She had taste—in furnishings, if nothing else. Charlotte looked about her, admiring the contrast between the dark cherry woods and the pale bed coverings and bright light streaming through the windows; the disparity between the simplicity of the naked, gleaming wood floor and the intricate style of draping over the large windows; and the austere white color scheme paired with rich, sumptuous, textured materials.

Charlotte glanced at Addy, who smiled knowingly. "I knew you was going to like it," she said. "Reminds me of the house of Legare Street. Before."

She didn't need to say before what. Their fall from grace was too painful a subject to be spoken of directly.

But now Charlotte began to hope that perhaps

their luck had turned. What couldn't she accomplish with the thousand dollars Dewhurst owed her? She might restore the house in Charleston. Buy back the family business. Buy Addy a servant so the woman who had worked so hard for Charlotte and her family could finally be taken care of herself.

Charlotte sat on the bed, then lay back, feeling the plush mattress sink deliciously under her weight. She rolled over, snatched a pillow, and hugged it to her. For the first time in months—in years—she began to feel hopeful. She reminded herself again that it would not do to become too used to Dewhurst's home or Dewhurst himself. But she could enjoy it for the moment. "Addy, come lie here with me. It feels heavenly."

Addy scowled. "Dewhurst gots me a good bed in the servants' quarters. I gots no time for lazing about."

"Oh, hush," Charlotte said. "I'm not being lazy, I'm . . . adjusting to my new surroundings."

"Is that what they call it?" Addy said, and Charlotte tossed the pillow at her. Addy threw it back, and Charlotte sent a volley of pillows at her, jumping up and running to the opposite side of the bed to avoid Addy's retaliatory strike. She was laughing so hard that even Addy smiled, and Charlotte, overcome with giddiness, collapsed once again on the bed.

"Oh, Addy. I have a very good feeling about

this. Two days ago we were on a ship with nothing. Now look where we are! Our luck has turned."

"Hmpf. I hopes so, Miss Charlotte. But yous still have to get along with that man."

"Not a problem, Addy. We had a small discussion today, and I think he finally understands who has the upper hand in this 'marriage.'"

"Hmpf," Addy said again, and kept dusting.

Chapter 6

In her explorations that day, Charlotte had discovered that not only were she and Dewhurst to sleep in close quarters, their bedrooms were actually attached via a dressing room door between them.

That night Charlotte sat on her bed, still in her black bombazine gown, and stared at the closed door. She'd locked it, not that she need worry her husband would throw it open and ravish her. She'd heard nothing but silence from his room and could only assume that meant he was still with his mistress.

And why that should bother her, she did not care to consider. It was not as though she wanted the mistress's place in his heart. She wanted no part of his heart.

But a small part of her wondered if any woman had ever touched him deeply. She'd seen him go from warrior to fool to lord and back again. Who was the real Dewhurst? The devastating charmer who'd made her feel like laughing for the first time in years? The lord who made her so angry she wanted to kick him? The warrior who would never let his guard down because any sign of vulnerability was seen as a defeat?

She sighed. How was she going to protect Cade from a man like this? A man who would be relentless in his hunt and ruthless in his execution of "justice."

She heard the door to Dewhurst's bedchamber open and held her breath. She'd heard the valet go in and out before and did not automatically assume Dewhurst was home. And then she heard his voice. He was speaking to Wilkins, issuing directives, telling a story, exchanging ripostes. Charlotte crept to the dressing room door and tried to make out his words. Did he mention Cade? Had they caught him?

What about the mistress? Was she out of Dewhurst's life?

Then all was silent, and Charlotte cursed under her breath. Now she'd never know. Unless . . .

She unlocked the door and turned the knob, ignoring the voice in her brain telling her, *Turn back! Turn back!* Charlotte crept forward, through the dark dressing room, and stopped before Dewhurst's door. Still no sound.

She glanced back at her room, all white and misty in the darkness, then turned and rapped on Dewhurst's door.

For three heartbeats there was silence, and on the fourth, his door swung open and Dewhurst, dressed in black trousers and a white shirt, open at the collar, stood before her.

He cocked a brow and then inclined his head. "Lady Dewhurst. To what do I owe the pleasure of your company?"

Charlotte wanted to cut him with a sharp rejoinder. Instead she found she could not take her eyes from the bronze skin of his chest, visible in the V of his shirt. She could not help but stare at his hair. The soft curls glimmered in the candlelight. And then her gaze drifted lower to the tight pantaloons, the muscled calves, and his bare feet.

Charlotte's gaze shot back to his eyes and saw he was watching her, allowing the perusal. "Have you seen enough?" he said with a half smile. "Or did you come hoping for more?"

Charlotte stammered, her mouth unable to form a reply. *Cade,* she thought. *Ask about Cade.* But when she found her voice, what came out was, "Did you dismiss your mistress?"

His eyes widened and he seemed taken aback.

Charlotte shook her head. "No, I meant to ask about Cade. I—I don't care about the mistress."

"Don't you?" Dewhurst said, and his eyes were amused. "I think it bothers you that I've spent the evening with Josephine almost as much as it bothers me to know you've been thinking of dear Pettigru."

"But I wasn't thinking of Cade. I mean, I was, but not in the way you imply."

"And I wasn't with Josephine. It didn't seem appropriate on the day of my marriage, though I can't say I expected you to agree to much of a wedding night." His emerald eyes swept over her, making her body throb everywhere his gaze touched.

"I'm not. What I mean is, I don't want a wedding night."

His gaze met hers again. "Then go back to your room and lock the door before I decide to see for myself whether you've got petticoats on under that dress."

Charlotte took one look at his face, turned, and did as he suggested. Once she locked the door, she leaned against it, wondering if she should pull the dresser in front of it, then decided that if he really wanted entrance, not even the dresser would keep him out.

The role of besotted husband did not suit him, Freddie decided the next morning at the dining room table. Having had nothing to do but sleep the night before, he was up at the ungodly hour of nine A.M. and was waiting when Mrs. Pots directed Charlotte to join him. Despite their heated exchange the night before, Freddie had every intention of treating her arrival with no more interest than he showed when buttering his toast. But inexplicably, the moment she entered, he pounced.

"Madam." He couldn't stop the word from escaping his lips or his eyes from raking over her. Disapproval lanced through him. She was dressed in the same tattered black gown, and though he knew she had nothing else to wear, it rankled him to see her in it. He did not like the idea of his wife, even a woman playing his wife, wearing rags. "I can see we will have to put a new wardrobe at the top of our priority list."

She eyed him from the doorway, half in, half out, gaze wary and defensive. "Not to worry, Your Baronship. I'm certain you'll still be the belle of the ball." She indicated his polished riding boots, buff breeches, and Clarence blue riding coat. Her lush voice ran over him like thick, warm honey. He might have retorted, but he was momentarily speechless. Dashed if he hadn't prepared himself for her irritating American accent. It was a jolt first thing in the morning, especially when he couldn't tear his attention from the way her full lips wrapped around the long, rounded vowels.

But she was more than ready for him this morning. Ready and willing to fight. Good. Her appearance in his room last night had thrown him.

He wanted to be back on solid footing. He was eager to spar, to show her who the true master was. He hadn't forgotten that she was a money-grabbing colonist who would stab him in the back the second she was faced with a choice between her lover Pettigru and her "husband." Freddie tried to speak and managed something resembling a growl.

"You're in a pleasant mood this morning. As usual," she said, raising a brow, then taking a seat opposite him.

He rose and signaled to the waiting footman, who approached with an offer of tea, coffee, or chocolate. Charlotte asked for coffee. When the beverage was before her, Freddie said, "As much as I enjoy trading insults with you, I have more important matters to attend to. As your failure at the lesson showed yesterday, your training will require a significant amount of time and effort, so I suggest we begin immediately."

Her eyes, whose color for some reason still reminded him of warm sherry, heated further, an indication—he was learning—that she was displeased. Selbourne's warnings and admonishments had not gone unheeded. This was a battle. It required strategy and finesse and a gentle hand. He'd need to reward her, subtly but effectively, when she bent to his will. But how did one reward a colonist?

Now, as Charlotte lifted her cup to sip the coffee, Freddie took the opportunity to slide the paper from under his napkin and peruse his notes.

Notes on the Training of an Upstart Colonist

1. Always remember that the colonist is the enemy. This is war. The colonist's extraordinary ~~beauty~~ deception, rather, is a weapon.
2. Colonists have an intractable side. Begin each training session by establishing you are the master.
3. Colonists prey on perceived weaknesses. Do not end a training session until you have ~~kissed her~~ reasserted your dominance.
4. Colonists are ~~attractive~~ simple. Introduce new and difficult concepts by breaking them into small chunks or sequences of steps.
5. Colonists *can* learn. Reward obedience; punish failure.

Freddie folded the paper and shoved it in his pocket. He must have been more tired than he thought to have made so many errors. Not that these errors meant anything even resembling Selbourne's insinuations of the night before. They were slips of the pen, not indications that he was by any means or in any way, shape, or form *attracted* to the girl. Ridiculous. She was a colonist, for God's sake.

At least the revised strategy sounded promising. Now to begin . . . He glanced back at Charlotte, trying to determine whether he'd established himself as master this morning. She raised a brow at him, then nodded at the sideboard. "Are we to have guests for breakfast, sir, or is all of that food to feed you and me?"

Freddie turned to the sideboard, covered with meats, cheeses, pastries, and fruits. There did not appear to be any more food than usual, but perhaps she was hungry and afraid of eating too much. Come to think of it, he couldn't remember when he'd last seen her eat. "You are welcome to have as much as you like," he said, then remembered rule five. Would not food qualify as a reward? "You may have as much as you like," he repeated, then added, "after you have mastered the order of precedence."

At his words, the hand bringing the coffee cup to her mouth stilled. It hung suspended between the table and her lips for almost a full minute before she slowly lowered the cup to the table, setting it silently aside. "Lord Dewhurst, forgive me. I cannot have heard you correctly." Her tone was sweet as peaches in cream, but when her eyes locked with his, he could see the kindling of a spark. "Surely you do not intend to imply that I am to be treated no better than a dancing bear, denied food until I've performed to your satisfaction."

Freddie heard a snort behind him, and looked over his shoulder in time to catch the footman valiantly working to suppress a smile. He made a mental note to lecture the chit on etiquette before servants, but as he obviously could not trust her at present, he waved the servant aside. "Thank you, Andrews. You may see to your other duties." The footman straightened, gave a stiff bow, and disappeared through the servants' door Freddie turned back to his wife. Hadn't he made his mastery abundantly clear? Dashed typical that he was saddled with a slow learner.

"Miss Burton—eh, Lady Dewhurst, I should say. In a few days, you will appear in front of the most powerful men and women of the world in the role of my wife. But for a slip of paper, you are indeed my wife. You sleep in my house, you breathe my air, you will wear clothes I have furnished and eat food I will provide. I am but a little familiar with the laws of your American colonies, but here in civilization, when a woman marries, she and all she owns become the property of her husband."

At the words her hand clenched on the table and color rose in her cheeks.

"Therefore, in the eyes of this household, the *ton*, and everyone who truly matters, you are mine. My chattel, to do with and treat as I will. If I say you will not eat until you have mastered the curtsy, then you will not eat until you curtsy as well as the Queen. If I say you do not sleep until you can recite the names of every member of the House of Lords, then you will not sleep until each gentleman's name is as familiar to you as your own."

Her jaw was set now, but Freddie could tell he had finally captured her attention. After this, molding her to his will would be easy. He strolled to the chair where she sat, determined to ram home his last point.

"And if I tell you to fall on your knees and polish my boots, you will do it or suffer the consequences." He winced a bit at the last. That had come out harsher than he'd intended, but it was more important to show strength at first. He could always praise and reward her later. He peered down at her, momentarily disconcerted at the stubborn set of her jaw, then her face softened, and he saw he had won.

"I see," she said, voice low and thick. "So you will not cease until you have me on my knees before you?"

He had not said it exactly that way, but now that the image was there, he was not opposed to allowing it to linger: the colonist on her knees before him, her head bowed, red hair spilling down her shoulders. His hand itched to capture a fistful of those fiery tresses.

"Well then," she said, lifting her coffee cup. "If

that is the way it must be, you leave me but one choice."

His heart stuttered in his chest as she slid her chair back. Was she going to fall to her knees before him right now? Should he allow it? Could he refuse? He gripped the table, mesmerized then perplexed as she reached out and dumped the hot, wet remains of her coffee cup down the fall of his buff breeches.

Charlotte set the cup down and brushed her hands. That would teach the arrogant man to treat her like one of his dogs. Lord, but she'd thought they'd established who had the upper hand last night. Was she stuck with a dim-witted husband? The dimwit was looking decidedly stormy, so she rose to leave, just as Andrews opened the door and announced, "Lady Dewhurst and Miss Dewhurst."

Dewhurst froze, a napkin clutched to his nether regions, and Charlotte blinked as two creatures frothed in muslin, lace, and perfume swept into the dining room. Now what?

"Freddie!" The older woman's voice held a note of censure and familiarity. Her gaze swept over Dewhurst as though she expected to see him changed into a lunatic with wild hair and mad eyes. But when she saw Charlotte, the woman halted and gasped, and Charlotte realized she'd become the spectacle here in Bedlam. Charlotte glanced at her husband for guidance, but he only groaned. She studied him, then the woman, then Dewhurst again. Both were tall, blond, and far too full of themselves. Dewhurst was wearing a stiff cravat, fitted tailcoat, and tight breeches—now accessorized with one coffee stain and one linen napkin—and looked every bit the flamingo. The woman—surely his mother—wore a pearl gray morning gown, a starched pelisse, and a bonnet with more feathers than a peacock.

Finally Dewhurst moved, intercepting Charlotte's arm before she could escape. "Mother!" he said in a tone that sounded contrived, even to her inexpert ears. "How good to see you. Tea? Scone?"

She glared at him in stony silence.

He, undeterred, pressed onward. "Lydia. Charming as usual. Apple tart?"

"Freddie," his mother said again, "I think you owe me an explanation." Her attention wandered to the linen napkin he had clutched to his crotch, and she gave a quick, concerned glance at the young woman with her. Charlotte assumed it was Dewhurst's sister. Like her brother, she had chiseled aristocratic features, golden blond hair, and heavy-lidded eyes. Charlotte's gaze swept over the trio, and the sensation that she was an outsider was so strong it almost knocked her over. What was she—plain, lackluster, daughter of a retired sailor—doing here among these golden angels, who had but to think of a wish for it to come true?

"Lydia," the older woman said, with a disapproving look at Dewhurst's napkin. "Wait in the coach."

"But Mama!"

"Do not argue, young lady."

"Dash it," Dewhurst said, squeezing Charlotte's arm with the force of his exasperation. "Any further squabbling and I will send you both back to the coach."

That unified the women, who gave him identical scathing looks.

"Now sit down, have some dashed tea and a scone, and allow me to explain."

The two women moved stoically to the dining room chairs, apparently forgoing the offer of breakfast. Charlotte, however, was much more favorably inclined to Dewhurst's offer. She had yet to eat anything, and she might need the sustenance if she was going to survive this ordeal. While everyone else angled for the table, Charlotte veered toward the sideboard, only to be propelled in the opposite direction and forcibly assisted into the chair next to Dewhurst's. "I'm hungry. I don't want to sit down," she grumbled.

He bent down in the guise of assisting her with the chair. "And I didn't want coffee scalding my inexpressibles, so it appears neither of us is going to get what we want."

He took the seat beside her, then caught her hand in his before she could snatch it away.

"Mother, Lydia," he began. "I have a surprise for you." He squeezed her fingers, and she frowned at him. That elicited another squeeze, and a dark look from his otherwise sunny features. Did the man actually want her to smile and pretend all was well? Charlotte returned his black stare, adding a challenge in her eyes.

Still smiling, he said, "This is not how I imagined this moment, but I am glad you two are here." He nodded at his mother and sister. "I know this seems abrupt and a bit hasty, but who among us can harness the power of love? I want to introduce my wife, Charlotte. Mother, Lydia, Charlotte Burton, now Dewhurst. Charlotte, this is my mother, Lady Abigail Dewhurst, and my youngest sister, Lydia." He inclined his head at the women. "I know, given time, you will come to care for each other as much as you do me."

He squeezed Charlotte's hand again, his smile as tight as his grip. *Think of Cade and the thousand dollars,* Charlotte reminded herself and was able to force her mouth to turn up at the corners. A little. She could see that her effort did not please Dewhurst, but he ceased the death hold on her fingers.

Dewhurst's words rang in the silence of the room, and Charlotte looked across the table to see both women looking more like buzzards than the hummingbirds they'd twittered in as. She swallowed and tried to remember how to address these members of Dewhurst's family. "How lovely to meet you, Your Grace," Charlotte said, and Dewhurst squeezed her hand so tightly she almost cried out. "I mean, Your Lady"—squeeze—"ship."

Dewhurst's mother had a look on her face very much like the one her son had shown when she'd made the gaffe about the earlette last night, but finally the woman cleared her throat. "I am sorry, Freddie. I must be mistaken." She smiled, almost laughed. "For a moment I thought you referred to this bedraggled, homely woman as your wife."

Charlotte's jaw dropped, and Dewhurst jumped in before she could respond. "Ah, Mother, I've always said you have a keen sense of humor."

"I have no such thing. In fact, as soon as I heard the twaddle about a marriage, I came here to hear the denial." She crossed her arms. "I'm waiting."

Dewhurst clenched his jaw and, worse, his hand over hers. "Mother, I can't—"

"Freddie, I am waiting for your denial, and I do not intend to leave without it."

"I'm afraid you're a bit too late."

"Rubbish," Lady Dewhurst announced, rising and staring at her son across the table. "Give the chit some money and send her back to wherever she hails. I have overlooked your dalliances with trollops and lightskirts in the past, but this is beyond the pale."

"Trollop?" Charlotte said before Dewhurst could stop her. "How dare you call me a trollop?" Before meeting this foolish flamingo and his family, she had never—*never*—in her life been treated as anything less than a lady. Now, in the space of a couple of days, she'd been mistaken for Cade's mistress, kissed and insulted as though she were a common tavern doxy, and now outright called a whore by a woman who seemed to think Charlotte was as easy to be rid of as a stray cat.

"I'll have you know," Charlotte continued, "that my father comes from one of the oldest families in Charleston, and we don't cotton to being treated worse than river rats."

Beside her Dewhurst groaned and looked as though he might cry, but whatever the cause of his distress—increasingly, Charlotte was coming to believe she was the source of his pain—she had to give him credit for holding fast to her hand and their ruse.

Dewhurst's mother was staring at Charlotte, by all appearances speechless, but his sister Lydia said, "I simply adore your accent, Miss—?"

"Burton," Charlotte said at the same time Freddie interjected, "Lady Dewhurst." That slip earned her another painful squeeze.

Lydia ignored the obvious tension. "Where are you from? I would guess Scotland."

Charlotte frowned at her. George, did this girl really believe she was from Scotland?

"I think Charlotte hails from an area rather more west," her husband said in a pained voice.

"Wales?" Lydia said, her cerulean blue eyes blinking rapidly. "Ireland?"

"Now I understand why some animals eat their young," Freddie muttered. Lydia gave him a predatory glare, and Charlotte quickly stepped in.

"I'm from Charleston," Charlotte supplied.

Lady Dewhurst threw an alarmed look at her son. "Where is this Charles Town, Freddie?"

Freddie scowled and Charlotte scowled back at him. Had he really hoped to keep her nationality a secret? He might be ashamed of it, but she was more than happy to announce her birthplace from the highest church spire.

Dewhurst slumped slightly, looking resigned. "I'm afraid Charlotte hails from the colonies, madam."

His mother looked as though she'd been hit by a strong wind, and she toppled into a chair.

"Colonies?" Charlotte said tersely, ignoring the woman's labored breathing and Lydia's confused expression.

Her husband looked heavenward. "Forgive me, darling. Charlotte is from the state—the Americans do not call them colonies anymore—of South

Carolina. Or perhaps North Carolina?" He looked at her for clarification.

"Oh, dear, how many Carolinas are there?" his mother said placing her hands over her heaving bosom.

"Just two, I think."

Charlotte bristled. "There are eighteen *states* at present, and I will have you know South Carolina was the first state to ratify the Articles of Confederation."

Dewhurst's mother appeared not to have heard. She looked at Charlotte, then Freddie, and shook her head. "But—but what can you have been thinking of? Marrying a colonist? The last I heard, we were at war with the colonies!" She looked to her son for confirmation. He nodded.

Charlotte reached for the teapot and refilled her cup. If this woman did not stop insulting her soon, she'd find herself in the same predicament as her son. Only this time one linen napkin would not be enough to hide the damage.

But surprisingly, before Lady Dewhurst or her son could attempt to toss her out on her ear, Lydia spoke up. "Well, I for one think her accent is charming, whether she's from Wales or Ireland or even France." She rose, came around the table, and knelt beside Charlotte's chair. "You're Freddie's wife, and that makes you my sister."

Charlotte smiled. Perhaps the British were not all bad. After all, her own mother had been

British, so the species couldn't be completely evil. Of course, Katherine Burton had given up her country and her nationality when she'd married George Burton, but there was still this girl, who Charlotte could not deny was perfectly charming. Her husband, on the other hand, looked ready to throttle his sibling.

Lydia put her hand on Charlotte's arm. "Oh, but I've always wanted a sister!"

"Lydia," Dewhurst said in an exasperated tone she was coming to recognize. "You have three sisters."

The girl tossed her hair. "I know how many sisters I have. The problem is the one brother too many."

Charlotte covered her mouth to hide a smile, but she could understand why Dewhurst was losing patience. His sister was sweet but not the brightest firefly in the night.

"Oh, do let's try to stay focused," his mother interrupted. "What are we to do about this crisis?"

Charlotte bristled. Obviously her husband had learned his manners from his mother. "I am hardly a crisis, Lady Dewhurst."

Freddie closed his eyes, while his mother widened hers. "On the contrary, young lady, you are becoming more of a crisis each time you open your mouth. Freddie, how could you do this to me—to us? A colonist? I insist you rectify this situation."

Charlotte lifted the teacup with malicious intent, but Dewhurst pushed her wrist back down and snatched the cup from her grasp. He sat back in his chair, looking like a man used to feminine ultimatums. "What would you have me do, Mother?" he asked, absently turning a fork up and over. "Divorce her?"

The look of horror that crossed his mother's features would have been comic, if not for the fact that Charlotte could see the idea had not been a complete shock to the woman. "Divorce is rather extreme, do you not think? I meant to suggest a more palatable solution."

"Annulment?" Dewhurst said. He did not look surprised by the suggestion, and Charlotte wondered if he hadn't expected this. Not that he would need an annulment as they weren't actually married, but he must have considered that the suggestion would arise. Charlotte half hoped he would take it. The more she was around him and his kith, the more meager that one thousand dollars seemed.

"Annulment on what grounds?" Dewhurst asked. "We're both of age and there are no previous impediments."

"I see," his mother said. "Perhaps we might apply on the grounds that you could not—ah, perform? We could—"

Dewhurst rose. "Do not say it, Mother. Out of the question."

Charlotte exchanged a look with Lydia, who

appeared equally bewildered. "Could not perform what?" Charlotte asked.

"It is not a consideration," Dewhurst repeated.

"Freddie, what is that stain on your breeches?" Lydia asked.

"I poured coffee on him," Charlotte explained.

"Whatever for?"

"A small argument. He was getting too worked up."

Dewhurst's mother gasped, and Dewhurst said, "I was not. That is not what she means."

Charlotte snorted. "That is exactly what I mean. Lady Dewhurst, I'm sorry to say it, but your son has a very hard head."

The woman merely stared at her, mouth agape. Stubbornness was not a pleasant trait, but Charlotte did not think it would upset his mother quite so much. "What I mean is," she began, "that he thinks I will kneel before him whenever—"

"Enough!" Dewhurst roared just as the dining room door swung open again and Addy marched inside, trailed by an irate looking Wilkins.

"Miss Charlotte!" Addy hollered so loudly it caused Charlotte to flinch. "This here man is mighty confused, and I has had enough. Get your things. We is going home."

Charlotte rose. "But Addy—"

"That's right," Wilkins said. "Run away, you she-devil. That will teach you to dare touch my iron and cravat starch."

Addy rounded on the small, pale man, who skittered back a step. "I don't know what you is talking 'bout, and I don't care. That maid Hester is worthless, so I was forced into pressing Miss Charlotte's underthings. Her stays—"

"Addy! We have company," Charlotte said, grabbing Addy's hand. "This is Lord Dewhurst's mother and sister."

"Eek!" Wilkins stumbled backward. "Lady Dewhurst, Miss Dewhurst, I cannot begin to apologize enough. Please accept my humblest, my most fervent, my sincerest—"

"Oh, stubble it, Wilkins," Dewhurst muttered.

"My lord!" the valet cried. "What has happened to your breeches? You must remove them at once."

"Good idea, Wilkins." He grasped Charlotte's hand. "Come wife, you still have a lesson to learn."

Before she could argue, he yanked her out of the room, Wilkins and Addy followed, while his mother yelled, "Freddie, do not touch her. Remember you must prove impotent for the annulment!"

Chapter 7

Freddie plowed through the house, tugging Charlotte in his wake. "Wilkins," he barked at his valet, who was scampering up the stairs behind them. "I do not wish to be disturbed the rest of the afternoon. No." He stopped suddenly and Charlotte collided with him. "The rest of the week." He looked at his wife meaningfully. "We have work to do."

He might not relish spending even one more moment in his wife's company, but he needed her to capture Pettigru. There were worse assignments than squiring a colonist about and pretending to be smitten by her. He couldn't think of any at the moment, but he was certain there had to be worse.

"Work to do. Yes, my lord," Wilkins wheezed,

finally reaching the top of the stairs. "But we must change your clothes. If I do not see to that stain immediately—"

"Dash the bloody stain, Wilkins!" Freddie dragged Charlotte along the corridor until they reached his room, then he burst in, surprising a maid who was tidying the bed. "Out," he said, and she scurried past Wilkins, almost knocking the slight man over.

Charlotte wrenched her arm free of Freddie's hold. "That was certainly entertaining." As usual, her voice was dark and slow and damnably unperturbed. "What do you do for an encore?"

"I'll catch a spy." Color rose in her cheeks, but he cut her riposte short. "Stubble it," Freddie said, rounding on her, feeling more perturbed than he had in a long, long time. "If we made a scene in there, the fault lies with you, madam."

"Me? *Me?*" She put a hand over her breast as though she'd been stabbed. "First you insulted me, and then you allowed your mother to do the same. You are fortunate you escaped with merely a stain on your breeches."

"And you're fortunate I'm a gentleman and a patient one at that. Had you used even a modicum of the manners I spent hours attempting to drill into you yesterday, we wouldn't be in this position. Further, if your maid had any sense of civility—"

"Don't you dare bring Addy into this!" She shook her finger at him. "Blame me if you must. I expect nothing better from you, but no Southern gentleman—no American—would disgrace a lady so."

Freddie made a show of looking about the room. "Is there a lady present? I haven't seen her."

There was a gasp, and behind Charlotte Freddie saw Wilkins take a startled step back. Freddie glared at the valet, who retreated farther, and shut the bedroom door. Unfortunately, his wife had abandoned her position in the corner of the room and was now steadily advancing on him.

"No amount of money is worth this treatment! I want out of this so-called marriage and out of this godforsaken country as well."

Freddie shook his head, quelling his impulse to yell back at her. "Why do you hate us so much?"

"You killed my family!"

"Do you blame the whole country for the actions of a few?"

She looked away, and Freddie walked toward her, stopping a foot away. "I'm sorry for your loss, but I am not responsible. Hating me will get you nowhere."

"I don't hate you," she said, still not looking at him. "But I know your kind, and I don't like you, either."

Freddie raised a brow. "My kind? I'm a patriot, motivated by allegiance to my country, as are you. Are we truly so different?" He reached out and fingered a lock of her hair.

"Yes, we are different. You—you're a warrior. You won't stop until you win. My father was like you. He never listened to reason, never considered compromise. You call me prejudiced, but tell me honestly, is there any room for doubt in your mind that Cade is innocent?"

Now Freddie looked away.

"I play at being harder than I am, but how else am I to protect myself? I've lost everything. I have to harden my heart. It's all I have left. But you have everything. What are you so afraid of?"

He looked at her, alarmed that she seemed to see through him so easily.

"Why are you so unwilling to let your guard down? Afraid you might feel something more than disdain for a lowly colonist? Afraid all your pride and lofty words mean nothing when your heart is exposed?"

Freddie's chest tightened. She hadn't hit the target, but she was not far from her mark, either. What was it about her that unnerved him? Was it the unexplained thrill of opening his bedroom door to her the night before? The need to protect her from Society's barbs—a need he couched in lessons and lectures? Or was it the yearning to kiss her, to touch her that he felt every time they were in the same room? And what if he were to act on those needs? What then?

She scared the hell out of him. Defenses up, he struck back. "It would take more than you—a dowdy excuse for a woman—to expose *my* heart."

Freddie glanced at her just in time to see the blow coming. Years of training had honed his reflexes, and he caught her fist without thinking. The impact jarred him and stung his palm, but he had her. She tried to pull free, and there was a momentary tug-of-war, and when Freddie looked into her face her eyes were shooting angry sparks at him.

His hand stung. Someone had taught the colonist to throw a punch. Now he'd show her that her actions invited equal and opposite reactions. He'd show her that she was nothing more to him than a means to an end. Hand still wrapped firmly around her wrist, he yanked her to him. She tried to back away, but he held fast, then slipped one arm about her waist, pulling her close until she was flush against him and breathing hard.

"You can give it but you can't take it, is that it?" he said, his own breath coming in choppy bursts now as well. His flesh might be heated, but his heart was firmly shielded.

"I can take anything you bastard English throw at me. Or have you forgotten the War for Independence?"

His hand flexed on her waist, the threadbare bombazine hiding nothing of the sweet curve of her back and the swell of her hip. She was warm—as hot as the fire in her hair. And he could feel those silky tresses against his hand as well. Her hair had come free sometime during their skirmish, and now it tumbled down her back and teased the skin of his hand and arm. "So this is to be war between us?" he asked, his voice little more than a whisper.

"What else? Neither of us can forget what the other is," she retorted, but her rich voice was even lower now. Ragged and husky and full of sweltering days and sweaty nights.

"I'll make you forget. I'll make you surrender." He bent his head close to hers, brushing his lips against hers with just a hint of pressure. She inhaled sharply and tried unsuccessfully to pull away.

"Only if you surrender first."

"Never." And this time he did not check himself. He took her mouth with his in a relentless kiss. She gasped, and her body went rigid with shock, but he gave no quarter. He took her full, honey-thick lips, parted them, and swept inside her mouth, teasing her tongue with his own. And still she resisted.

But he'd brook no retreat. He pushed her to the limit, bending her body back, pressing her hard against him, and molding her mouth to his until she returned the kiss with a violence equal to his own. His adrenaline surged, and he was heady with the smell of victory. He possessed her now, and all talk of exposing his heart was ridiculous. It was she whose heart was in danger.

And then suddenly he was no longer restraining her. She moaned deep in her throat and ceased all resistance. His hands were wrapped in her hair, caressing the skin of her neck and cheek, and her own hands were like small, kneading paws against his chest. Pushing and caressing and demanding more of him. He gave it, kissed her with the passion and violence, and still she did not back down. Now she was pushing him, and he was not at all certain he wanted to let her any farther inside. But at the same time his mind resisted, his body ached for her.

He took a step back, moving toward the bed and taking her with him. He wanted her on the velvet counterpane, her hair spread out beneath her like a fiery halo, and her pale skin an enticing contrast to the scarlet fabric.

He angled directly for his bed, and she went willingly, not seeming to notice where she was or what he was doing. But he knew, and his mind sounded the cannon to cease the charge. He could not do this. He would not.

Her hand slipped inside his shirt, somehow finding the chink in his armor, and he drew in a sharp breath as flesh met flesh. Oh, dash it all to hell, he thought, bending to sweep her into his arms and thus onto the bed. And then she was beneath him, all softness and curves and her sweet feminine smell. He wanted to drive into her, to press his body even more intimately against her, to surrender to his need for her.

At the thought, a shock rippled through him, and he reared up, backing away from her. Slowly she opened eyes hazy with desire, and it took all he had to resist returning to her arms. She blinked, ran a tongue over her swollen lips, and then, thank God, he heard a pounding on the door.

He jumped up, and for the first time since they'd entered the bedroom, his mind was working.

"Alfred William Dewhurst!" his mother bellowed from the other side of the door. "Do not touch that woman! You are impotent, do you hear me? Impotent!"

Freddie looked at Charlotte—sprawled on the bed, her skirts ruched to her knees, her hair in wild disarray, her face flushed with passion—and for once he wished his mother were correct.

Charlotte opened her eyes and looked at Dewhurst. "We're not finished here," he promised, then crossed to the door, opened it, and stepped outside. Alone, Charlotte slumped back into the bed's mattress. Every muscle in her body was trembling and her heart was pounding so hard she was afraid it would break free. What had she been thinking? George, here she'd meant to assault his defenses. Instead he'd battered hers. What would she do if he broke through? What would be her fate if she began to feel for a man incapable of returning any of her sentiments?

She hated him, and yet she burned for him, too. How was that possible? Just like an Englishman, he had to make everything complicated.

Rising, she went to the door of the dressing room between their rooms, opened it, and stomped through, careful to lock her door when she closed it. "Ridiculous, preening flamingo!" she muttered. "I can't stand him or his peacock mother!"

"What you gots against birds, Miss Charlotte?" Addy asked, rising from the rocking chair near the far window of Charlotte's room.

"Birds? Nothing. Preening English aristocrats, however, are the bane of my existence." She flopped down on the bed, throwing one arm over her eye. "And the servants here! Hester never knocks before barging in, Mrs. Pots still hasn't shown me a menu, and the cook all but chased me out of the kitchen this morning!" Charlotte lowered the arm from her eyes. Addy was not coming to comfort her. Addy *always* came to comfort her. She looked around and found her maid still standing beside the rocking chair at the window. Charlotte propped herself up on her elbows. "What's wrong?"

Addy scowled out the window. "I gots problems of my own, Miss Charlotte. That man 'bout to drive me batty as a drunk pig."

Charlotte frowned, trying to remember if she'd ever seen a drunk pig.

"He walk around here like he own the place. Like he own the world."

Charlotte nodded. "He does, doesn't he? Ooh, his arrogance is so galling!" She sat up and clenched her fists.

"You ask me, it 'bout time he put back in his place. Who he think he is?"

"Who indeed? Vain flamingo!"

"Skinny-legged, pasty-faced fool!"

"What?" Charlotte said. "I actually thought his legs were rather nice."

"Nice?" Addy rounded on her, turning her back to the window. "They skinny as all get out. Like twigs."

Charlotte shook her head. Dewhurst's legs weren't at all like twigs. In fact, they were far too muscular, too finely toned and shaped for her comfort. And what was Addy doing looking at Dewhurst's legs anyway!

"And his manners leave a mighty something to be desired."

"Yes, they do."

"The way he done snatch that starch right out my hand this morning. Ooh, Miss Charlotte, if I weren't a lady, I'd have smacked the holy—"

"Addy! Wait a moment. Are you talking about Lord Dewhurst?"

Addy shook her head. "Please, Miss Charlotte.

That there man is your problem. And if I could trade you, I would. I like Mr. Dewhurst."

"Then who are you talking about? Wait. Are you still angry at Mr. Wilkins about the starch and iron?"

"Oh, now it be *just* starch and an iron. Hmpf. We'll see how you feel when there ain't no starch nor no iron to be had and your dress is limp as a—"

"Addy!" Charlotte held up her hand, not at all certain she wanted to hear the completion of that analogy. "I understand that you don't like Mr. Wilkins. He's . . . different, but we have to try and get along with these people while we're here. We have to make the best of a bad situation."

"I'm pleased as Punch to hear you say so."

Charlotte whipped around. Her husband was standing by the wall, arms crossed, lazy smile in place.

"How?"

Dewhurst stepped aside. "I have a key." He held up a shiny gold key, allowing it to dangle from his finger before opening his hand and making the key disappear.

"Parlor tricks, Alfred?" she said. "How quaint."

His smile grew lazier, if that were possible, and Charlotte's stomach fluttered with butterflies. "I knew you'd enjoy it, but don't expect me to pop over uninvited often"—he winked at her as though recalling her visit the night before—"I only came to tell you that Madam Vivienne, the best mantua maker in London—if my sister has the right of it—has been sent for. She should soon be on her way to outfit you."

Charlotte glanced at Addy, who sighed heavily. "I's going. I's going."

"Miss Addy." Dewhurst bowed as she passed him. "Always a pleasure, madam."

When she was gone, Charlotte turned back to Dewhurst. His green eyes, their color now softer, swept over her shabby dress. He had changed out of his stained clothing, and Charlotte could only blink at the rapid transformation. How did the man manage to go from scruffy to stylish so quickly?

Under his scrutiny, she suddenly felt more like a street urchin than a well-bred Charleston lady. Her dress was wrinkled and ill-fitting. Her hair had come loose and was streaming down her back. And though Dewhurst had been through the same ordeals as she this morning, her husband stood before her looking more the archangel than ever.

"My mother and sister will be here to see you through," her husband said. "I trust their choices and expect you to defer to their judgment in all matters. I want a full report when I return."

"Return?"

"I'll dine at my club tonight. If you refrain from assaulting my cook again, I'm certain he will make whatever you request."

"Assault? I merely asked the man if he had any lemon water."

Freddie waved a hand, dismissing her. He began to close the door behind him, but Charlotte pushed it open.

"You're leaving, sir?"

"As you see." He indicated his clothing, and Charlotte finally registered the reason for the quick change in his attire. He'd traded the soiled breeches for riding breeches, a charcoal tailcoat, and boots black as night. His hair, which she'd succeeded in loosening from its queue during their morning parlay, was once again restrained and tamed into some semblance of order. She frowned, thinking she liked the golden mass free and curling against his neck.

Much as she hated the English and their aristocratic ways, she could not deny that this man looked every inch a prince. More than his attire, his bearing suggested refinement and majesty.

And she was no princess. As high an opinion she'd had of her social dexterity, she knew now she was sorely outmatched when it came to London and its *ton*. She really did need Dewhurst and his stupid lectures if this ruse were to work. And she needed it to work. Perhaps that's what vexed her the most. Guilty or not, she would not abandon Cade to rot in an English prison or to stand trial for treason, and she would not give up her one thousand dollars. To give up the money would mean letting Addy down and returning to Charleston with nothing. She could not go back to the ruins of the life her father had left for her. She could not go back to those whispers and pitying smiles.

But if this—at this point she could only think of it as a madcap scheme—were to work, she would need more than a gaggle of feathered dresses. She'd need to survive in London Society until Cade came for her. For that, she'd need a husband. Or at least she'd need these people to believe Dewhurst was her husband, and that meant he had to appear to be in love with her, to want to be with her, to be so swept away with love that he *had* to have her, even though she was a—what had he called her?—an uncouth colonist.

Charlotte looked into Dewhurst's eyes and frowned.

He frowned back. "What?"

"I think it's better if you stay." Because of their charade, Charlotte reminded herself. Not because she cared what he did or who he saw. "Your running out to see your mistress or dine away from me does not smack of marriage."

He snorted. "Women's idea of marriage perhaps, not a man's."

She put her hands on her hips. "Oh, really? Well, perhaps that is the case for other husbands, but I won't tolerate it from mine."

He crossed his arms over his chest. "And I

won't tolerate a wife issuing me rules and orders. I'll spend my time how and where I want."

"And with whom," she said, narrowing her eyes.

"Correct."

Charlotte turned her back and shrugged. "Well, then I see no real reason to see this Madam Vivienne. If you can't be bothered to spend one day at home with your wife—the wife you fell madly in love with and married, even though she's naught but an uncouth colonist—then what I wear won't matter. No one will believe this marriage were I dressed like a queen."

Silence. Charlotte glanced over her shoulder at Dewhurst. "That is the story you and your poetic cousin concocted, is it not?"

He glared at her, his eyes sharp and hard like emeralds now. She raised a brow, and his look darkened. "I see what you're trying to do, Charlotte, and it won't work."

"What I'm trying to do?" she said. "I'm trying to save my friend and ensure my one thousand dollars."

"It's one thousand *pounds*. And that's your only objective?"

"Of course. What else?" She stared at him, saw the way he scrutinized her, and couldn't help but let out a loud laugh. "Oh, heavens. What were you thinking, Alfred? That my pleas for your presence at home were a ploy to get you to fall in love with me? To capture your heart and your title in truth?"

He didn't respond, but she saw the faintest flicker of affirmation in those emerald eyes. Good. She'd set him straight. Set herself straight as well.

"Allow me to let you in on one tiny, little secret." She sashayed up to him in her best imitation of a Southern belle. "Believe it or not—and I'm sure you do not—I am not interested in your heart or your title." She reached up and traced a finger along the stiff cravat knotted at his throat. "I am not interested in London or your *ton* or all your silly rules. What I am interested in, sir, is my friend Cade Pettigru and getting back to Charleston. I am interested in the one thousand dollars you owe me, and I intend to be paid."

He stared at her, face hard and expressionless as she wound two fingers around the cravat's knot, circling it tightly.

"So you go out to your clubs and your women and your fancy society, but I will get what I want—one way or another." She released his cravat and turned to sashay away, but Dewhurst gripped her shoulder and spun her round.

"You're playing a dangerous game, Charlotte," he growled. "One you don't know the rules to and against an opponent you've sorely misjudged. I don't play to lose."

She looked him straight in the eye. "Nor do I, sir."

He nodded. "Very well. Let the games begin."

She smiled. "Oh, they already have." He released her shoulder and turned back to the dressing room door. "Oh, and Mr. Dewhurst"—she neglected his title deliberately—"if I'm to be sleeping so close to you at night, I really must insist on owning the key for this door. If you would please hand it over, I would be much obliged to you, sir."

He stopped mid-stride and looked back at her. "And I would be obliged if you would call me *Lord* Dewhurst, but we can't all get what we want, can we, Charlotte?"

And he slammed the door.

Chapter 8

Charlotte would have laughed if Dewhurst hadn't made her so angry. As though a pampered British aristocrat could even conceive of the notion of not getting what he wanted.

She had not been born into a wealthy family, but her father and mother had worked hard and improved their position until they were one of the well-to-do families in Charleston. Charlotte's mother had been from an aristocratic British family and was the niece of a former governor of Georgia. When she'd married Charlotte's father, they'd taken her small dowry, invested it, and built from there. By the time Charlotte was born, their wealth—all new money, which in Charleston was not the same as old money and never would be—had gained them an entrée into some of the best circles. From all accounts, life for the Burtons had been perfect.

And then the first of the cracks in their porcelain life had appeared. Charlotte had been too young to remember the illness that took her mother. She remembered only snatches of her—her voice, her smell, her laugh. As expected, her father took the loss of his wife hard, but his remedy had been to throw himself into his work. Burton & Son Shipping grew and became one of the most successful companies in South Carolina. When Charlotte had come out at sixteen, she'd done so in the company of young women from the best families. And she had not disappointed. She had glittered and dazzled like the best of them.

And then the porcelain had cracked again.

Her father, whom she had loved more than anything—excepting her brother, Thomas—had begun coming home drunk or not at all. And then one night Cade Pettigru had pounded on her door in the middle of the night. She'd thrown on a wrapper and ushered him into the parlor. His face had been ashen and his eyes dark and haunted.

"What is it?" she said, coming to sit beside him on the settee. "Is it Thomas?"

He shook his head. "No," he said gruffly. "It's—let's have a drink first, Charlotte. Do you have any brandy?"

She gave him a surprised look but rose to fetch it. Thomas was away on one of the company ships, a routine trading run to New York that was scheduled to return late next week.

"Pour yourself a glass as well," Cade said from behind her, and a flood of fear swelled and threatened to overwhelm her. She did as he asked, and when she was again seated beside him, took a slow, measured sip, trying to hide the growing trembling in her fingers.

"It's not Thomas," he'd said, after draining his glass. "It's your father. Charlotte, I just came from Adelaide Cooper's."

Adelaide Cooper was the proprietor of a whorehouse and casino in town. Charlotte knew her father often gambled there. Cade loosened his neck cloth and looked down at the empty glass in his hands. Without a word, Charlotte went to refill it. When he'd warmed the liquid between both hands again, he said, "He's lost it, Charlotte."

Charlotte inhaled sharply. "What does that mean, Cade? Lost what?"

Cade sighed heavily, putting his head in his hands. "The business, Charlotte. Perhaps the house by now as well."

Charlotte stared at him. His words made no sense to her. She understood them, but it didn't seem possible that her father—the man who'd caught her effortlessly to prevent her childhood falls, the man who'd danced with her at her debut, the man who'd always left a lamp burning during thunderstorms because he knew without being told that they terrified her—that man had let her down. That man had let them all down.

The remainder of the night was mostly a blur to Charlotte. She'd blocked out much of it because she did not want to remember the things she'd seen. She'd gone to Adelaide Cooper's and helped Cade drag her father home, and then she'd sat up all night and most the rest of the day, nursing his overindulgence in play, women, and drink. And when he'd finally sobered up, she'd held him while he cried and apologized and begged her forgiveness.

She'd little time for apologies. Charlotte had gone to the shipping offices and began to put things in order. By the time Thomas had returned, she'd liquidated all the assets her father hadn't lost and convinced several of her father's good friends to loan her money. But no matter how much she and Thomas pleaded, the men her father owed would not accept substitutions for what they'd won. Half of the business—her father's half—went to Beauford Porcher, one of her father's competitors in the shipping industry, and her brother retained control of his own fifty-one percent only through sheer force of will. They held on to the house because Cade's family owned the bank and was willing to overlook a few missed payments on the mortgage, but Charlotte had had to sell almost everything of value to salvage the family share of the shipping business.

In the end it had been sheer desperation and shame that drove her father and brother to attempt to run the British blockade with smuggled goods. If they'd succeeded, the profits might have been enough to restore the family to something of its former standing—monetarily, if not socially—but their failure and death had been a worse blow than any measure of poverty she'd ever had to endure.

After her father's death, Charlotte had made a last effort to salvage the family business. She'd gone to Porcher and told him she had several investors abroad interested, and if he gave her perhaps six months, she'd have the funds to buy back what her father had lost.

Porcher was no fool, and he said immediately, "You thinking of Cade Pettigru. Is that it?"

Taken off-guard, she'd nodded.

Porcher had sat back, lit one of his long, sweet cigars, and said, "Do you know where he is? Do you even know if he has any money?"

"You leave that to me, Mr. Porcher," Charlotte had said. "All I want from you is your word that if I return with the money, you'll sell my father's share of the business for what it's worth."

He was silent for a long moment—long enough for Charlotte to hear the creek of the cedar boards in the grand house and the call of a pine warbler, and smell the light fragrance of a magnolia tree—then he said, "I've always liked you,

Miss Burton. You take after your mother, and she was a fine lady, even if she lacked taste in her choice of partner. Further, Eliza Lou has always been partial to you."

He gestured at the French doors with his cigar, and Charlotte glanced out to see his daughter walking the grounds with a cluster of her friends, their parasols brushing against the profusion of roses twined among the wrought-iron gates.

Porcher smiled and added, "I myself have always been partial to you as well. You have spunk, Miss Burton. And that's a quality we need if this country is going to stand on its own two feet. The British haven't beaten us yet, and if the next generation has as much spunk as you, the damned redcoats never will."

Charlotte had smiled and gone away with assurances that, were she to return with ample funds, Beauford Porcher would sell her the Burton business back. She had no such assurances that Cade would be able to help; regardless, she and Addy had packed their meager belongings and set off for England.

Charlotte blinked and registered the gray, foggy view from Dewhurst's window. And now she was here: the London town house of a British aristocrat. One thousand dollars. Was it enough to endure the next few hours with Dewhurst's family and friends? Enough to endure Dewhurst himself for God knew how long?

Her thoughts were interrupted by a sharp rap on her bedroom door, which promptly swung open, admitting Lady Dewhurst, Lydia, and a petite, fine-boned woman with dark hair and exotic eyes.

"Here she is!" Dewhurst's mother said when Charlotte turned from the window.

"*Mon dieu!*" the dark-haired woman exclaimed. She paused to look Charlotte up and down. "*C'est terrible*. You said is to be much work, but this . . ." She gestured feebly at Charlotte.

Charlotte's first impulse was to tell the Frenchwoman where she could put her opinions, but she held her tongue, and was surprised to see Lydia Dewhurst step forward.

"Well, Madam Vivienne," Lydia said, appearing to admire her tan kid leather gloves, "we called on you because everyone who is anyone says you outfit all the incomparables. But if this is too much for you, we can call on Madam Bichon. I am certain *she* can work wonders."

The Frenchwoman's eyes grew small and slitted, and Charlotte decided that Madam Bichon and Madam Vivienne were perhaps not the best of friends. Not only that, but Lydia Dewhurst was not as insipid as she might first appear.

"*Attente.*" Madam Vivienne raised a hand. "I have not said I cannot outfit the pretty mademoiselle. She has—*ce qui est le mot*—many attributes. Not the hair. Not the skin. But the figure *c'est trés bon*. You wait. I will make her into *un diamant*." Then she added more quietly, "I do much better than *la chienne*—Madam Bichon."

Charlotte wasn't certain whether she should be pleased or insulted—pleased that Madam Vivienne could make her into a diamond but insulted that the woman thought the task so difficult. Charlotte's French was elementary, so she could not follow a great part of the discussion that ensued as the three women conversed in a jumble of French and English. It appeared, however, that they were discussing what colors, fabrics, and styles would suit her. Charlotte's attention went from Lady Dewhurst to Lydia to Madam Vivienne and back again while the women debated, conjectured, and suggested. Apparently, Charlotte's own opinion was not needed.

A few moments later, she was hustled onto a padded, satin footstool that seemed to have appeared with Madam Vivienne. There she was stripped to her plain petticoat, turned this way and that, measured, prodded, and poked with fingers and elbows and pins. Madam Vivienne was a virtual whirlwind, everywhere at once and with hands to spare. She always had a measuring tape, pins, a bolt of material, and a sketchbook and pencil at the ready.

When Charlotte's legs began to tire and the muscles of her arm ached from holding them extended, she ventured to inquire—very politely, she thought—whether they might soon be finished. She was quickly set to rights on that account.

"Charlotte!" Lydia exclaimed. "We've only just begun. We've measured you for opera dresses, theater dresses, and evening dresses—"

"*Non, non!*" Madam Vivienne said. "Keep the hands out. *Comme ceci.*" She extended her arms again, and Charlotte sighed.

"But why do I need theater dresses and opera dresses?" Charlotte said. "Won't the same dress work for both?"

All three women stared at her for a moment, uncomprehending.

"Well?" Charlotte demanded.

"Actually," Lady Dewhurst said, "We were to cover dinner dresses next."

Madam Vivienne jabbed Charlotte with another pin, and Charlotte sighed in resignation. An hour later, she'd been fitted for not only the dinner and opera dresses, but morning dresses and carriage dresses, walking dresses and riding dresses, promenade dresses and garden dresses. Her eyes were glazed over with talk of muslins and silks, when she looked up and spotted Dewhurst lounging, shoulder jammed against the far wall of her room.

She shrieked and dropped her arms to cover her thin petticoat. Madam Vivienne, startled by Charlotte's outburst, jumped as well, sticking Charlotte in the arm with a pin. Charlotte jumped again, this time in pain, then pointed to Dewhurst. "What are you doing here?" she screamed. Then, looking at Lydia, "Why is *he* here?"

Lydia glanced at her brother and gave a delicate shrug. "Oh, he doesn't trust anyone's taste but his own. You're not needed here, Freddie," she called to him. "We are almost done."

"We are?" Charlotte was momentarily relieved, then remembered Dewhurst. "Sir, I must insist you leave. I am not fully dressed."

Dewhurst gave her petticoat his infamous lazy smile. "Nothing I haven't seen before, my dear."

Charlotte felt herself blush from the roots of her hair to the bottom of her feet. Even her toes were bright pink when she stared down at them. She would have flown from her perch and donned a dressing gown, a curtain, anything . . . but Madam Vivienne held her hostage with pins, tapes, and laces.

"In any case," her husband said, "I *am* needed here. You can't possibly think to dress her in that blue or that green. Those colors suit Lydia's complexion, but will do nothing for Charlotte."

"Freddie—" his mother began.

"No!" Madam Vivienne poked her head out from behind Charlotte. "Listen to this man. He knows of what he speaks. Monsieur, this is what I was saying. Put her in the russet or the gold. Copper, too, will bring out her coloring."

"Exactly so." He circled her, seeming to study her from every angle. She blushed even harder, her skin so hot that she felt that she might burst into flame. "Those colors will do well for evening, but I'm thinking yellow and peach for morning. Perhaps burgundy for a riding habit. No blue," he said decisively, stopping in front of her and cocking his head to the side. "Blue will do nothing for that cinnamon hair and those sherry eyes. Keep her in dark, brazen colors. Those will suit her best."

There was silence in the room as everyone stared at him. Charlotte's jaw was hanging open, but she was too surprised to shut it. She had cinnamon hair and sherry-colored eyes? She would look best in dark, brazen colors? George Washington, but he was making her sound like some sort of temptress! She wanted to be offended. She wanted—once again—to slap him hard across the face until that lazy smile was permanently removed. Instead she found herself strangely flattered. He thought she was bold and dramatic. A temptress.

Then she remembered where she was and her state of dress—or rather, undress—and she tensed again.

The silence was finally broken by Madam Vivienne. Beaming, she danced out from behind the footstool, her little feet flying like bumblebees. *"Oui! Oui, monsieur! Exactement!"* She looked up at Charlotte with new admiration. "*Votre mari est si à la mode. Entre nous,* you are *une femme chanceuse.*"

Charlotte's gaze met Dewhurst's, then he turned and strode to the dressing room door. He paused, winked at her, and was gone.

Freddie closed the door to the dressing room and almost collapsed against it. It had been a mistake to enter Charlotte's room, a mistake to risk seeing her in a state of dishabille. He'd thought he was safe. His mother and sister were in the room with Charlotte, dash it. But the pope could have been in attendance and it would not have tempered Freddie's arousal at the sight of her in a paper-thin petticoat and nothing else.

He'd seen many women undressed. He'd seen many beautiful women undressed, but he'd never experienced such a jolt of arousal as he had upon entering Charlotte's room. She stood on a white pedestal, a lick of fire rising out of a cool winter snowbank. The room's froth of white decor surrounding Charlotte had served as a cold contrast to the warmth of her peachy skin and the cherry spill of her hair. Arms outstretched, eyes slightly closed, lips parted, she was the most innocently sensual creature he'd ever seen.

And that was before his eyes had fallen on her generous curves, the sweeping, lush landscape of her body. The mourning dress she'd been wearing had been more ill-fitting than he'd realized. It hid the creamy slope of her breasts, rising above the rounded neckline of her petticoat. It hid the small circle of her waist and the proud jutting of her hips. The petticoat was tattered and old and undeniably alluring. It was so thin he could see the shape of her legs through the material, and if his eyes—already dazed by the assets displayed before him—were not mistaken, her legs were long and round, tapering into a sweet derriere.

Dash it, but if he did not remove the image of his half-naked wife from his head soon, he might end up married in truth.

He should have gone to his club. He should never have listened to a foolish American who knew nothing of the inner workings of the *ton.* And he would have gone—if her reasoning hadn't made so much sense. How many times had he seen a newly betrothed couple at a ball or dinner party and known the match was at the wish of their parents? How often had he watched married couples at the theater, sitting next to each other and yet virtual strangers?

That would not do for him. If the story of their marriage was to be believed, Freddie could afford no doubt, no question as to his affections for Charlotte. And yet somehow he had to keep those affections a ruse. He had to keep his emotions toward her in check. Already he thought of her too often. Reacted to her too intensely.

He needed to temper all of it, regain control of himself, and play his part to the hilt. He would make Society believe his unlikely match was genuine. The gossips and social commentators would talk loudly and freely of the stylish baron and the fiery American. And then Pettigru would find her. The spy would not slip through Freddie's fingers again. He would have the man, and he'd do whatever it took to catch him.

Chapter 9

Charlotte smiled when she learned that Dewhurst had decided to change his plans and spend the evening at home. So he would not be visiting his mistress after all.

It had been a long time since she'd thought of dressing for dinner. For the past few years she'd mainly been concerned if there was to be any dinner, but fortunately Madam Vivienne had left several gowns behind to hold Charlotte over until her own gowns were made.

Charlotte pulled several dresses from the armoire and tried to remember which were which. She discarded a pretty muslin frock as a day dress and a heavy gown with as much embellishment as a ball gown, and that left her one choice.

The gown had obviously been made for an

older woman and was, Madam Vivienne assured her, only a temporary selection as Lord Dewhurst had not seemed to think she would shine in green. But Lady Dewhurst had called her son's pronouncements nonsense. Her one concern with the gown was that the vibrant green-colored crepe over the ivory satin slip was too matronly.

Charlotte thought an objection to the neckline might be more appropriate, but when she'd slipped the gown on for a few alterations, no objection had been forthcoming. Now, with Addy's help, Charlotte donned the gown again, then went to the mirror to observe the effect. The neck was still objectionable—round and low, the mantua maker having explained that the current style was to show as much of the bosom as possible—but the sleeves were full and slashed. Charlotte liked the sleeves and only wished that some of the overabundance of material gathered there had been used to form the bodice.

Looking in the mirror, she pulled the dress higher in an effort to keep her breasts from spilling out, then adjusted her mother's emerald necklace, which actually looked nice, set off by the color of the dress. Addy came to stand behind her, shaking her head and pursing her lips. "That dress ain't proper, Miss Charlotte. How you going to go around showing so much flesh? You be put in jail for a loose woman."

Charlotte frowned in the mirror. "First of all, Addy, I won't be out and about in the city. I'm having dinner downstairs with Dewhurst. Secondly," she said as she settled behind the dressing table and handed Addy a brush and several hairpins, "I am supposed to be a married woman. Married women are allowed more liberty in their dress than unmarried women. Lastly, if you had been paying any attention to the conversation between the Dewhursts and Madam Vivienne, you would know—ow!" Charlotte put a hand to her stinging scalp, where Addy had just ripped through a particularly vicious tangle.

"Oh, sorry, Miss Charlotte. I forgets you're such a tenderhead."

Tenderhead, my foot, Charlotte thought. Even a woman in a wig would have protested at that harsh treatment. It had been some time since she and Addy had engaged in this ritual. Hairdressing had seemed unimportant when they were faced with so many other obstacles in their daily lives, but Charlotte had no doubt Addy, who had been dressing hair for longer than Charlotte had been alive, had not slipped with her hairbrush.

"As I was saying," Charlotte continued when she'd blinked away the tears and the burning in her scalp had receded to mere smoldering, "you would know that ladies in London have different standards and styles of dress. What is fashionable, even appropriate here, is not necessarily what we in Charleston would consider appropriate. But when in Rome . . ."

Addy snorted. "We ain't in Rome, Miss Charlotte. But we ain't in Charleston no more neither."

"Addy, I have to try and fit in here. This is what the upper-class ladies in London wear."

"It ain't right."

Charlotte didn't answer. It was all well and good to dress the part of a fine lady, but she wanted to show Dewhurst and all his snobbish friends that her blood ran as blue as theirs. As yet, she'd few encounters with the loftier class, but the sketches and styles Madam Vivienne had shown her had been eye-opening. From what Charlotte could tell, the ladies went about the city practically naked, the cuts of their dresses so low that the necklines provided no cover for their often abundant bosoms. The fashionable materials were light and clingy, leaving absolutely nothing to the imagination. On top of this, apparently most ladies wore only a thin wrap or none at all. Charlotte did not see how they could stand it in such a cold, damp climate.

Looking at Dewhurst and his male servants, Charlotte had ascertained that the male fashions were just as bad—pantaloons so tight the men could barely walk and certainly not bend over, cravats and stocks starched as stiffly as a chaperone's spine, and colors so glaring and mismatched that Charlotte could do little but gawk.

Addy continued to sweep Charlotte's hair into a simple style, and Charlotte stared unseeing into the mirror and sighed. There was nothing for it. It was she who had coaxed the reluctant Addy into coming to Europe, she who'd been the one to go without in order to scrape together the funds, and she who had made this deal with Dewhurst even the devil would think twice before accepting.

She was well and truly mired in a quicksand of her own making, and she'd only sink deeper if she couldn't make this work. She needed that one thousand dollars. Addy stuck the last pin in Charlotte's hair, stepped back, and said, "Oh, my."

"What is it?" Charlotte glanced at herself in the mirror and then stared.

"Oh, my," Addy said again. "I always knew you looked like her, but I never seen the resemblance so strong."

Charlotte nodded, her voice having deserted her as she stared at her own reflection—a reflection that looked so much like the portrait of her mother that had hung over the mantel of their house in Charleston that Charlotte thought for a moment that she was actually looking at that painting. She took a deep breath, and her gaze met Addy's.

Addy's eyes were cloudy and watery with tears. Addy had been Katherine Burton's maid and confidante long before Charlotte had even been born, and Charlotte knew Addy still mourned Katherine Burton's passing. Charlotte could only imagine the despair she would feel if she lost Addy, who was practically the only mother she could remember, and she saw the pain and loss reflected in Addy's weathered face in the mirror.

Charlotte wished there was something she could do to comfort her friend, but she couldn't bring her mother back any more than she could have stopped her father from gambling away his portion of the business or convinced Thomas that the benefits of running the British blockade were not worth the risks. But through it all, she'd kept the family together, then taken care of herself and Addy, and she would take on the whole of London if that's what it took to restore her life to even a shadow of what it had been.

"Addy," Charlotte said, reaching back and taking her friend's hand. "We're going to get back. Just you wait. We'll sail home in style, march into Porcher's library, slap Dewhurst's money on his desk, and buy back what was always ours. The business, the house, everything. Before you know it, we'll be back on top of the world. Just give me a week or so." Charlotte rose and straightened her skirts. "I'll get these British titles and rules down if they kill me. You'll see. Proper English lady." She shook her head. "How hard can it be?"

She walked to the door, threw her shoulders back, and started for the dining room. As the door closed behind her she thought she heard Addy murmur, "Lord help us now."

Freddie had paced the dining room from top to bottom exactly seventeen times, when Charlotte threw open the door and stumbled breathlessly inside. He paused mid-stride, a scathing reproach on his tongue for her tardiness, but one look at her and his voice failed him.

She caught his eye and straightened immediately, brushing a strand of her hair back into place. "Please forgive my late arrival, Lord Dewhurst."

Freddie raised a brow. She was using his title.

"I'm afraid I got a bit turned around and ended up in the library. But no need to worry. Andrews found me and showed me the way."

Freddie glanced at the footman holding the door, then looked back at Charlotte.

And looked.

"What?" Charlotte said, turning to glance first at Andrews and then down at her gown as if there were some defect. "What have I done now?"

Freddie wished she had done something wrong. How the devil was he supposed to wrest control of his emotions if she kept surprising him? First the tantalizing view of her fitting with Madam Vivienne. Now the sight of her in all her glory.

Freddie wished her gown was ugly or prim or a

yard too big. He wished he hadn't a very good idea of what the gown concealed. As it was, the emerald gown highlighted all her assets and hid her flaws—if there were any. The gown was cut so that he had an excellent impression of her figure, and he had yet to find an imperfection in her lush form. If anything, she was too perfect—too much the epitome of the women he always found himself drawn to.

There was the hair—that cinnamon color sprinkled with gold and dancing in the candlelight. There was her roses-and-cream complexion—offset to perfection by the lustrous green satin of the gown. Finally there were her eyes—dark and warm, like a good sherry. He followed a loose curl of her hair down her cheek, past her rosy lips, down her almost-bare shoulder, past the small cut emerald she wore at her neck, and rested his gaze on the swell of her breasts, rising like ripe half moons from the low-cut bodice of the gown. He allowed his attentions to drift lower, over the folds of the gown, draped so that they hinted at the lush treasure beneath.

Freddie took a long, deep breath. "You've done nothing wrong," he said, his voice sounding low and gravelly in his ears. "You look—" Words failed him momentarily. She looked alluring, sensual, like a ripe fruit begging to be peeled and savored. He had to remember her association with

Pettigru. She was the enemy, and her allure was part of her armory. "You look . . . appropriate," he finally managed.

Her eyebrows came together. "Appropriate? How generous."

Freddie nodded at the chair at the far end of the table. "Please, be seated."

Andrews moved to pull out the chair for her, but Freddie waved him away. Instead he himself slid her chair out with a flourish and made a sweeping bow. "Your servant, my lady."

She raised a brow but took the proffered seat, and he took the opportunity to walk behind her, running a hand over the curve of her chair so that his fingers slid against the silk sweep of her hair. He paused to take in the enticing view of her décolletage his vantage point offered, then proceeded to his seat.

Dawson, his butler, was waiting, and as soon as Freddie's fingers touched the chair, the footmen with the first course appeared. As was the custom, the soup tureen was placed before Charlotte, and the fish—a large eel tonight—was set before him.

The footmen stepped back, and Charlotte gazed down at the tureen with a perplexed look. Freddie was sorely tempted to issue instructions for ladling the soup, but he kept quiet. Once in Society, he would not always be present to smooth her way. Better if she learned now to rely on her own wits. Charlotte lifted the top of the tureen and sniffed. "What is this?" she asked, making a face. Freddie prayed her grimace would not be relayed back to Julian, his cook.

Freddie lifted the carving knife and sliced into the eel. "Soup," he answered. He placed a portion of eel on one of the Wedgwood china plates and handed it to the footman to carry down the table to Charlotte. She sniffed the soup again.

"As your housekeeper ignores every request I make to see the day's menu, can you enlighten me as to what kind of soup?"

Freddie hadn't bothered to look at the menu, so he glanced at Dawson for assistance. Dawson cleared his throat and said in an authoritative voice. "The soup tonight is *la garbure aux choux.*"

Charlotte nodded. "I see. Sounds delicious."

To Freddie's relief, she lifted the ladle and began spooning the broth into a bowl. The footman placed her slice of eel before her and took the bowl of soup to deliver to Freddie. He smiled. Perhaps the chit was not hopeless after all. She waited until he lifted his soup spoon before sampling her own, and as Freddie brought the first sip to his lips, he closed his eyes and inhaled.

"Hellfire and damnation! Cabbage!"

Freddie jumped, dropped his spoon, and soup splattered all over the fine tablecloth, the rug on the floor, and his waistcoat, shirt, and breeches.

Dash it! Wilkins was still in a pet about the soiled breeches from breakfast. How was Freddie going to show him this mess?

"Yech. Yech. Yech." Charlotte had her napkin to her mouth, her complexion almost as green as the broth.

"What is the matter?" Freddie yelled and immediately swore under his breath. He was supposed to be in control. He was the master. "Swearing like a sailor is not appropriate behavior."

Charlotte dropped the napkin and downed her wine instead. Freddie raised his brows. That was expensive French burgundy—hard to come by with the war on.

"I'm sorry," she gasped after finishing off the wine. "You didn't mention cabbage. I have a violent reaction to cabbage."

Freddie shut his eyes and prayed for patience. "That is what *aux choux* means. With cabbage."

Charlotte shook her head. "I don't speak French."

The footmen had moved in to remove the soup bowl and spoon as well as dab away some of the residue from his clothing. Freddie brushed the napkin Andrews wielded away from his ruined waistcoat. "No French? Not even a rudimentary understanding?"

Freddie felt his stomach heave, much as it did whenever he boarded a ship. Everyone in the *ton* knew French. Whole conversations were often held in French, and many of his favorite bon mots were impossible to appreciate without a thorough understanding of both languages. This disastrous turn of events he had not foreseen. There was no means to hide her lack of the language from those who came into even casual contact with her.

Freddie rubbed the bridge of his nose. His head had been steadily drumming since he'd met this Yankee chit, and he had a feeling relief was not in sight. What could he do? Could he teach her French in the space of a few days?

He thought about the precedency fiasco and discarded that idea. Perhaps they could pretend she was deaf. Or maybe he could tell everyone she was insane and locked up in his attic. Hmm. Now that idea had some merit.

"Of course I have a rudimentary understanding of the language," Charlotte said, interrupting his thoughts.

Freddie brightened. Thank the Maker. All was not lost.

"I know *oui*, *merci*, and *arrivederci*."

Freddie groaned aloud. Dash it all to hell. He was doomed.

"Now what's the matter?" Charlotte demanded, and Freddie noted with unease that she poked the eel uncertainly as she said it.

"*Arrivederci* is not French," Freddie mumbled. "It's—what in blazes are you doing to that fish?"

She stopped poking it and looked up at him. "I'm poking it. It seems . . . slimy."

"It's not slimy. It's sauced, and it's delicious, so stop poking it and eat it."

She frowned. "What type of fish is it? I haven't seen a fish like this before."

Freddie speared a portion and put it in his mouth. He savored it and swallowed. "It's eel."

"Eel!" Charlotte pushed the plate away with a force so strong it almost toppled to the floor. The ever-adept Andrews caught it and whisked it away.

"On the contrary, it's quite good, as you would find for yourself if you would eat it instead of throwing it on the floor," Freddie ground out.

"How many courses remain?" she said dubiously.

"Not many," Freddie said, then mumbled, "And at this rate, we may never eat again."

Julian would not be pleased to see so many of his dishes returned untouched. Freddie would have to pay the cook handsomely to keep him from leaving. Not only were the servants going to be unhappy, but Freddie himself was in dire jeopardy of losing yet another training session. He had to remember rule four: colonists are simple. Perhaps he had overwhelmed her with table manners. Should he break the lesson into smaller, more digestible portions?

Freddie speared another bite of his eel, but he could not enjoy it with Charlotte staring at him, lip curled, from the top of the table. Finally he waved at the footmen to take the eel away and bring the next course. As soon as he saw it, Freddie gritted his teeth, reached out, and intercepted the footman carrying the calf's head to Charlotte's end of the table.

"Andrews, I'll do the honors tonight," Freddie said. He'd seen some women balk at carving a calf's head, and he was taking no chances.

"What is it now?" Charlotte asked, and Freddie was relieved the table was long and covered with enough flower arrangements, wines, pots, platters, and sauceboats to obscure the calf's head.

"It's beef," Freddie answered, cutting into it. "You do eat beef?"

Charlotte sipped her wine again, and Freddie noted that, though she only sipped this time, she appeared not to realize her glass was refilled each time she drank. He continued carving, giving her the best, most delicate parts. Andrews took her plate away, and Freddie began carving his own portion. A gasp from the end of the table jolted him, causing his hand to slip and cut a finger.

"Dash it! Now what?" Freddie yelled, standing up and clutching his napkin to his bleeding finger.

"There's an eye in my food," Charlotte said, standing with hands fisted. Her face was ghastly white now.

"It's a calf eye. A bloody delicacy, you daft woman!"

Charlotte threw her napkin on the table. "Me, daft? You're the one serving eel and calf eyes and—" She poked at the other item on her plate.

"Neck," Freddie said and watched her sway. He started toward her, but she gripped the back of her chair and seemed to recover. Mumbling something unintelligible, she turned on her heel and marched past Dawson.

"Madam," Dawson began, but she shot him a glare, then opened the door behind him, striding straight into the butler's pantry. Freddie put his uninjured hand over his eyes and shook his head.

"My lord, do you think she'll realize—?" Dawson began and then was interrupted when the door opened again, and Charlotte reemerged, looking sheepish. Freddie had to give her credit. She held her head high as she strode to the correct exit.

Freddie watched her go, then checked the progress of his finger. The bleeding had slowed, but when he looked down, he saw that he'd gotten blood on his tailcoat and added red splotches to the greenish cabbage soup stain on his breeches. "Bloody hell," he growled and followed her through the door and into the entrance hall.

"There he is! My lord, come tell this misguided miscreant that I have first rights to this tub. I must prepare your bath." Wilkins was standing in the middle of the foyer, on the first step of the stairs, playing tug-of-war with Charlotte's servant. Two maids who had obviously been assisting with the chore of carrying the tub upstairs cowered on a third step.

"Now, Mr. Wilkins," Charlotte, who appeared to be attempting to restore order, said, "we've discussed this before. Please try and remain civil."

"Civil?" Wilkins howled, yanking viciously on the tub. "Civil! Try telling that to this madcap rudesby."

Freddie blinked. "Madcap—?"

"She all but snatched the tub from my hands."

"Now, Miss Charlotte, that ain't nothing but a bald-faced lie," Addy bellowed from her position on the second step. "I hads the tub and these here girls were helping me to carry it to your room so I coulds prepare your bath, when this here skinny-legged fool tried to snatch it away."

"Perhaps you could prepare my bath after Lord Dewhurst has finished," Charlotte said tentatively. "Or I could bathe in the morning. In any case, it appears Lord Dewhurst needs a bath far more than I."

She glanced back at him, her eyes resting on the bloody napkin about his finger and the sundry stains on his clothing.

"Egad!" Wilkins cried, jumping back, releasing his hold on the tub, then wheeling his hands to keep his balance on the steps. "My lord, now what have you done?"

Freddie's stomach dropped as it hadn't since

he was eight and had been caught using a mirror on a pole to look up the maids' skirts. He had the strange urge to stare at the ground and shuffle his feet before he remembered that Wilkins was not his guardian and that the man, in fact, worked for him.

"Now's our chance!" Addy screamed at the maids. "Grab the other end and be quick about it."

The maids rushed past Wilkins and grabbed the tub, and Addy began herding them upstairs. Wilkins watched, apparently torn between establishing his dominion over the tub and rescuing his master's second-best tailcoat from further ruin.

To Freddie's surprise, the valet opted for the tub and scampered after Addy and the maids, calling, "Stop! Thief! Tub pilferers!"

Charlotte stared after the rowdy group and then turned back to him. "Do you have any more of that wine?"

Chapter 10

Freddie chuckled. It appeared they'd arrived at a temporary truce, and he wasn't going to question it. She wanted a drink, and that he could certainly supply.

"Follow me." He led her through the hall and opened the double doors to his library, holding them wide until she'd passed inside. When he'd closed them and turned around, he found her looking about, wide-eyed and slack-jawed.

"This is magnificent," she cooed, her eyes all but caressing the towers of books extending to the top of the twelve-foot ceiling. In the middle of the room was a fireplace, the fire burning low and orange and casting shadows about the wall of books. Two couches faced each other on either side of the mantel. At the far end of the room, situated before a huge octagonal window that extended past the rest of the house and provided a stunning view of his garden when the sun shone, was Freddie's desk. Intricately carved and highly polished, the desk was the centerpiece of the room. The wood was gorgeous—mahogany from the wilds of the Caribbean—and the ornate carvings were the perfect embellishment to the imposing room and its glorious window. "This is truly magnificent," Charlotte repeated.

"A man must have his sanctuary," Freddie answered, crossing to the table beside one of the couches, where several decanters glowed in the firelight. He poured himself a healthy dose of his best port and splashed out two fingers of brandy for Charlotte. He probably should have given her the claret, which was far more suitable a drink for an English lady, but thus far she'd exhibited no signs of ladylike behavior, and she definitely wasn't English.

He didn't know what they drank in America, but he had a feeling one dose of brandy would not put his colonist under the table.

She took the glass from him, sipped the brandy, and nodded her approval. Freddie watched her, wondering just when she'd become *his* colonist. Certainly he had some rights over her—perhaps *rights* was not the correct word, but definitely responsibilities—but she was in no conceivable way his. A few weeks more and she'd be back in

America, back in her precious Charleston, a thousand miles and a god-awful sea between them.

He should rejoice at the mere thought of so much distance separating them; instead, the prospect made him feel lonely. His life these past two days had been turned upside down, his sober, efficient household set on its ear. And yet there was something exhilarating—and not a little scary—in the uncertainty his wife and her sidekick brought into his ordered life.

She turned again to survey the room, and he mentally shook his head. What was he thinking? Did he actually want the little hoyden to stay? She belonged in her backward barbarian land, and he belonged here in the height of culture and civility.

She started for the octagonal window, navigating past the desk, and Freddie held his breath. She did not walk so much as sway her hips while moving forward. Her skirts swished from side to side as her sweet derriere swung back and forth. Silently he thanked Madam Vivienne for her artistry. The gown had been made with seduction in mind.

When Charlotte reached the window, she bent over to get an impression of the lawns outside, and Freddie's heart thumped in his chest. He had a perfect view of her round, wiggling rump. Finally she turned back to him.

Freddie swallowed, but his throat felt like someone had stuffed his cravat down it. When he tried to wet his lips with a sip of port, he found his glass unaccountably empty. "This is a beautiful room," she said in that low, sultry voice he was coming to know so well. "I had no idea you were such an avid reader."

Freddie followed her gaze over the rows and rows of books, most of them purchased by his father and grandfather. "I'm not an avid reader. Not a reader a'tall, if you must know."

She glanced back at his desk and the small stack of books on the corner. Two were open and his stopping point on the others was clearly marked. "And those books on your desk?" she asked.

"Part of the illusion." He took a seat on the couch and motioned for her to follow, but she shook her head.

"Exactly what illusion are you attempting to perpetuate, Alfred?"

"My persona, when I go out in Society, is that of a dandy." She wrinkled her brow. "A fop, a fribble, a—"

She shook her head, uncomprehending.

"A popinjay. Oh, dash it! A man with interests in fashion and little else."

"And this is a persona?" She ran her eyes down his starched, perfectly tailored clothing, immaculate except for the cabbage, the wine, and—oh, yes, the newest addition—the blood. "You're quite convincing."

He inclined his head. "Years of practice,

madam. Am I to assume that you are an avid reader? Do colonists know how to read?"

She gave him a wan smile. "If I follow the page with my finger and sound the words out."

Freddie raised a brow. The chit could be amusing when she wanted.

"But to answer your question, no, I am not an avid reader, much to my father's disappointment, I'm afraid." She gave the room another wistful perusal. "He would have adored this room. He would have taken up residence and then refused to be moved until he'd read every book twice."

"Rather a frightening prospect, but I've known worse fathers-in-law."

She was quiet, her face full of grief for a moment.

"You're thinking of him," Freddie said quietly. "I'm sorry."

"As am I."

Freddie shifted on the couch, uncomfortably aware that he wanted to go to her. She looked so forlorn, standing in the center of his massive library like a little girl lost. He wanted to take her in his arms, tell her everything would be all right, but how the hell did he know that everything in her life would work out? Still, he couldn't stop himself asking, "Is that why you need the thousand pounds? Debts left by your father?"

She gave him a curious look, then turned her face away, mumbling, "Something like that."

Freddie set his glass of port on the side table.

"Then you need the money." She made no indication of hearing him, and he said, mostly to himself, "And you aren't likely to give up."

Her gaze whipped back to meet his. "Give up? Never, Lord Dewhurst. I will make this scheme work and clear Cade's name."

"Ah, and we've returned to the topic of the infamous Mr. Pettigru. What exactly has he done to garner your loyalty? Tell the truth. You don't care if he's guilty. You'll fight for him regardless." He clenched his hand into a fist, not liking the image of her with Pettigru, and liking his own jealous reaction even less.

"I will fight for him. He was my brother's friend, and he's been another brother to me. He used to tickle me until I screamed for mercy, teased me about the boys I had crushes on, and he even danced with me at my first ball."

Freddie reached for his port, drank it down. He could well imagine Charlotte at her first ball. Young, innocent, beautiful. He would have fallen hard and fast. Freddie poured himself another drink. "Join me?"

She raised one graceful eyebrow. "I hope I have not driven you to drinking, Mr. Dewhurst."

Freddie clenched the glass. "You'll have me on the cut in no time if you insist upon lowering my rank at every opportunity."

Charlotte smiled, and he could have sworn she'd intentionally called him mister.

"It's *Lord* Dewhurst, my lady," he reminded her.

"That's what I meant," she said airily, and his hackles rose. He needed to put her back on the defensive. He didn't like feeling out of control.

"Yes, that response will go over well when you're addressing the Prince Regent. 'I meant to say Your Highness,'" he drawled, imitating her Southern twang.

"You're not nearly as amusing as you seem to think," she retorted, the color rising prettily in her cheeks. "I'm making every effort."

He snorted. "Ha! I might believe that if I still thought you had windmills in the head, but you obviously have some intelligence. So? Explain. Is there some reason you feel the need to constantly demote me? No one's yet broken their teeth by calling me lord."

"I find titles repulsive, Alfred. Most Americans do. Unlike you Brits, we value equality among all men."

"Really?" Dewhurst said, leaning back on the couch and stretching his legs out. His polished boots brushed against her dainty white slippers. "Does that include all men or just white men?"

"It includes neither Negroes nor women as yet, sir, but I trust that will change."

"I see. Then you admit that in your country not everyone is equal?"

Charlotte shifted from one foot to the next, obviously not liking his insinuations. He didn't sympathize. She had started it, after all.

"Our system is by no means perfect, sir, but—"

"Neither is ours," he said, sitting up and grasping her wrist. She jumped at the unexpected contact, and he was able to take advantage of the moment and pull her to him. "But everyone knows his or her place. And if I am to escort you about Town, I must insist that you keep the line." He could feel the pulse beating in her wrist now, and knew he was causing the reaction.

"Keep the line?" Charlotte asked, twisting her wrist in his grip and glaring at him.

"Quite right. Address your betters as such." He kept his tone light, but he was deadly serious. She would have a hard enough time as it was without ignoring the rules governing Society. And he would jeopardize neither his cover as a dandy nor his assignment for one stubborn American.

No matter how rich her auburn hair, how full her lips, or how voluptuous her body.

"My betters?" she hissed, yanking her arm but not freeing it. Instead Freddie pulled her toward him until she was bent forward. In hindsight, it was not the best move he could have made. When she bent over, he had a tantalizing view of her ample cleavage. Worse, he could smell her. Smell the faint but undeniable scent of . . . honeysuckle?

He swallowed. "This discussion is a mere taste of what you will encounter when you finally make your entrée, so if you're going to kick over the traces every time some cake of an earl or duke unwittingly insults you, it were better that you stay home." His eyes burned into hers, but she met his gaze defiantly.

"I think, like most Englishmen, you underestimate my American sense of determination, sir," she bit out.

"Good," he said, releasing her and sitting back to give the appearance of never having touched her at all. His body—the thrumming in his loins, the residual heat from her skin on his—told a different story. "And as to your dilemma concerning my title, Dewhurst will do just fine."

"I can think of several other more colorful—"

Freddie raised a brow. "Now, now. Language like that hardly befits a lady. Or were you hoping for a language lesson?"

She pursed her lips. "Hardly. When am I to make my entrée? Shouldn't we begin to plan the time and place?"

Freddie rolled the glass of port in his hands. "You're not ready. You still have more—"

"Lessons. Yes. That's what you always say. What are these finer points of etiquette I'm missing? Is it just the titles? Because I do know them."

Freddie would have loved to test her on that point, but he refrained. "The titles are the least of it, madam. There's your deportment, your manner of speaking, your"—he looked down at his soiled clothing—"table manners, your—can you even dance?"

She blew out an angry breath. "Of course I can dance, and there's nothing wrong with any of the rest of it, either."

"That is a matter up for debate, so let's end it." He put the port aside. "Let me see you make a sweep."

She stared at him. "Pardon?"

"Curtsy," he said sharply.

"You mean bow?"

"No, men bow. Women curtsy. Give it a go."

She shook her head. "I prefer to shake hands."

"You can shake hands with friends and equals. You curtsy to those with a higher rank."

"Higher rank? I just told you that I value equality—"

"Humor me," he growled. She glared at him, but finally she curtsied. Freddie winced. "What was *that*?"

She put her hands on her hips and scowled. "My curtsy. If you're just going to make fun of me—"

"Not a'tall. Though that particular attempt was a bit cow-handed. Do it again."

"Did you just refer to me as livestock?"

"No, I said it looked cow-handed." He stood and crossed to the fireplace mantel. "It means clumsy."

"Oh, really?" she said jerking her chin up. "This

curtsy, which you, sir, call clumsy, attracted every beau for three counties in South Carolina."

"Is that so?" He finished the port and set the empty glass under a portrait of his great-grandfather.

"Yes, it's so." She glanced away. "Mostly."

"I can see why it was popular. You're bowing so low you're likely to display all your assets in an evening gown."

Charlotte gasped, her jaw dropping open. "How dare you, sir!"

Freddie flicked her protests away. "If you want my assistance I'll have to be honest. None of that flummery you may be used to."

"Flummery?"

"Just do it again, and keep your back straight this time." He watched her take a deep breath, from the look on her face no doubt battling a murderous rage coursing through her. Finally she complied, her back so stiff he thought it might break.

"No, no," he exclaimed. "You're not going to be addressing the Queen. Not so low. Here"—he strode to her—"try it like this." He placed one hand on her back and the other on her abdomen below her breasts.

She inhaled sharply, then without looking at him, curtsied.

"That's all the go," he praised. "Again."

She did so, then turned with bright eyes for another word of approval. He hadn't expected the movement and found himself staring into her hopeful, sherry-colored eyes. Almost involuntarily, his hands on her stomach tensed, and he felt the fullness of her breasts press against his chest.

He looked down at the cool rosy pink expanse of flesh, his eyes tracing her curves from the swell of her breasts to the slim lines of her bare neck. Her skin there was pale and beckoning, and he couldn't resist trailing a hand up her spine until he could caress the warm flesh at her nape with two fingers. Soft as silk. Would she taste as sweet and sultry as she sounded? Her eyes flew to his mouth and, unable to resist, he bent to brush her mouth with his.

He intended to end it there—a quick taste and then a retreat. But as soon as his lips touched hers, all thoughts of retreat vanished. The velvet softness of her lips on his, the warmth of her flesh pressed against him, the taste of her . . .

Before he could think, Freddie had one hand on the nape of her slender neck and another caressing the small of her back. He pressed her lush little body against him, then parted her lips and swept inside, his tongue meeting hers.

Bloody hell, but she tasted like honey. Even the shyness and surprise in the way she kissed him back was sweet. Sweet and tempting and driving him to new heights of need.

"Dewhurst." She pulled back, staring at him,

her eyes dark now and wary. "I don't think that is such a good idea."

Freddie wanted to agree. In fact, he *did* agree. He agreed wholeheartedly that not only was kissing her a bad idea, but this whole scheme, from start to finish, was a dreadfully appalling idea.

But he couldn't say it. He couldn't agree with her because, as much as he wanted to agree, when she'd spoken the words, her rich, low voice poured over him, warming him in places that hadn't felt heat in years—if ever. "On the contrary," he heard himself say, "it's a very good idea." And he bent to kiss her again. She put a hand between them and pushed him back.

"Why?"

He frowned. "Why?"

"Yes, why?"

Dashed if he knew why. He wanted to kiss her, he wanted to feel her heat fuse with his, he wanted to take her upstairs, strip her down to her petticoat, and ravish her until they were both thoroughly sated. That was why.

And he wanted to run screaming from the room because it was completely unacceptable that he should feel this way. She was a *colonist*, for God's sake! He should throttle her, not kiss her.

"Because it will help our cause," he murmured. What in bloody hell was he doing? Why was he trying to convince her to go along?

She wrinkled her brow, and he smiled at the

way her nose wrinkled, too. She was terribly cute when she did that.

Dash it! No, she was not cute. She was a barbarian colonist, devil take him, and he had to stop this seduction immediately.

"How will it help our cause?" she asked.

He opened his mouth, then shut it again. Dashed if he had any idea how it would help the Foreign Office if he took her on the floor, hard and fast, right here and now. But the idea was not without its appeal.

"Wait, now I see," she added. Freddie held his breath. What exactly did she see? "It will help because it will lend authenticity to our marriage, correct? It will make us seem more . . . ah, intimate."

Yes! Yes! "Exactly," he said, his voice sounding remarkably composed. "Authenticity is key. We cannot be *too* authentic." He leaned in to kiss her again, his lips just brushing hers, when she spoke again.

"But neither should we get too carried away."

He had no idea what she was saying, only that he had to settle for nuzzling her neck because her lips were still moving. Surprisingly, nuzzling her neck was an altogether pleasant endeavor indeed. Her scent—he was certain it was honeysuckle now—was stronger here, close to her hair. It was delicate and sensual and driving him to the brink of arousal.

"Dewhurst!" she said sharply as his tongue flicked her earlobe. "I said we shouldn't get carried away."

"Why not?" he whispered and had the satisfaction of feeling her shiver in his arms. "I *want* to get carried away." He turned her in his arms then and kissed her, pressing his mouth hard against her, claiming her and ceasing all possibility of further protest on her part.

Not that she was protesting. No sooner had his lips caressed hers again than her earlier hesitation was gone, and she returned the kiss with passion and an intensity he hadn't expected. This time, before he had even fully accustomed his mouth to the feel of hers, she'd slipped her tongue between his teeth and slid it along his.

Every hair on the back of Freddie's neck reacted, and he couldn't stop himself from pulling her tighter against him, crushing her breasts to him, feeling her softness, smelling her scent, tasting her raw sensuality.

She broke the kiss first, parting from him and gasping for air. Her breasts heaved against him, and he bent to kiss her jaw, this time allowing his tongue to snake down her neck and over her heart. When he reached the mounds blossoming from her bodice, he opened his mouth and pressed against the ripe flesh.

Her reaction was sharp and immediate. She let out a small cry, then pushed him back.

"What's the matter?" he said, and his voice sounded slurred and fuzzy even to him.

"Sir, I must ask you to cease. I understand that a few kisses might be in order if we are to appear . . . ah, authentic, as you said, but this goes too far. Despite the illusion, I am *not* your wife."

"Thank God," he mumbled, and she tensed. "Dash it!" he added quickly. "No, that's not what I meant. I mean—" Her scent had enveloped him again, and he was finding it almost impossible to form a coherent thought other than the ubiquitous *I want her.* Why was he even fighting it? "Charlotte," he said, looking into her eyes, which turned out to be a mistake because they only served to distract him once again.

"Yes?" she prodded.

He shook his head to clear it. "I want you, and I think you want me as well. This . . . arrangement between us does not have to be unpleasant. Not if we make the best of it."

"Are you implying—?"

"No," he said quickly, having had experience with women and their use of the term *implication.* "I'm not implying anything, other than that I enjoy kissing you, touching you, and if you allow me, I'll make sure you enjoy it, too." Before she could argue, he bent once more to her full breasts, scraping his tongue down the valley between them. She gasped and tried to push him away.

"Sir, I don't think—mmm, I—oh!"

Freddie knew a capitulation when he saw it, and he rode the momentum of his temporary victory, seeking to prolong it. Moving his hands from her waist to cup her breasts, he pushed her fullness into his mouth and allowed the heat to penetrate through the layers of silk. He ran a thumb over the hard peaks of her nipples, now detectable under her light stays.

She gasped again, arched, and in one movement and a few deft flicks of a hand, he had her bodice loosened and slipped down to reveal those stays hampering his progress. A moment later, he had those free, and he was cupping her soft flesh in his palms, taking her hard, rose-colored nipples in his mouth and rolling them over his tongue.

She moaned, a moan of pure pleasure, low and throaty like her voice, and unbelievably arousing. He took her other nipple in his mouth, using his hand to tease and tantalize the second. It grew rigid between his fingers, the hot flesh pebble-hard and, judging by her reaction, extremely sensitive. Freddie sensed victory and pushed her bodice lower, wanting to see more of her, wanting to bare more of her creamy flesh to his gaze. She whimpered, and he could almost hear the war raging between her body and her mind.

Her body won, and she arched her back, thrusting her breasts into his waiting hands—hands that were suddenly and as agreeably filled as his every sense was with her.

He bent to kiss her again, to take more of her into his mouth, and he heard, "Pish-posh, Dawson. I don't need to be announced. His Lordship is always home to me."

Freddie jerked away from Charlotte so quickly that she stumbled and pinwheeled her arms to steady herself. He caught her elbow, then, in once swift motion, righted her stays, pulled her bodice back in place, and put the space of a dozen men between them.

"And so the duke said, 'If I'd wanted a biscuit, old boy, I could have fetched one myself!' " Freddie laughed uproariously as the library doors opened. He gave Charlotte a look full of meaning, and she managed a weak smile before Sebastian Middleton sauntered into the library.

"Felicitations, coz! I see you've been busy."

Chapter 11

Charlotte's cheeks fired so hot, she was afraid she might emit steam. George Washington! It was Middleton again—and this time she was rather glad to see him. And rather mortified at the thought that he knew what she and Dewhurst had just been doing.

She didn't even want to know what she and Dewhurst had just been doing!

Freddie's cousin strode toward the couch where they were standing, and Charlotte noticed that today he wore not only an Elizabethan doublet, but a ruff as well. "I hear you've gone and gotten leg-shackled, coz," Middleton said with a wink. "Say it's not true."

Dewhurst glanced at the double doors where Dawson was still waiting. He dismissed the man with a nod. "'Fraid you are going to have to congratulate me, Middleton, and allow me to introduce my lovely wife, Charlotte, to you. Charlotte, my cousin, Sir Sebastian Middleton," he said with a last glance at Dawson.

Middleton stepped forward, playing his part admirably, and took her hand in his, kissing her knuckles. "'If I profane with my unworthiest hand this holy shrine—'"

Dewhurst stepped between them and took her hand in his own. His touch still burned her, and his husky voice made her shiver. "'My lips, two blushing pilgrims, ready stand to smooth that rough touch with a tender kiss.'" Their gazes met and held, and Middleton finally broke the silence.

"Is it warm in here?" He pulled at his ruff. "I find I need a drink."

Charlotte took a deep breath, flutters still dancing in her belly. She glanced at Middleton. "Thank you, Sir . . ." She paused and glanced at Dewhurst for guidance. Was it Sir Sebastian or Sir Middleton? Oh, she'd never get all these titles right.

Dewhurst mouthed *Sebastian*, and she knew she should finish her greeting before the pause dragged on too long, but the way Dewhurst's lips moved sent a shiver of pleasure through her. Not a moment ago, those lips had been on her mouth, her neck, her breasts. She shivered again, and the spell was broken only when Dewhurst finally spoke for her.

"Sir Sebastian," he interjected into the silence. "I'm afraid my wife hasn't quite mastered all of the differences between our two cultures."

Charlotte gave Sebastian a tight smile, and he smiled back, his eyes soft with understanding. Oh, why couldn't she have had to pose as Middleton's wife? He seemed eminently more reasonable than her current spouse. Even if he did take the role of the lovelorn Romeo a bit too far.

"No worries, my lady. You'll catch on in no time. And you shall have the opportunity to practice sooner than you think. I have a box at the opera tomorrow night."

"No," Dewhurst said. "Absolutely not. She's not ready."

Middleton helped himself to a large glass of brandy. "She'll have to be ready. We can't afford to wait any longer."

"We can't afford *not* to wait. I'll be laughed out of Town when she calls some cake of an earl or duke mister or stumbles over her feet when she curtsies. And the gowns I've ordered for her won't arrive until next week at the earliest. She's not ready."

"Well, Pettigru is."

Dewhurst stilled, and in the sudden silence, Charlotte was certain the sound of her heart pounding was audible throughout the house. Cade had been spotted? He'd been seen again? Perhaps somewhere close. But Charlotte bit her cheek to keep the questions from spewing forth.

"Are you certain?" Dewhurst asked. "Have *you* seen him?"

Middleton glanced at her, and she quickly directed her gaze to the floor. *Try to look uninterested,* she told herself. *Pretend you don't care.*

"I have it on good authority that he is in Town, and looking for Miss Burton. The *best* authority."

Charlotte bored a hole in the rich burgundy carpet with her eyes. They were talking about another spy—they had to be. And they didn't want her to know whom. But Cade was in London, and that was the most important thing. Middleton was right. It was time to stop playing at teacher and student and seize the opportunity to find and warn her friend.

But Dewhurst was shaking his head. "We need more time. We haven't discussed how to approach him, where to approach him, and Charlotte hasn't yet established herself in Society."

"Society," Middleton scoffed. "Pish-posh. She's the hottest topic since Wellington at Vittoria. If you don't bring her out soon, our demure Society ladies will storm your door."

That at least elicited a smile from Dewhurst. He took a seat on the couch and leaned back. He appeared resigned to his cousin's plan. "Very well. Do you think the opera is the best place for her entrée? Pettigru is unlikely to be there."

"True," Middleton said, coming around to the couch opposite Dewhurst and seating himself in it. "But it will give credence to the rumors that the Miss Burton he knew in America is the same Miss Burton who married you. And we might use the opportunity to establish a rendezvous more amenable to our purposes."

Charlotte had slowly sunk back, out of the light and the men's vision, but now she pressed forward again.

"Very well." Dewhurst nodded. "What do you have in mind?"

"We make it widely known Charlotte will be attending a ball."

"Which ball? I have a pile of unopened invitations—"

Middleton was shaking his head. "No need. I have already acquired an invitation for both of you." He extracted a slim, creamy white card from his waistcoat pocket and handed it to Dewhurst.

Dewhurst read it, then raised his eyes until they met hers. "This will do very well," he said. "Queer that the ball is in two days' time, and I hadn't received an invitation until now."

Middleton shrugged. "You might say this is a special ball, contrived to suit our purposes."

"But Lady Brigham? She's hardly capricious enough to pull this off. She goes into hysterics if she is even five minutes late. This tardy announcement is not like her."

Middleton smiled. "Perhaps the beau monde will assume her flighty daughter put the idea into her head." The two men exchanged glances full of meaning, but the language was incomprehensible to Charlotte.

"You'll attend, then?" Middleton asked.

"It's a start," Dewhurst said. "And not a bad one, though I do have my concerns."

Charlotte took a deep breath. The look he was giving her reminded her of Miss Crudsworthy again. It was the same look her primary school teacher had given the class when she was about to call on one of the students to recite in front of the class.

Oh, no. Much as Charlotte wanted to stay and hear any additional tidbits Dewhurst or his cousin might drop, she decided to flee and cut her losses before they became insurmountable.

"Excuse me," she said, backing toward the doors. "I am feeling a bit tired, and I believe I shall retire."

Both men stood and bid her good night. Dewhurst's gaze rested on her a bit longer than she found comfortable, and for a moment she thought she detected a flash of the ardor she'd seen in his eyes when he held her in his arms. She fled through the double doors, up the stairs, and into her bedroom.

A half hour later, she was sitting in warm, soapy water, listening to Addy hum as she prepared Charlotte's room and nightclothes. Charlotte closed her eyes. Cade was close now. For some reason, knowing he was so near made her pine for home.

In her mind, she saw the long pastel piazza from her house in Charleston—her favorite spot. She'd curl up in her lounge chair and watch the last rays of the afternoon sun filter through the trees, extending long, dying fingers to touch the petals of flowers in the high-walled garden below. The garden had been one of the finest in Charleston—at least she had thought it so.

The garden had been surrounded by wrought-iron gates so covered with verdant foliage the metal appeared to be alive. She remembered walking beside that gate, her parasol brushing the honeysuckle blossoms when she paused to admire pink roses with blooms as big as her hand.

She remembered standing under one of the old magnolia trees, its shade a welcome relief from the heat of a summer day in Charleston, and she recalled James Huger. He'd put his hand on the tree trunk behind her, then leaned forward and kissed her, his tongue igniting a passion in her that she'd never known existed.

She remembered pulling away from James, then clutching his coat and pulling him back. She looked into his face—those lovely emerald eyes, that lazy smile, that tousled blond hair.

Charlotte sat up so suddenly water sloshed from the tub. James had had brown eyes and chestnut hair. George Washington! She was thinking of Dewhurst again.

She had to put him out of her mind, but every time she did so, the thought of the heat in his eyes, that sensuous mouth, the feel of his tongue when he flicked her nipple, made her achingly aware of him again. She looked down to see her nipples standing out, hard and erect. She might try to forget him, but her body would not.

She sank lower in the tub and tried to think what to do. She did not want to feel anything but hatred and loathing for Freddie Dewhurst. He was a warrior and would never allow himself to feel anything for her. Not to mention, he was British, and as such, he was not entitled to any of her softer emotions—dislike, antipathy, aversion. She would not allow an Englishman, who just happened to know how to use his tongue, to sway her from that conviction.

She sighed. There. The matter was settled. She would not think of Freddie again.

Freddie . . . the name suited him. It had a charming, boyish sound that reflected his personality. She wondered what he would do, what he would say were she to whisper, "Freddie" in his ear.

"Dash it!" She sat up again. "Goddammit! Now he's got me saying it!"

"Miss Charlotte?" Addy called from the other side of the partition. "You okay?"

"Oh, fine, Addy! I'm almost done in here."

"No rush, Miss Charlotte." Addy's low voice wafted through the partition. "That skinny-necked fool think he own this tub. No how. No way. We'll keep it as long as we like."

Charlotte sighed. Thank God Cade was close because she couldn't take much more of this war between Addy and Wilkins. Cade. She had to focus on Cade. Dewhurst and his cousin claimed he was a spy. Was it possible?

Charlotte sighed. She knew it was, but she owed these Brits no loyalty. Had she been in Cade's place, she might have done the same. Her goal from now on would be not to think of Dewhurst at all. She would find Cade and warn him about the dangers awaiting him. But first she had to get through tomorrow night.

The opera turned out to be no small affair. The box Middleton had acquired for them was to be occupied not only by Dewhurst, his cousin, and her, but also Dewhurst's mother and sister Lydia. Charlotte had worn her green dinner dress again as she had no opera gown ready, but Dewhurst had not commented, so she supposed she did not look too unsuitable.

Hester, Dewhurst's maid, volunteered to style Charlotte's hair, and Charlotte reluctantly agreed, hoping the maid had more of an aptitude for hair-dressing than she did for cleaning. Hester, lazy and usually rude, had found her forte as a hairdresser, and for the first time Charlotte thought her red hair looked pretty. Not that the dress or the coiffure would survive the night.

It started on the way to the opera. She was squeezed next to Dewhurst in his gleaming black Town coach, which, although spacious, was overcrowded with five passengers—Charlotte, Middleton, and the three Dewhursts.

Quarters were so close, she had practically been forced to sit on Dewhurst's lap. He was in full dandy persona, and while she tried to forget her discomfort, he complained endlessly about the possibility of her crushing his cravat. She had wanted to thump him over the head with her reticule, came very close to it in fact when he told her she looked "all the crack."

Lydia assured her he meant it as a compliment, but Charlotte had seen his eyes dip to the low-cut bodice of her dress. She'd wanted to wear a wrap to cover the excess cleavage spilling out, but Freddie had snatched it away, remarking that it was not at all the thing. Charlotte had asked if catching her death of cold was more fashionable, but her husband had been unperturbed, flashing his lazy smile at her.

Despite Freddie's comment, in the end Charlotte had been glad she'd left the shawl at home. She was not cold; in fact, the opposite was true. The heat from being jammed in the carriage and then crammed tightly in the crowds once they reached Covent Garden was almost too much. No wonder the British women never wore wraps despite the cold weather; there were simply so many people about that they packed up against one another and generated heat that way.

When they finally made it through the crush, as Dewhurst had called it, and arrived at the box reserved for the evening, Charlotte took a deep breath and slumped in her chair. She was exhausted, and the evening had barely begun.

But as Charlotte gazed about the theater, all her fatigue melted away. Covent Garden was absolutely the most beautiful place she had ever seen. The stage was large, hidden by a rich crimson drapery, and ornamented by an elegantly paneled arch. On each side of the arch rose two female figures represented in relief, who looked as though they had just stepped out of an ancient Grecian temple. Above her, the elaborate ceiling of the theater was painted to give the appearance of a cupola, the painting depicting an ancient lyre. Just looking up at the vast domelike ceiling made her dizzy.

When Charlotte had her fill of what was before her, she began to marvel at the wonderful boxes the upper classes were beginning to fill. There were tiers and tiers of boxes, one on top of the other, with intricate carving on the wood between. The seats were covered with a light blue cloth, and even though it seemed these Brits preferred being crushed together, the theater boxes were quite spacious. Separated from its neighbor by gilt columns, each box was illuminated by chandeliers of cut crystal suspended from the tops of pillars. To Charlotte, the chandeliers sparkled like tiny stars against the sky blue background of the boxes.

A refined, charming city in its own right, Charleston had its share of beautiful feats of architecture, but Charlotte had never seen anything to rival this. She turned absently to the person seated beside her to comment breathlessly on the splendor before her and was discomfited to find her husband seated there.

Of course he was, but, oh, why could she not get away from him!

He was watching her closely, a strange look on his face. And when their gazes met, the look in his dark green eyes sent heat rushing to her face.

Charlotte did not know how long they stared at each other—it seemed like an eternity—before his mother leaned over and inquired what she thought of the theater.

Charlotte tore her eyes away from Freddie's and answered, "Oh, it's just stunning, madam. Quite grand."

"I am sure you have nothing in Charles Town to match this," the woman said smugly. Charlotte smiled, letting the woman have her moment of glory. It seemed to mean so much to some people that others were impressed by their grandeur. She saw no harm in giving Dewhurst's mother a moment's pleasure, especially when Charlotte was finally impressed.

But the mention of Charleston also brought Cade into her thoughts, and Charlotte turned her attention back to the theater with a new purpose.

She began scanning the patrons, looking for his black hair. She turned to scan the boxes and in so turning, Charlotte again met Freddie's lingering gaze.

Lord! The man was still watching her! What *could* he find so interesting? Knowing him, he was probably adding up every mistake she had made so that he could fully enumerate them later.

"Mr. Dewhurst," she began, intentionally omitting his title. He gave her a look of annoyance, and she began to wonder what else she could she say to keep that searing look from returning to his eyes. "Are there many officers in attendance this evening? I have seen several red coats."

His eyes scanned the theater with affected ennui. "Suppose I see a few officers. Worried?"

Charlotte shrugged. "A British officer might not like the idea of an American, the enemy so to speak, in such close proximity."

"Fustian nonsense, m'dear! I hardly think a British officer would have any ill will toward *you*."

She didn't know why not when she certainly held a great deal of ill will toward them. But she did not comment right away. Instead she narrowed her eyes at Dewhurst. He was quite good at playing the dandy role. His voice was higher than she was used to hearing it, his movements overblown. Charlotte caught a flash of black hair and, pointing to the man, said, "Who is that?"

"Couldn't say," Dewhurst answered.

"What about him?" Charlotte said, pointing to another black-haired man.

"Dash it if I know," was his response. "Look how he's dressed, Middleton. You want a theatrical tragedy? Look at that tailcoat."

Charlotte raised a brow, realizing she was unlikely to learn much with Dewhurst in this mode.

"Ah, yes," Freddie continued, "but take Colonel George Hanger there. Complete to a shade. And the Duke of York. The cut of that coat doesn't suit him, but he's usually bang up the prime. Can't think where he got that coat, though. Dreadful color, too."

Charlotte sighed. She was learning nothing of any interest, except that the Duke of York had poor taste in tailcoats. If Cade really needed her help, Lord help them all.

"Are there any Englishmen who can speak on a subject other than fashion?" Charlotte mumbled irritably.

"I can speak on love," Middleton, who must have been listening to their conversation, put in. "'Love goes toward love as school boys from their books; but love from love, toward school with heavy looks.' "

Freddie smirked, but before he could make some rejoinder the majestic curtain rose, and Charlotte turned her attention to the stage. She quickly realized she was the only theatergoer who had done so, as the conversations around her did not cease, merely increased in volume to carry over the music.

She had forgotten to ask which opera they were seeing, not that Dewhurst would know much more than which tailor had made the costumes, but she found the overture enchanting.

A few minutes later an actor entered and the audience applauded. His voice swelled as he began a light aria. The libretto was in Italian, which Charlotte did not understand, but she felt the raw emotion in his voice. It shot through her, and she felt her throat constrict with emotion.

As the opera continued, a tragic love story unfolded. And when the two lovers sang of their passion for each other, Charlotte wept at the beauty and unfairness of it all. Freddie handed her a handkerchief, and it was such a nice thing to do, such a sweet gesture when she was trying so hard not to think of him, not to put him in the dashing role of the opera's hero, that she started blubbering all over again.

Freddie was actually rather relieved Charlotte was too wrapped up in the opera to notice him.

He did not think he would be able to hide the look of pure amazement on his face.

Since the moment he'd seen her that night, he'd been hard-pressed to take his eyes from her. Once again, she looked ravishing in her low-cut, green crepe dress. The lines of the design molded to her sumptuous body, emphasizing the fullness of her breasts and hinting at the curve of her hip. As if the sight of her had not been temptation enough, she had then been squeezed beside him in the carriage, her sweet curves pushing against him, arousing him to no end.

But it was her face that drew his glance again and again once they were seated in his box. She gazed at everything with the innocent wonder of a child. Her smile was beatific, her eyes sparkled, and in those moments, he knew her to be the most purely beautiful woman he had ever known.

And she continued to amaze him. Not only was she actually watching the opera when the *ton* merely went to the opera to see or be seen, but she seemed to be enjoying it. Her face betrayed her every emotion—she flinched at the actors' pain, laughed at their successes, wept at their defeats. This behavior was certainly unprecedented in his circle, and looking around, he saw more than one member of the upper classes had noted her unusual behavior and were commenting on it behind raised palms or fluttering fans.

She seemed to recover slightly by the intermission, and Freddie offered to fetch the ladies refreshments. When he returned, the box was almost too full for him to enter. Apparently Sebastian had been right about the *ton*. They couldn't wait to meet Charlotte.

When Freddie had waded through the crowds, he caught sight of the Selbournes beside Lydia. Lucia, Alex's wife, was laughing at something Lydia was saying, and Alex was silent and brooding, as usual. Freddie caught his eye, and Selbourne nodded at Charlotte appreciatively. For some reason, Selbourne's—any man's—admiration of Charlotte set his bristles up. He felt a very uncharacteristic stab of possessiveness.

Selbourne moved closer to Charlotte, who was smiling and nodding at Sebastian, and Dewhurst found himself holding his breath. Selbourne was not the real test, of course. That would come tomorrow night at the ball, but if Charlotte could not hold her own on friendly soil, they were all doomed. Sebastian noted Alex and made the introductions, whereby Selbourne bowed, took Charlotte's hand, and kissed her gloved fingers. Charlotte's eyes met Freddie's over Selbourne's shoulder. She seemed to know he was evaluating her performance, and she gave him a saucy smile.

Straightening, Alex slanted a glance at Freddie. "You must be the American Dewhurst can't stop talking about," he said.

"I hope he has not found too much fault with

me, *Lord* Selbourne," she said, still watching Freddie.

Impudent girl. He shot her a look of warning.

"Considering your marriage not only flouted convention but"—with a glance at Dewhurst's mother, Selbourne lowered his voice—"probably needled his mother as well, he has nothing but praise for you. Which, as I'm sure you concur, is as it should be."

Charlotte looked a little surprised by that statement, but Lucia took Freddie's chair, saving Charlotte from a reply.

After the requisite introduction, Lucia said warmly, "Your accent is wonderful, Lady Dewhurst. You make every word sound coated in honey."

"Thank you, Lady Selbourne," Charlotte said. "Yours is the first kind word I've had regarding my accent."

Lucia smiled. "Oh, I imagine everyone is just jealous but too proud to admit it. And please call me Lucia. Freddie is such a good friend that I've almost adopted him as a brother. I want us to be like sisters."

"Thank you. Then you must call me Charlotte. I so dislike the formality of titles," Charlotte said with a knowing look at Freddie.

Freddie ignored her jibe, focusing instead on her smile. She was practically beaming at Lucia. He couldn't recall seeing her smile so warmly before, and the effect was truly stunning. With the lights glinting off her copper hair and her wide, full lips and entrancing eyes, she was ravishing. Freddie realized that, if she hadn't already been his, he would probably be paying her as much court as the other men clambering for a position inside the crowded box.

"How are you enjoying the opera, Lady Dewhurst?" Selbourne asked. And Freddie was grateful someone was listening to the conversation.

"It's entrancing. The score is so beautiful and"—she paused, glancing behind her—"the costumes divine. Don't you agree, Lydia?" Everyone turned to Lydia, who Freddie realized had been pouting at the lack of attention. Now that Charlotte had found a way to involve her, she smiled and began a long speech on her opinions.

After Lydia had gone on a moment, Lucia leaned over to Charlotte, and Freddie edged closer to overhear their confidences. "I hope we can find a few moments to chat at my mother's ball tomorrow night. I would so love to hear about life in America. I fear I have inherited a love of other cultures and peoples from my mother."

"Oh, of course. I did not realize Lady Brigham was your mother."

"Oh, good Lord, yes. The night is sure to prove extremely tedious, but my mother is on a mission, and that ranks above all else."

Charlotte raised a brow. "Mission?"

Lucia nodded. "To marry off my twin brother. He's fighting the nuptial knot as hard as he can, but once my mother gets her apron strings firmly round his neck, he'll be doomed."

"Your mother sounds like a formidable woman."

Lucia closed her fan in her palm. "Oh, you do not know the half of it, Charlotte. But, I have to say, she is a kind woman and does everything with the best intentions."

Freddie frowned. Lady Brigham was an interfering harpy with a mania for Italy. She was more selfish than kind, and he doubted she'd ever done anything with any intention but her own in mind. But, as usual, Lucia seemed to have a talent for casting others in a sympathetic light. In the past on more than one occasion, he'd spied a bit of muslin he'd liked to have known better, only to have Lucia deter him by making him feel guilty.

He missed the transition into the next topic, but he caught the look Lucia gave him. He wondered what strokes she was using to paint him. What did she want Charlotte to see? And what did his little Yankee see when she looked at him? His money, his title, his dandy persona? Or could she see something of the man lurking inside?

"I suppose we must be going," Lucia said, glancing at Selbourne. "Like you, Charlotte, I adore the opera. And while Italian is not Selbourne's favorite language"—Freddie smiled when Alex scowled at his wife, who laughed merrily—"I think he is enjoying this one as well."

Lucia rose and gave Freddie her hand. She leaned forward, ostensibly to kiss his cheek, but whispered instead, "Don't muddle this one up, Freddie. You worry about whatever your little mission for the Foreign Office is and leave the romance to me. I have a plan." Freddie stiffened as apprehension, icy cold, washed down his spine.

"Lucia—" he began, but Alex came up behind her.

"Come wench, I have matters pertaining to Italian to discuss with you." Lucia laughed and winked at Freddie as she exited the box. He frowned. One would have thought that after seven years living with the dourest man in England, Lady Selbourne would have adopted some restraint. But underneath the title and the fortune, she was still Lucia Dashing—concocting harebrained plans and kicking up larks.

The remaining invaders were beginning to disperse as well, and Freddie was finally able to reclaim his seat beside Charlotte. As he did so, his mother leaned over and whispered, "Lord and Lady Selbourne's notice of you is quite an honor, Charlotte. They are extremely wealthy, and despite the matter of their elopement, eminently respectable."

"They seem very happy," Charlotte replied.

"Theirs was a love match," his mother informed her.

"Love match!" Freddie interjected turning around. "More like an exercise in humiliation. Selbourne made an absolute cake of himself over her."

"He seems to think it was worth it," Charlotte observed.

"Hmpf," Freddie replied.

The strains of the orchestra rose again, and Freddie glanced surreptitiously at Charlotte, wondering just how much effort she was worth.

Chapter 12

Freddie waited until Charlotte had gone to her room before seeking out her servant. Fortunately the woman hadn't yet retired to the servants' quarters, and he found her discussing the benefits of frequent polishing of the silver with his butler, Dawson.

"Miss Addy," Freddie said and gave a sweeping bow. "May I have a moment of your time?"

She gave him a weary look then shrugged. "I s'pose."

He led her into the drawing room and indicated she should take a seat. She shook her head. "I know what this is about. That skinny little man is complaining about his starch again. Well, you just tell that little weasel that I's got a right to the starch, too."

Freddie stared at her for a long moment, watching the frantic way she clutched at her ragged shawl. "Madam, I have no notion what you are going on about, but I assure you that whatever it is, I will rectify the situation."

Addy snorted. "Nothing's free."

Freddie inclined his head. The woman was no fool. "All right. Then I will make sure you have—?"

"Starch," she supplied. "A lot."

"A lot of starch if you give me a bit of information on your mistress."

Addy crossed her arms and stuck her lip out. "Oh, no. Miss Charlotte's like my own child. I couldn't betray her."

"Oh, I'm not asking for any information like that. I just want to see that we get along better and make sure she's happy here." And that was all it was, wasn't it? There was nothing to his request. He simply wanted to make their sham marriage appear more real. "I just want to know what she likes," he continued. "What flowers and jewels does she prefer, for example?"

"Hmpf. You won't get far offering her jewels. She wear that necklace her mamma gave her, and she don't never take it off."

Freddie nodded. "Good to know. I think you earned yourself some starch, Miss Addy. Now what else can you tell me?"

Addy gave him a long hard look. "I likes you, Mr. Dewhurst. Lawd knows why because you dress prettier than most girls I know. But I thinks you're good for Miss Charlotte."

"Then you'll help?" Freddie smiled. Now this was the effect he was used to having on women.

"Oh, I'll help," Addy said. "But you goin' have to give me more than starch."

She lifted up a corner of her ragged shawl, and Freddie sat back to listen.

Charlotte heard the carriage wheels clatter over every cobblestone in the streets between Bruton and Berkeley Square, where Lord and Lady Brigham lived. It was the night after the opera, and they were en route to the Brighams' ball. It was a short distance, but the crush of traffic slowed their progress to a crawl, and by the time they arrived, Charlotte's nerves were frayed and she was ready for the ball—the entire charade—to end. But she'd frozen that polite smile on her face, and she would not remove it until she found Cade.

But as soon as she and Dewhurst stepped over the threshold of the Brighams' spectacular town house, Charlotte realized the charade had only just begun. Here all of London was on stage. Dewhurst led her deep into the foyer and through the receiving line, pausing before a tall woman with short, springy platinum curls.

"Signora Brigham," Freddie said bowing gracefully. He was deep in his element now.

"*Buona sera,* Lord Dewhurst," Lady Brigham

said so loudly that Charlotte almost stepped back. The woman had a high-pitched tone that must have carried into every room of the mansion. "And who is this lovely *signorina*?"

"Lady Brigham, may I present Lady Dewhurst, my wife. Charlotte, Viscountess Brigham."

Charlotte curtsied. "Good evening, madam."

"Oh!" The woman's eyes widened. "But you're not English."

"Lady Dewhurst is from Charleston," Freddie supplied.

"Charleston?" Lady Brigham's blond brows furrowed. "Is that near Norwich?"

Norwich? Charlotte was appalled. How could this woman not know where Charleston was? "Certainly not, madam. It's—" Charlotte began.

"Near the Scottish border," Dewhurst finished for her. She gave him a sharp look, and his jade green eyes glinted playfully. Now what game was he concocting?

"*Mamma mia!* Lord Dewhurst, I had no idea you were acquainted with anyone who lived so far *north*." Lady Brigham fluttered her fan rapidly. Charlotte opened her mouth to protest, but before she could do so, the party was interrupted by Dewhurst's cousin.

"Dewhurst. Fashionably late as usual." Middleton strode into the foyer. He had obviously attempted to put his Elizabethan dress aside for the evening, but now he wore wide, baggy mauve trousers, lavender waistcoat, and green tailcoat he wore. It hurt Charlotte's eyes to look at him.

"Good God, sir," Dewhurst said. "Did you fall and hit your head? You look like a zany." Freddie took his cousin's arm. "Do sit down. You might have a concussion."

Middleton grinned and shook off Freddie's arm. "I hear the ladies like bright colors. 'Sides, I don't care a fig if Beau Brummell's here. I'm a connoisseur of love, not fashion. It's the ladies I want simmering with lust when they spy my Cossack trousers," he added in a conspiratorial whisper.

"Simmering with lust, eh?" Dewhurst muttered.

Middleton turned to Charlotte, who was still trying to understand the appeal of such a vibrantly colored outfit. "Lady Dewhurst—" Undoubtedly he was about to spout Shakespeare, but his words were lost in the loud gasp her husband let out. A few guests had gathered to watch the antics of these pinks of the *ton*, and Charlotte saw more beginning to crowd around.

"Selbourne, old boy. Has someone died?" Dewhurst called.

Charlotte turned to see Lord Selbourne—she rarely had trouble remembering *he* was a lord—and Lucia, arm in arm, approaching. Lucia was smiling, but Selbourne scowled. "Don't start, Dewhurst."

"But, I say, the last time I saw so much black was

at the funeral of my great-aunt Agatha. You remember, Sebastian?"

Middleton nodded sagely.

Charlotte actually thought Lord Selbourne looked quite nice in black breeches, a black velvet waistcoat, and an ebony tailcoat of superfine. His basic cravat was stark white, and the simplicity was refreshing next to Middleton's profusion of purple.

"At least I don't look like a puffed-up peacock," Selbourne retorted.

"Peacock! You wound me, sir! This color is referred to as Spanish blue. Peacock blue does not suit me a'tall."

That earned a laugh from the onlookers.

"I suppose now that you have an audience, I'll never escape without some remark concerning my cravat. Make it so that I may escort my wife inside."

"Audience! Sir, I think it is you who enjoys an audience. Why, I half expect you to propose marriage to my new wife at any moment."

Charlotte blushed, and there was more laughter. Lucia slapped Freddie playfully on the arm. "Be nice, Freddie."

"Madam, I am always nice."

"No, you're not. You antagonize Alex, and then I have to smooth his ruffled feathers."

"Ah, who is the peacock now, Selbourne?"

Charlotte didn't hear Alex's response because

Lucia stepped in to save her. "Lady Dewhurst, what a pleasure to see you again. These boys may insult each other all night. We needn't wait for them. Please, come with me inside. I'll enjoy squiring you about and introducing you to all the bucks and beaux."

Lady Brigham was immediately at Lucia's side. "*Mia figlia,*" she whispered. "Do you think that is such a good idea? Lady Dewhurst is *Scottish.*"

"Oh, *Mamma,*" Lucia said walking away and pulling Charlotte with her. "Don't be silly! Charlotte's not Scottish. She's an American!"

"*Mamma mia!*"

Lucia was as good as her word, and Charlotte was introduced to so many people that she was sure she'd never remember half of them. She was belatedly glad of Dewhurst's lesson on titles, but she found she couldn't remember who was a duke and who a viscount. Lucia helped her without being obvious, and Charlotte could have kissed her for being so kind.

"Kind?" Lucia said with a laugh later, when they had gone into dinner, and Charlotte tried to express her appreciation. "I am not being kind, Charlotte. I have ulterior motives." Lucia whispered the last conspiratorially and gestured to Charlotte to take a seat beside her at the table. The dancing was just beginning and the crowds at the tables laden with rich offerings were thinning.

"I don't believe a word you say. You've rescued

me more than once this evening, Lucia, and I am certain smoothing over my social blunders is not how you wished to spend your evening." Charlotte felt her cheeks heat, thinking about the plethora of mistakes she'd made in the last hour; often she was in the middle of a faux pas before even realizing it.

It was all so different from Charleston. She'd never faltered at social occasions during the Charleston Season, but now she understood why Freddie had scoffed at her comparisons. London was nothing like Charleston, and Charlotte had to admit that she was out of her league here in London. While her family did hold a prominent position in Charleston society, they had never been part of the upper echelons.

Charlotte straightened her shoulders and glanced in one of the long, rectangular mirrors lining the room. It amazed her that she still resembled the girl who'd danced at balls in Charleston. In five years she'd changed—become a different person—as different as her first ball gown from the one she wore now.

Light yellow satin with a V neck and full shoulder sleeves, the gown tapered to a hem embroidered with small white and yellow flowers. Below the exquisite hem peeked dainty white slippers adorned with silver rosettes. Lady Dewhurst had given Charlotte a small ivory fan decorated with white and yellow flowers that perfectly matched those of her dress and the small flowers peeking from the curls in Charlotte's hair. The last touch was a strand of lustrous yellow pearls draped around her white neck. Charlotte felt uncomfortable without her mother's emerald necklace, but Addy promised to keep it safe until Charlotte returned and could exchange the pearls for her most prized jewel.

"I knew this color would be perfect for you," Dewhurst's mother boasted. "You shall not see many ladies tonight in yellow. Their complexions would appear far too sallow, but with your coloring, it is perfect. And do not touch your hair!" she ordered, slapping Charlotte's hand away. "That Hester is a genius."

Charlotte had to admit the lazy maid was a talented hairdresser. She'd made a mental note to change the girl's duties. Mrs. Pots wouldn't like it, but Charlotte was gaining authority with the housekeeper, too. If only she could see the menu . . .

Charlotte took a deep breath. She must remember that all this finery was merely illusion. Underneath the silk and the lace, she was still Charlotte, the American wholesaler's daughter. Soon she would find Cade and the pretty illusion would end.

"You have a very serious look on your face, Lady Dewhurst," Lucia said, breaking Charlotte's reverie. "I'm terribly sorry, but sober thought is not allowed at *ton* balls. We are all about folly and frivolity, so put your insipid smile back in place."

Charlotte laughed. "Very well, then, but you have to promise not to report me to Freddie. If he finds out I've broken another rule, he'll quiz me until my head explodes."

"Agreed. On one condition. Tell me what had you looking so distraught."

Charlotte glanced down at the fan, the tassel of which she was twisting around her fingers. "I was thinking of home, of my first ball, and my father and brother."

Lucia put a warm hand on her arm. "Freddie tells me they died recently. I'm sorry for your loss."

Charlotte nodded, unable to speak for a moment. Then she said, "Lady Selbourne, thank you for escorting me about tonight, but I am certain you must wish to return to your husband."

"Alex? At a ball? Oh, I assure you I have no wish to see my husband tonight."

Charlotte frowned. Almost all she'd thought about since Lucia had led her away was Freddie—what he was doing, where he was, with whom he was dancing. She didn't want to think of him, but no matter how hard she tried, each time she heard a man's voice or a laugh, she turned in search of her golden angel. But wherever he was, it was not where Lucia had taken Charlotte.

"All I wish to do at a ball," Lucia was saying, "is

dance and laugh and drink champagne. All Alex wants to do is grumble and drink gin. He is a far better companion in the country." Lucia popped the last small cake on her plate into her mouth.

"But if you wish to dance, then you should do so," Charlotte said. "You mustn't let me stop you."

"Oh, you're not," Lucia assured her. "In fact, I have a confession to make, Charlotte."

Charlotte raised a brow. What deep, dark secret could this sparkly blond doll be hiding? Lucia looked around her, and apparently seeing no one she need worry might overhear, said, "You see, I had not realized how distracting having an American at the ball would be to Mama. She is so busy worrying what everyone is saying about you that she's had no time to think of me."

"I don't think I understand. Why don't you want your mother to think of you?"

Lucia sighed and looked at her hands, folded in her lap. "Because I cannot bear another conversation about the prospect of grandchildren. You know that my mother has actually started trying to give me . . . hints. It's absolutely *mortifying*." Lucia's gaze did not meet Charlotte's as she spoke, and she'd linked her fingers together now.

"You don't have any children then?" Charlotte asked gently.

"No, and I'm beginning to think that we never will. And I am coming to terms with that possibility, Charlotte, really I am."

"And Lord Selbourne?"

A shadow of pain bruised Lucia's porcelain face. "Alex says I am enough. We have three nephews and a niece we see quite often, but my mother . . ." Lucia sighed.

Charlotte took her hand and held it tightly. "You want children, don't you?"

Lucia wiped a tear away and glanced around to see if any lingering guests had observed her. "Desperately sometimes," she whispered, her eyes watering a little. "I love my niece and nephews, but I would so much like one of my own."

Charlotte squeezed her hand. "Do not give up hope yet."

"But how can you say that when it's been seven years?"

"Because my father and mother had difficulty conceiving, and even after my mother bore my brother, it was another thirteen years before I was born. Addy, that is the woman who raised me, always says that 'God didn't put no salt in the sweet pie.'" Lucia's brows furrowed, and Charlotte explained. "That means that everything happens for a reason. If it's meant to be, it will be."

Lucia's lips curved in the shadow of a smile. "I don't know that I'm a great believer in fate."

"Neither am I." For the most part, Charlotte believed in making her own destiny. "But what is the creation of life if not a roll of the dice? Boy or girl?

Blond or brunette? For once, matters are taken completely out of our hands."

Lucia nodded, and her engaging smile was back. "How did you become so wise, Lady Dewhurst?"

"Oh, it's not me. It's Addy."

"God didn't put any syrup in the pie. Is that it?"

"No, it's 'God didn't put no salt in the sweet pie,'" Charlotte corrected, playing up her accent. "And as Addy would say, 'You'd best to remember that.'"

"Oh, I will—"

"Lady Selbourne?" a harried servant interrupted apologetically. "I'm sorry to interrupt ye. A 'undred apologies."

"What is it, James?"

"Lord Brigham, my lady. He's looking for ye."

"Thank you." She rose. "Well, Charlotte, are you ready to meet my father?"

Charlotte wasn't sure she liked the twinkle in Lucia's eye.

Like his daughter Lucia, Lord Brigham was tall and handsome. A prominent member of the House of Lords, he took politics quite seriously, as Charlotte discovered when he blustered a quick greeting and turned back to argue heatedly with another peer—a rather rotund gentleman twirling a quizzing glass about one finger.

Lucia curtsied to the two men, murmuring, "Father. Lord Alvanley. This is—" But her father did not wait for her to finish.

"Just a moment, Lucy. Now see here, sir. Your opinions regarding the war are little more than a barrel of horse—" He stopped himself, glancing apologetically at his daughter, who only raised an innocent eyebrow. "Well, they are preposterous. By God, Alvanley, if Bonaparte still thinks he can conquer England after Wellington's decisive stroke last week at Vittoria, he is an even bigger ass than I thought."

Charlotte allowed her eyes to roam about the ballroom. It seemed that in London, every new venue was more beautiful than the last. The walls were painted to resemble white marble, the cut-crystal chandeliers glittered and bounced light off the shimmery heavy gold draperies, which were tied back from the French doors, and the ladies and gentlemen in attendance radiated wealth and style.

Charlotte glanced at Lucia, wondering what it must have been like to grow up in a home like this, to be surrounded by such opulence. Lucia was still trying to get her father's attention, but suddenly standing beside Charlotte, the corner of his mouth quirked in a half smile, was Freddie Dewhurst. He bowed slightly when their eyes met, and Charlotte stiffened. All night she'd been hoping to see him, but now that he was here she felt uncomfortable—too warm, too aware, too . . . everything.

"Father, I—" Lucia tried again to get her father's attention.

"Now, just a moment, Lucy. And about America, sir. If those colonists think to take us on, then I say let 'em come, sir! By God, let them come! We'll send 'em home whimpering."

Charlotte's head whipped around so fast that she heard the tense muscles and joints crack.

"I put little stock in the American forces," Alvanley drawled, lifting his quizzing glass to peer at Freddie's cravat with disdain before turning back to Brigham. "But they are one more diversion Napoleon will use to his advantage."

"Diversion!" Charlotte gasped. "How dare you call—"

"Dash it if my head doesn't swim with all this talk of politics," Freddie interrupted, yawning. "I always say that at a ball one should confine one's conversation to what is really important: how much lower ladies' necklines will plunge and whose are plunging on the lawn as we speak."

"Yes, that would be the extent of your intellectual capabilities, Dewhurst," Alvanley sneered. "That and how to snatch one's mistress from right under a man's nose."

Freddie shrugged. "At least I don't try to steal a man's valet. Now that, sir, is truly hitting below the belt."

Lucia quickly stepped in before the argument

grew any more heated. "Did you need to speak with me, sir?" she asked her father.

"By God, I do, Lucy. What's this I hear about you gallivanting about with Americans? I won't have it!"

Lucia's eyes met Charlotte's, and Charlotte, never willing to allow another to shield her, said, "I think you must be speaking of me, Lord Brigham." Charlotte held out her hand. "I am Charlotte Bur—" Freddie's soft curse was audible to all. "Lady Dewhurst, I mean," she finished.

Brigham did not take her hand. "I see. So you are the American that has got my wife in a tizzy? Well, you look harmless enough. Dewhurst, twirl your wife around on the dance floor once or twice."

Freddie bowed obligingly, holding out his arm, but Charlotte ignored him. "I suppose you believe all Americans harmless, do you not, Lord Brigham?"

Lucia's father threw a puzzled glance at Freddie, then answered, "No, I do not, madam. You colonists can be quite a pain in the . . . neck when you choose to be."

Charlotte took a deep breath of air and opened her mouth, but Freddie's voice drowned hers out. "Dash it if the contredanse is not about to begin. My lady, if you would be so kind?" He glared at her, holding his arm out again.

"I am afraid I cannot dance, sir, when my country is being insulted." She turned back to Lord Brigham. "Colonists, sir? I believe we won the War for Independence." She shook her head slightly to show her disdain. "We are no longer your colonists, and I must say that we are all the better for it. We Americans value freedom and liberty for all."

Freddie began clapping. The music had just ended, and his hollow claps echoed throughout the large room. "Beautiful, Lady Dewhurst. Your patriotic sentiment almost moves me to tears. Almost."

Charlotte turned and shot him daggers. And although his face retained its bored expression, his eyes flung bullets right back.

"Almost, sir?"

"Yes, almost. Alas, I fear I must correct you, madam. Your country has not advanced so far as you might think. You value freedom and liberty but not for all. At my last count, freedom was still the sole province of rich, white American men. You *Americans*"—he said the word derisively—"speak of equality, but I have to wonder: where is it? No, madam, your country is quite the contradiction."

"Well, at least we are not overbearing, arrogant, and vain," Charlotte threw back. She knew it was weak, but she hoped it would hit a nerve.

Freddie raised a dispassionate eyebrow. "No, you are merely foolish."

"Clarify yourself, sir!"

"Take the current war."

"Yes, do. Your puffed-up, egotistical governmental attempts to dictate policy to the United States are at an end. We are a sovereign country with trading privileges that—"

"Your trading privileges have been reinstated. The Orders in Council were revoked, madam."

"Oh, yes, and that paltry gesture came far too late. We suffered one grievous insult after another."

"If you hate the British so much, my lady," Alvanley interjected with a mischievous glint in his eyes, "then might I inquire as to why you are in our country and married to an Englishman—our Dewhurst here?"

Charlotte's mouth shut quickly.

"Ah," Freddie said straightening his cravat. "Thank you, once again, Alvanley, for putting your two pence where it is not wanted. But, as usual, you have the situation all wrong."

Alvanley raised his quizzing glass in curiosity, and even Charlotte wondered what the man could have gotten wrong. It seemed to her the plump man had the situation exactly right.

"You see," her husband went on, "it is not Charlotte's views toward England that have changed, rather it is my own views toward the United States."

Alvanley's brow rose above the quizzing glass,

and Lucia reached over and pinched Charlotte excitedly.

"What the devil do you mean by that statement, Dewhurst? By God, it's a pile of rubbish if I ever heard one," Lord Brigham blustered.

"I only meant," Freddie said, his air casual and unconcerned, "that my dear wife has a point. The United States did win the war—that is a fact, no matter how much we seek to deny it. And they have reason to oppose us now—or at least they did before we revoked the Orders in Council. There is a new world order, gentleman, and that order advocates equality and liberty for all. England would do well to take note. We can no longer dictate policy to the rest of the world. We can no longer keep such a sharp, unwavering focus on foreign affairs. We have our own issues—riots, poverty, inequality—right here at home."

Charlotte blinked. Had Dewhurst just defended America? Even worse, had he just defended her? Why? Did the man realize how much harder this would make it for her to hate him? The small party stood in silence for a moment, presumably digesting Dewhurst's discourse, then Lucia—apparently adept at smoothing over the rough moments—stepped in.

"Well," she began, clapping her hands together. "Charlotte, I simply must introduce you to the Duchess of Richmond. She can be quite . . . amusing." Lucia grabbed Charlotte's arm, and Charlotte stumbled ungracefully away with her.

When they were well away from Freddie, Alvanley, and Brigham, Lucia grabbed two glasses of champagne, handed one to Charlotte, gulped her own, and then began to laugh. Charlotte merely stared, her glass untouched. "Why are you laughing?"

"Oh, it's not at you, dear Charlotte. I have not seen my father so flabbergasted in a long time, and for once it wasn't with me. Oh, and Freddie! Did you see his face? He was furious! I *loved* it!"

"Furious with me!" Charlotte retorted.

"Nonsense. If there's one thing I know about Freddie, it's that he's loyal to the last. He's one of the best men I know."

Charlotte's jaw dropped. She had begun to trust Lucia's judgment in these matters, but now she began to wonder if Lucia was altogether sane. "Lucia, he's an arrogant, egotistical, spy!" Charlotte seethed. "I abhor him!"

"Of course you do." Lucia laughed again. "Now have a sip of the champagne. Champagne always makes everything seem better."

Chapter 13

Charlotte took Lucia's advice and sipped her champagne. Now that her temper was cooling, she regretted her words to Lord Brigham. She'd never been very good at keeping her emotions under control when arguing politics. She took after her own father too much, and his motto had been "My way or no way." She downed the champagne, and Lucia, smiling, fetched her another.

By her third glass of champagne, Charlotte was also able to laugh at Lord Brigham's shocked expression when she'd countered him and at her own overreaction. She wasn't yet able to laugh at her defeat and subsequent salvation at the hands of Freddie Dewhurst, but she could smile ruefully. When Lydia, Freddie's sister, joined them, Lucia left in search of Lord Selbourne.

"I have just been dancing with Lord Westman," the young girl squealed breathlessly. "He dances divinely."

"I am very glad to hear it," Charlotte said, at a loss for any other comment. Had she ever acted as silly and excited as Lydia? She sighed. Probably she had, but it seemed a lifetime ago. Charlotte watched the forms of the dance on display before them and tried to conjure a carefree feeling of excitement. Perhaps if she could regain that lost freedom, then she'd stop worrying so much and just enjoy herself.

Lydia sighed dramatically. "Westman is so handsome. He's the son of an earl, you know."

"Oh. Is that good?"

Lydia sighed impatiently. "Yes, that's good. It would make me a countess if we married."

"Oh, yes. I always have trouble with that one."

Lydia's pretty blue eyes clouded in confusion, but Charlotte wasn't really paying attention. The champagne was making her head swim, and the music and the swaying dancers all seemed a bit too much suddenly.

Lydia clutched Charlotte's arm, forcing her to focus. "Here he comes!" Charlotte frowned. How long was she to stand here, smile, and pretend interest? And where was Dewhurst?

"Excuse me, Lydia," she said. "I need to—" She needed to what? She didn't finish, but Lydia was focused on Westman and didn't seem to notice.

Charlotte made her way to the open windows of the ballroom. She had drunk too much champagne, and she knew she walked a little unsteadily. But if she could just step outside for a moment, she would be in the fresh air, away from the music and the crowds. She was exhausted—mentally and emotionally—and no matter where she turned she was surrounded by the enemy. And despite the crowds, she'd never felt so alone.

Charlotte felt tears prick at her eyes, and for once she allowed the rivulets to stream down her cheeks. It had been so long since she'd allowed herself to cry, to mourn the large losses in her short, small life. She'd been strong for so long, and she just didn't think she could do it anymore. But the terrace of the Brighams' town house was perhaps not the best spot for her breakdown. She needed to find a place inside where she could be alone. She began moving against the wall of the town house, but her head was spinning, and she stumbled every few moments.

Feet scraping on gravel, Charlotte saw a faint light, like a beacon, pouring into the garden a short distance away. She lurched toward it and peered inside. For once she was in luck. The room had to be the Brighams' library. She looked more closely, noting that three or four candles had been lit and a fire burned low in the hearth, but the room was still empty. Perfect.

Charlotte turned the handle of the French door,

fully expecting it to be locked, and pitched inside when it opened easily. She closed it quietly behind her, shutting out the insistent cold and welcoming the low warmth of the fire.

It was a man's room, all dark wood and heavy furnishings. Books lined the walls from the hardwood floors to the elaborate crown molding running the length of the ceiling. The room was dominated by two pieces of furniture, a dark burgundy velvet couch and a massive polished mahogany desk. The simple decor of elegant tapestries and imported rugs testified to the wealth and position of the Brighams.

She leaned against the French door, put her hands to her face, and sniffled. Half of her wanted to laugh at the idea of her—an American—in the bosom of British Society, the other half wanted to dig a deep hole and cry.

She was so tired of being alone. So tired of struggling, clawing, and pushing to get what her family needed and wanted. She sniffled and put a hand to her mouth, allowing a trickle of the silent sobs to escape. Oh, God, would she ever feel secure again? Would she ever be able to close her eyes and drift to sleep without a thousand worries pressing down on her like a mountain of boulders? Was she destined forever to be alone?

"You're not crying, are you?" A familiar masculine voice floated across the library.

* * *

Freddie set his crystal glass of brandy, now half full, on Brigham's mahogany desk, just before Charlotte's shriek. The chit howled when he spoke, then jumped back so quickly she hit her head on the door. Freddie rose from the desk chair, where he'd been taking a brief respite from the ball—that was, avoiding the sight of his lovely, tempting bride. Freddie's retreat had served another purpose as well, however. He'd met with Sebastian and Alex in the library, where Sebastian announced that he'd seen the man they suspected of being Pettigru's contact in London at dinner. Surely the news about Charlotte's marriage and her presence in London would reach Pettigru's ears soon.

Freddie's friends had just exited when his wife slipped inside and began to whimper. He hadn't meant to scare her or hurt her, but now she was rubbing the back of her head, and he winced in sympathy.

"*You,*" she whispered in a tone one might use with a mongrel. He glanced behind him, but not a spaniel in sight. Was he the mongrel in this scenario? A big, fat tear trickled down her cheek. Freddie went rigid. He hated it when women cried. Detested tears above all else. Flay him, torture him, scald him with hot coals, but do not saddle him with a teary-eyed woman.

"Dash it! You *are* crying. Here, take my handkerchief." He fumbled for the piece of cloth.

"Don't cry!" he ordered thrusting the handkerchief into her hands.

She stood there, staring at the fine linen. Then she murmured, "I'm not crying."

Freddie narrowed his eyes skeptically. "Your eyes have gone all misty, and you're sniffling."

"I'm fine."

Freddie raised a brow. "Oh, really?" He reached out and ran the back of his hand gently across her lashes, capturing one of her tears with a finger. He held it up triumphantly. "Then what is this?"

Charlotte touched her cheek where his fingers had skimmed across it, then stepped back, rattling the French doors. "It—it's cold outside, and my eyes—"

Freddie's gave her a quelling look. "Madam. It is July."

She took a deep breath and seemed to cast about for another excuse. "I don't feel well," she said quickly. "I feel . . . faint!" She put a hand to her forehead, and when Freddie peered closer, he decided she did indeed look peaked. She swayed, and he caught her elbow to steady her. Instinctively it seemed, his other arm wound around her, catching her waist and pulling her closer than he'd intended. It wasn't a sensual embrace, but the feel of her warm, soft body against his jolted him into awareness nonetheless.

"Dash it, Charlotte. Do not faint." He urged her gently to the dark velvet couch. She sank into its plush cushions and closed her eyes. He frowned down at her. Her cheeks were flushed and her hair slightly mussed, but that might have been from waltzing.

Whose arms had she been in?

Freddie pulled on the sleeves of his tailcoat violently. Logically Freddie knew she would be asked to dance at the ball, but he hadn't anticipated his reaction to the notion of her in another man's arms. He didn't like it.

Strange, considering that he was not a proprietary man. Horses, women, the blunt in his pocket: share and share alike had always been his motto. Tailcoats and a fine valet were another matter entirely. But with the exception of the time Alvanley had wooed Wilkins away—something the dandy had yet to allow Freddie to live down—and the few instances when Brummell's tailcoat had been far superior to his own, Freddie had never once felt a twinge of envy. When he felt it, he was not inclined to be reasonable. He'd acquiesced to Wilkins's demand for an exorbitant salary, and he'd accidentally spilled claret on Brummell's tailcoat—one reason he and Brummell were on shaky terms to this day.

And here he'd been tonight: defending the colonies and seething over the idea of Charlotte dancing with another man. He'd needed space. And then, just when he was feeling reasonable again, the contrary chit had found him.

Now he was all at odds again and every semblance of reasonableness had gone the way of the codpiece and Elizabethan ruffs. He shook his head. Why did he feel so disconcerted when in her presence? Tonight he'd been steadfast in his resolve not to let her affect him, but how was he to temper his reaction to her when, even red-eyed and runny-nosed, he wanted her?

His hands burned to caress her graceful neck, wrapped in glossy pearls, then trace the curve of her jaw and brush his thumb against her wide mouth until she opened it and . . . Painfully he noted the perfect hair, still his favorite color. He wanted to run his hands through that hair, pull it down, hold it to his nose and inhale the scent of honeysuckle.

He reached up to run a finger inside his tight cravat, and she finally opened her eyes. She dabbed the last drops of moisture away with his handkerchief. Her sherry gaze focused slowly on him, darkening the longer she stared.

"Dewhurst. You're still here."

Freddie took a long, slow breath. That accent, the lilt, the low, rich tones. He'd forgotten how much he enjoyed the sound of her voice, even—and this he would never admit—when she antagonized him by calling him Mr. Dewhurst. "Are you feeling better?" he asked.

"Wha?—oh, no. I think we should go home."

She smiled, a wobbly smile that seemed out of place on her.

He peered at his pocket watch. It was barely eleven. Lydia would not be pleased to quit the ball so early. But he said, "Of course. I'll order the carriage."

She sat forward, swayed, and had to grip the arm of the couch to steady herself.

"Good God. You're not well a'tall." He strode quickly to the side table and poured three fingers of Brigham's brandy, then pressed the crystal glass into her hands.

"No, I don't want it." She handed the glass back, but before she could loosen her grip, he wrapped his fingers around her wrist. He felt her pulse thrum under his touch, and she stared up at him.

"Do not argue, Charlotte," he said, thrusting the glass under her nose before he did something dreadfully unfashionable and which he would surely regret in the morning. "Drink it," he murmured.

Eyes wide, she stared at him. "But I can't. I mean, I don't think—"

He tightened his hand around her wrist. She was dashed stubborn. "Very well," he said, releasing her. "Then we wait. I won't have you fainting in the hall. I might be forced to catch you. It may sound romantic in novels, but such gestures are devilish hard on the cravat and tailcoat."

"Oh, George Washington forbid I wrinkle your precious tailcoat!" she exclaimed.

Freddie stifled a smile. "There's no call for blasphemy."

"You are the most irritating man I have ever known! I don't know why I ever married you." Before he could remind her that they were not truly married, she snatched the glass from his hands and held it up. "You are going to regret this." She downed the brandy and set the glass on the end table. Only she misjudged the distance, and it splintered against the polished wood floor.

Freddie's jaw dropped. His little American hellion was not feeling faint, she was drunk. And now he had likely made her more so. He cursed himself for not noticing before—dash it if all the signs weren't there: the wobbling, the high color in her cheeks, the slight slurring of her words—but the idea of her being foxed had not crossed his mind. Ladies of her supposed ilk did not over-imbibe. *Supposed* was obviously the operative word. She was no lady. He knew it, but how was he to keep the rest of the *ton* from the latest *on-dit*—the fact that his wife, Lady Dewhurst was an uncouth, uncultured—he shuddered—*American*? If the chit wasn't so integral to the capture of Pettigru, Freddie would never have borne this.

The American knelt unsteadily on the floor to collect the shards of glass, but he quickly hauled her up again. What was he going to say if someone walked in and saw his wife crawling about on the floor? To her he said, "Leave it be. You'll cut yourself."

"Oh, hellfire," she muttered as he hoisted her back onto the couch, where she promptly fell back onto the cushions. Hellfire was right, he thought. What was he to do with her now? She was drunk, disheveled, and . . . completely at his mercy.

Freddie started, alarmed by the direction of his thoughts. He had to send his mind on a detour—and quickly. But Charlotte was a sight to tempt any man—sprawled on the couch, hair in disarray, lace at her bosom trailing down the swell of her breasts. The dress was snug across her generous curves, and his fingers curled in an effort to curb the urge to loosen the gown, once again caress her ripe breasts, and feel the nipples harden against his palms.

Freddie clenched his jaw. He needed to remind himself that he didn't even like this Yankee. Her manners were incurable, she had no subtlety, no style. Dash him if she hadn't stood in the ballroom beside Lord Brigham and faced them all down like a common laundress.

Laundress or not, he respected her passion and her loyalty to her country. He had damned near taken her into his arms and kissed her right there in the ballroom. Her eyes had been burning so brightly that he had wanted to see them when overtaken with passion of another sort.

And now she was drunk. Damned little fool!

Without thinking, he crossed to her and yanked her up. She swung forward unsteadily, and he grasped her arms, half out of anger and half to support her. "Why the devil didn't you tell me?"

"Tell you what?" she stammered, trying to squirm out of his arms. He tightened his hold, fingers curling around the deliciously bare flesh above her sagging gloves.

"Why didn't you tell me you were foxed, you little fool? Now we've only made it worse."

"I told you I didn't want the brandy, but you wouldn't listen." Her sherry eyes flashed fire.

"I would have listened had I known the reason. I thought you were just being stubborn. As usual."

"I'm not stubborn." She swayed slightly in his arms, and he pulled her back down on the couch beside him. The cushions were so plush that she practically fell against him. God help him to endure this temptation.

"How dare you call me stubborn. *You* are the stubborn one, but I suppose you think all Americans are stubborn." Her voice was muffled from being pressed against him.

"Do *not* start that patriotic rubbish again," Freddie ordered tiredly. "I call a truce for the rest of the night." As he spoke, his lips moved against her velvet cheek, soft as the material of the couch underneath him. He closed his eyes. "Darling," he whispered because he was unsure of his voice. "How did you become so foxed?"

"What's a foxed?" she murmured, and he could feel her voice resonate through him.

"Drunk. How did you become so drunk?"

She pushed away from him. "Drunk? I have never been drunk in my life. I'm simply in-in-invitriated."

"Inebriated?"

"Oh, just forget the whole thing. I don't care. I just want to find Cade and go home."

Freddie heard the catch in her throat before she turned her head away, and he grasped her chin between his thumb and forefinger and tugged her face to his. The couch sloped inward, and they were thrown quite close together.

"Buck up now, Charlotte. None of that blubbering."

Her lips were trembling, and she gave him a shaky smile. Freddie's gaze darted to the tip of her tongue as she ran it quickly over her lips, and he had to restrain himself from brushing his fingers against her mouth. A mouth that was too big for her face, a mouth that he could imagine doing wicked things to him with that little pink tongue.

He pulled his hand away, resisting temptation.

"You are the bossiest man I have ever met," Charlotte complained, laying her head on the couch cushions behind her. "First you tell me how to speak, then how to dress, and now I'm not even allowed to cry."

Freddie couldn't stop a small smile at her pitiful tone, but his thoughts did not tend toward sympathy. Underneath the lustrous yellow pearls she wore, Charlotte's neck was slender and vulnerable. Was she trying to tempt him by arching it so? Was she tempting him earlier with the flick of her tongue?

Lazily she rolled her head toward him. "I am so in-in—drunk. Everything is spinning." The words were so slurred, Freddie could barely make them out. She closed her eyes. "I wish I were home."

Her voice was so full of anguish that Freddie gathered her in his arms without thinking. He pulled her close, and then her tears began in earnest.

The smell of honeysuckle overwhelmed him. It was in her hair, her clothes; it seemed to emanate from her skin like a part of her. He closed his eyes and pulled her closer, willing her tears to stop. She wasn't sobbing uncontrollably, just the tears of someone who was exhausted physically and mentally. Someone homesick. He remembered the feeling. When he'd first arrived at Eton, he'd cried and pined for his mother and father and home. The older boys had toughened him up quickly enough, but he never forgot the sick feeling in the pit of his stomach or the pang of yearning.

Freddie pulled her snugly against his shoulder and stroked her hair. Fire and small white flower blossoms swirled around his fingers. Like molten lava, her hair glinted in the candlelight.

Soothed and quiet, she snuggled into the crook of his shoulder. His hand strayed from her hair to the nape of her neck, smooth and delicate, bending gracefully like a willow and with that hidden strength as well. How much strength this woman must have to be sitting in Lord Brigham's library with him even now. How much must she have overcome?

And how great would be her reward? A thousand pounds. She wanted his money, not him. She wanted no Englishman.

But quite suddenly he realized that he wanted her.

Freddie stiffened involuntarily, coming back to his senses like a man bowled over by a wave from the ocean. She was getting too close. He was beginning to find it more and more difficult to keep her at a distance.

Were her actions calculated? Did she have some ulterior motive? And dash it if he couldn't get the idea of her warm supple body arching beneath his in the firelight out of his mind. He wanted her.

"You're ruining my hair," she murmured, her breath tickling his neck.

"I'll stop," he said, moving to separate their bodies, but she did not relinquish her hold.

"No," she said. "I like it. I feel . . . safe for the first time in . . . oh, never mind." She peered up at him, thick lashes wet with tears. "I need a hero, Freddie."

He tensed at the sound of his name on her honeyed tongue.

"I need someone to save me. Just once. I'm so tired, so tired of saving everyone else." She shook her head, peered into his eyes. "Why you?" she asked.

He frowned. "Why me, what?"

"Why does it have to feel so good in your arms? Why do you make me shiver every time you touch me?"

He shivered himself at her words. "Do I?"

"Mmm-hmm." She nodded and licked her lips again. He took a fortifying breath, then raised his hand again to the nape of her neck, fingers sliding slowly upward to cradle the base of her skull and test the weight of her hair. The intimacy of seeing her with her hair down was beginning to affect him. Only husbands and lovers had this privilege.

Charlotte leaned into his touch. "What else do I do to you?" he said, voice husky as his fingers trailed down her neck to trace the delicate arch of her jaw.

"You make me warm," she said softly. "You make me feel like there's a fire pooling in my belly and sliding down—all the way to my toes."

He rubbed the pad of his thumb across her

lower lip, feeling it give gently, feeling the inviting warmth of her lips and mouth.

"Do you like the fire, Charlotte?" he said. "Do you want to burn hotter?" She nodded, and he whispered against her lips, "Show me."

Charlotte met his gaze, then reached up, cupped a hand around his neck, and pulled his mouth to hers. Lips met lips, tenderly at first. Testing, then exploring.

At first Freddie thought that he must be the one who was drunk. Everything about the experience of kissing her intoxicated. He was engulfed by her scent. He was sinking in her skin, relishing the taste of her abundant lips and the feel of her ample breasts pressed against him.

His tongue flicked her lips, and she opened for him. The lush feel of her tongue mating with his sent his senses reeling. He felt like a man who has been numb all his life and has suddenly learned how to use his senses. It was as if he'd been wearing thick gloves for an eternity and they were suddenly and unexpectedly ripped off, and he could *feel*.

He was suddenly alive. Alive in the moment but alive inside as well. The feel of her, the tentative touch of her tongue, sparked something in him—something he hadn't felt in a long time and something he didn't want to let go of again.

An urge to possess her ignited within him, and instinct, feral and primitive, took over.

In one swift motion, he lifted her onto his lap so that her legs straddled him. When she might have protested he deepened the kiss, stroking her hot, wet mouth with his tongue, bruising her lips with the force of his passion, and tangling his hands in that flaming hair. He explored the recesses of her mouth as he wanted to explore her skin, showing her how he would please her with his body, making her breathing quicken and her body shudder.

He felt her tremble, and it only made him want her more. Was he the first? If he entered her now, hard and fast, would he find her untouched? Desire ripped through him at the thought, and he took her mouth hard. She gasped, and deep within, Freddie knew he should draw back. But he was so far gone, so hard under her, his body seemingly composed of corded sinew and steel. Freddie had a reputation among the ladies of the *ton* as a skilled, aloof lover. But his need for Charlotte would not allow any pretense. He could not play a part with her. His longing was too intense and possessive. Too dangerous.

He tried to force himself to be more gentle, fearing she'd push him away or cry out in protest. But as soon as he drew away, she made a moan of disapproval and pulled him hard against her again. "Don't stop," she groaned and pushed against him.

The effort Freddie had to exert to stop himself from toppling her onto the floor and taking her right then was immeasurable. He was as taut as a wire, and all control threatened to break. Oh, the safe, comfortable façade was definitely gone now, perhaps beyond any recovery, and Freddie was exposed—raw and fierce. He dared not allow this to go any further, and yet he ached to see passion light her face. He needed something, some memory to get him through the long, lonely nights when she was gone.

Keeping one arm about her waist, he pushed her skirts high on her legs until he could look down and see the creamy skin of her thighs. He ran his hand along the top of one leg, feeling the silky skin smolder under his fingertips. With a deft flick, he pushed the bulk of her skirts away until she was bare before him. "Open for me," he murmured, fingers teasing the juncture of her thighs to entice her. She did not move and he glanced up at her.

God, she was a vision. Her flaming hair and flaming cheeks were the perfect picture of every male fantasy. She looked debauched. Wanton. Freddie's need for her reached new heights.

"Open for me," he whispered, and she did, revealing her wet, pink flesh. Hand shaking, he reached out to stroke her. At the first touch, she cried out and bucked against him. He stroked her again, his touches longer and more deliberate. Then he entered her with two fingers, felt her close tightly around him, heard her whimper in pleasure.

She was breathing hard now, her breasts heaving, her eyes wild. He lifted his hand to cup her, stroked her again until she clenched hard around him and cried out, arching her back and thrusting hard. Then she slumped against him, her heart beating so hard and fast he could feel it in his own chest.

"You shouldn't have done that," she said a moment later. "It's not proper."

Freddie smiled and tilted her head back so he could see her. "I thought I was the one giving the etiquette lessons."

She looked as though she would argue but what came out was a moan. Freddie narrowed his eyes. That did not sound like a moan of ecstasy. "Are you all right?" Freddie asked cautiously.

"No," Charlotte croaked. "I think I am going to be sick." Her hand flew to her mouth, and her wide eyes scanned the room frantically.

Freddie had her off his lap and across the room in mere seconds. He dragged her to the French doors and pushed her outside where she promptly began retching, quite loudly, into the bushes of the garden.

"Oh, good God," Freddie groaned. He had better get her home and without anyone seeing. He glanced back out the French doors and saw that she had stopped retching and was now just moaning, and he crossed to the front doors of the library, opened them a crack, and peered out. It didn't look as though anyone was about. He eased the door open farther, poked his head out, then realized his mistake.

"Freddie!" a gaggle of female voices called. "There you are! We've been looking for you."

Freddie stepped back into the library and slammed the door shut again. How had they found him? Worse than just his scatty sister Lydia, all four of his sisters had been hunting him, and now they'd cornered their prey.

The library doorknob turned.

Chapter 14

Freddie threw a quick glance at the French doors, wondered if he had enough time to close them and keep Charlotte out of sight, but the library door opened and several women poured in on an endless ruffle of silk.

Not just any women—his four sisters.

"Freddie!" Meg, his eldest sister, exclaimed. Unlike the rest of the family, she had dark hair and eyes, and they flashed at him now. "Where have you been? I want you to have a word with Lord Oxbow about his plans for the south fields at Downsleigh. He simply will not listen to reason and insists on planting corn."

"I see," Freddie began, wondering how he had become enough of an expert to advise his sister's husband on crop rotation. "Perhaps I could—"

"Freddie," Lydia interrupted. "First I need you to speak with Mama. I promised Lord Westman the first dance at Lord and Lady Winterbourne's ball the day after tomorrow, and Mama says she has no intention of attending."

Freddie frowned over his shoulder at the French doors. How could he get his sisters out of here before Charlotte began retching again or stumbled in through the doors? "Ah, why not tell Westman you'll see him at the theater or Almack's on Wednesday?"

"Freddie!" Mary said, bustling forward. She was two years younger than he, pale, and quite short. "Lydia cannot tell Lord Westman she will not be available to dance with him at the Winterbournes' ball. Do you want her to end up a spinster?"

Freddie opened his mouth and closed it again. "I fail to see how the two—"

"Oh, you never see!" Lydia cried. "You don't need to see, just speak with Mama."

"He will," Meg said, "after he speaks with Oxbow."

"Now girls," Jane, the peacemaker in the family and five years Freddie's junior, said. "Freddie will have time to speak to Oxbow and Mama. There's no need to argue."

Mary sneered. "You think if you're sweet to him now then he'll talk to Fitzherbert for you, is that it?" she accused Jane. "Don't listen to her, Freddie.

She's angling for a new town house, and she wants you to plead her case with Fitzherbert."

"That's not true!" Jane said.

"My problem with Oxbow comes first," Meg said.

"But what about Westman? I hate being the youngest," Lydia cried. "I never get any attention."

"Oh stubble it, Lydia," all three girls said in unison.

There was a moment of stunned silence, for it was not very often that the sisters agreed on anything, and in the momentary quiet Freddie heard the sound he'd been dreading. The hinges on the French doors creaked, and Charlotte staggered inside. "I don't feel very well," she groaned.

"What is *that*?" Meg cried and backed away.

Freddie rolled his eyes and wished he were somewhere else—an iceberg, a prison barge . . . Hell. "Ladies, might I introduce—"

"Charlotte!" Lydia screamed. "Freddie, what have you done to her?"

"Nothing. I didn't touch her," he answered automatically, then remembered she was supposed to be his wife. "I mean, she's not feeling well, and I was about to take her home."

"*This* is your new wife?" Mary asked, staring at Charlotte with unabashed curiosity. "She's not what I expected."

"Not at all," Meg chimed in.

"She looks very . . . sweet," Jane said helpfully.

Charlotte glanced at the three women, then at Freddie, and muttered, "This is all your fault. I told you I didn't want that brandy."

Jane gasped, and Mary and Meg's eyes got very large. Lydia scowled. "Freddie, is poor Charlotte"—she lowered her voice—"indisposed?"

"Ah . . ." Freddie looked from one sister to the next, then at his wife. "I think we'll just be going now." He took Charlotte's arm, but when she stumbled, he bent over, swept her into his arms, and carried her out of the library, past the guests loitering in the hallway and out the front door to find his coachman.

Do you like the fire, Charlotte? Do you want to burn hotter?

Charlotte massaged her pounding temples as Freddie's words ran through her head for the three hundred and seventh time that morning. Actually, it wasn't even morning anymore. Addy had long since come and gone with the breakfast tray, and from the sounds outside the window, it sounded as if it was now past noon. Not that she could tell from the position of the sun, as there never seemed to be any sun in this godforsaken city. Instead she lay in her ivory bed, under vanilla silk sheets, listening to the quiet patter of rain against the windowpane.

Her head ached and her stomach roiled and she was so confused that she didn't know where to begin sorting it all out. Her feelings, her thoughts: they were all such a jumble. Who *was* this man playing at being her husband? Just when she thought she had him figured out, he did something unexpected. Like kiss her senseless and then put his hands . . .

She blushed and turned her head into the pillow. Perhaps she remembered that part incorrectly. Perhaps that had been nothing more than a dream—a very intense, pleasurable dream—but she couldn't bear to think that she had behaved so shamelessly in real life.

And why would she behave so? She hated Englishmen. She hated Dewhurst.

Then, last night, he had kissed her. *Really* kissed her.

And she realized there was a depth to him she hadn't seen. The fierceness in him, the raw need she felt in the Brighams' library had set her on fire. It had left her shaken and wanting more. But even as she tried to be offended by the liberties he had taken in kissing her, she remembered another good quality.

He'd defended her. Defended her and her country in front of the whole of London Society, and she knew how much their opinions meant to him. What could have gotten into him? She was not his wife in truth. Could he feel a sense of loyalty toward her anyway? And Charlotte would never forget the tenderness in his eyes when she'd told him he made her feel safe, when she'd told him she needed a hero. And how could she ever shut out the raw, flagrant desire in his eyes when he'd ruched up her skirts and moved his hand tantalizingly between her thighs?

Charlotte shivered and pulled the covers to her jaw, but she could not shut out the memory of his fingers pressed tightly against her and the stirring sensations each infinitesimal movement elicited. And she couldn't help but wonder what it would have been like if they had continued. If he'd . . .

But certainly that was not what she wanted. She did not want to lose her virtue to an Englishman. Not when the English had taken so much from her already. And she certainly would not lose her heart to Lord Dewhurst. That, above all, was the true danger. Her body desired him, and her mind was intrigued by the contrast between his cool, fashionable exterior and his hot, passionate interior. But her heart . . . her heart melted when he smiled at her, said her name, stroked her hair. How was she to defend her heart against a man who described her plain auburn hair as cinnamon and her brown eyes as sherry-colored? If that was not evidence that he found her alluring, then nothing was.

George Washington! Perhaps he played the part of a fool, but what sort of fool was she if she fell in love with him? He was a warrior. If he even possessed any of the more tender emotions, he would never succumb to them. Becoming involved with Freddie Dewhurst beyond this business deal would leave her scarred and alone. And she was already that without him.

"Well, I see the princess is finally awake," Addy said from the doorway.

Charlotte glanced at her friend, then looked more closely. "Is that a new shawl you're wearing?"

Addy merely smiled. "Maybe it is. You going to get up or loll in bed all day?"

"I suppose I had better get up and, um . . ." What did she have to do when she got up? "See to the servants and the dinner menu," she finally said.

Addy harrumphed. "Every day you say you going to look at the menu, and every day I hear you arguing with that Mrs. Pots 'cause she ain't showed it to you."

Charlotte glared at her. "Thank you for pointing that out, Addy."

Mrs. Pots was proving quite stubborn, but Charlotte had no doubt she'd come around. After all, Charlotte had won the other servants over. Now that Hester was no longer simply a maid but also a hairdresser, she was far less lazy, and Wilkins hardly ever grumbled about sharing his starch with Addy anymore, and Charlotte had even convinced Freddie's cook, Julian, to experiment with some of her American favorites.

Everything was falling into place. Everything

except Freddie and Cade. To rid herself of one, she'd need to contact the other.

With Cade safe and her thousand dollars in her reticule, there'd be nothing to stop her from going home. Home. Where she and her heart would be safe.

Freddie's ebony walking stick made a pleasant clicking sound as he made his way through the thinning crowds on Bond Street to Gentleman Jackson's Rooms. Freddie was fond of pugilism and he wasn't bad in the ring, but he had no intention of participating that night. His first order of business was to find Sebastian and hear his report.

Freddie nodded to Lord Yarmouth, who was exiting Gentleman Jackson's as he entered. The rumor was that Yarmouth was the latest recipient of Josephine's ample charms. Freddie frowned, suddenly realizing that he hadn't thought of Josephine for days. He hadn't thought of any woman save one: Charlotte Burton.

Dash it if the hellion hadn't intrigued him—no, bewitched him—with her charms last night.

Wilkins had had to query three times which riding boots Freddie preferred this morning, and he had no idea how many times his housekeeper, Mrs. Pots, had inquired if his breakfast was satisfactory. Freddie couldn't even remember what, if anything, he had eaten for breakfast.

Two things played upon his mind constantly. One was that he had to have Charlotte Burton. He wanted her in the biblical sense of the word certainly, but he also feared that he might feel the need to have her in a more permanent way as well. As a mistress?

No, she would never agree to that.

Which left only—Freddie shuddered and endeavored, for perhaps the fiftieth time, to pretend the idea had never crossed his mind—marriage.

Leg-shackled. Tied the nuptial knot. Buckled.

He didn't know where such a thought came from or how to rid himself of it. He could only hope this irrational need to possess her would wane. He didn't know what was wrong with him. Never before had he even considered marrying a woman of his acquaintance. He was fond of the ladies he knew and courted, but he felt no great affection. Then there were his paramours, of course, but none of them would have made a suitable match. And neither would Charlotte, he reminded himself sternly.

And he'd be dashed if he couldn't imagine the tittle-tattle when Charlotte vocalized her very American political views again. He could not hope to keep her silent on that point. Of course, her loyalty was commendable, and Freddie knew without thinking that she was fiercely loyal to her family and friends. What might it be like to be the recipient of such devotion? For a man who had made a career of trusting no one, the idea was almost inconceivable. Could he trust Charlotte?

That brought him back to reality. What of Charlotte herself? Could he trust her to uphold her end of their bargain concerning Pettigru? And what of the money she demanded as payment? Was she just a mercenary, a money-grabbing chit like so many others he'd known?

Freddie's hand clenched around the gold lion's head of his walking stick. He did not want to think of Charlotte in those terms. It was much more pleasant to dwell on the memory of her lush body pressed against his. He knew enough of women's bodies to know that hers would mold perfectly to his. That he could easily lose himself in her satiny skin, her velvet curves, and the heady scent of honeysuckle. He imagined her cherry hair splayed on the white of his pillow, her sherry brown eyes half closed in pleasure, her—

Freddie's roguish smile was still on his lips when he saw Alex signal to him from across Jackson's Rooms. He made his way to his friend, who was lounging next to Sir Lumley Skeffington, odd pairing that, and belatedly realized the two were engrossed in a boxing match between Middleton and Lydia's beau, Westman. Gentleman Jackson, the retired pugilist and owner of the establishment, was shouting encouragement and directions.

Freddie took the empty space next to Skiffy, who then remarked, "Zounds! Middleton is giving Westman a beating. Poor chap. I never thought that chitty-faced fop had it in him." Freddie smiled crookedly at Skiffy's characterization of Sebastian as a fop. He could smell Skiffy's strong perfume three feet away and endeavored not to take note of the yellow satin suit he wore or the face paint.

Freddie glanced at Alex, but he seemed more engrossed in the fight than usual. That was to say that his jaw was clenched and his arms crossed. The day Selbourne shouted encouragement to one of the pugilists would be the day Almack's opened to the general public.

"What's got Selbourne all agog, old man?" he asked Skiffy, wincing as Westman threw a low right that hit its mark.

"Oh, he's got a monkey on this mill. Middleton, of course." Sebastian swung at Westman, but the punch went wild and Westman easily sidestepped it.

"And you haven't risked any of your own blunt?"

"Zounds, no, sir! I'm in dun territory as it is. Can't a fellow have a look-in on the Corinthian Path without having his windmill dwindled to a nutshell?"

Just then Sebastian brought up his left, and, in a

move Freddie knew well from experience, feigned a punch, then floored Westman with his right. The fight was over.

Alex uncrossed his arms and turned to Freddie. "Drinks are on me tonight."

"In that case, may I remark that I have always admired you, Selbourne," Skiffy exalted. "Always said you were the best of men."

Alex raised an eyebrow but didn't have a chance to respond as Sebastian came striding between the men. The other spectators were still calling their congratulations, and Sebastian was glowing from his victory and eager to recount the entire fight to Dewhurst.

After several moments of Middleton's detailed retelling, which bordered on reenactment at times, even the promise of free alcohol ceased to interest Skiffy, and he left to seek grander entertainments with Golden Ball Hughes.

Freddie listened with what patience he had, which was generally not much where his cousin was concerned, and just when Sebastian was relaying the coup de grâce, he interrupted.

"What can you tell me about our American friend? Has he heard of my wife's arrival in Society?"

Sebastian sighed. "You could have at least let me finish my crowing, especially as I've no word yet."

" 'Fraid I find that hard to believe. None of your contacts know of the man?"

"Nary a one."

Freddie looked contemplative, and Alex, who although not involved in their efforts on behalf of the Foreign Office was still reasonably informed, added, "We'll know shortly. If Pettigru doesn't get his hands on the new codes soon, the information he's passed to the French will be too old to use in deciphering Wellington's communiqués."

"How often does Wellington change the cipher?" Freddie asked.

"As needed," Alex answered. "And if the British codes have changed, Bonaparte will not be pleased. If Pettigru is as determined to contact Charlotte as you say he is, he'll make a move to contact her tonight or tomorrow."

"I say we all keep our ears to the ground tonight, and then make every effort to throw Miss—I mean, Lady Dewhurst—in his path tomorrow night at Winterbourne's ball," Middleton said.

Freddie sat up straight. "I don't know that I like the idea of throwing her in anyone's path."

"But that's the reason she's here," Sebastian protested. Freddie didn't respond. His cousin was right, but Freddie didn't want to be reminded of that fact. Once they apprehended Pettigru, Charlotte would be free to leave. He'd pay her the thousand pounds; she'd be out of his life forever. And perhaps that was for the best.

"Well, I for one have had enough pugilism for a day," Middleton said. "What do you say we set off for the club? I've got a taste for a bit of hazard."

White's was crowded and loud with the same men who'd been at Brigham's ball the night before. The greater part of London's *ton* were at their country houses for the summer, and Freddie felt the lack of variety. He wished he'd gone home, but he feared that without copious amounts of alcohol, he would not make it through the evening. He could not endure another night lying in his bed, knowing that Charlotte was sleeping just a few feet away.

The dressing room door he had barely noted before Charlotte's arrival took on a new significance with her on the other side. So far it had taken monumental resolve not to turn the knob. Freddie feared he was fresh out of resolve tonight, but he had wine, and perhaps if he drank himself senseless, he could forget the red-haired hellion sleeping in his house, playing the part of his wife, in all ways but one.

Freddie was well on his way to entering a drunken stupor when Alvanley and several of his cronies entered White's gaming room, where Freddie and Alex were drinking and watching Middleton lose a small fortune at the tables.

"Ah, there he is," Alvanley sneered when he spotted Freddie. "The traitor lover."

Freddie raised a lopsided brow. "What's got you chomping at the bit now, Alvanley?"

Alvanley raised a copy of the *Times*. "Your precious Americans are getting out of hand again, Dewhurst."

Freddie shrugged. The story of Mad Jack Percival had been in all the papers the day before. Percival was an uneducated American man who'd started his sailing career as a cabin boy. He'd been impressed into British service and even served on HMS *Victory* before escaping.

Then on July 4, he'd made an ass out of the British navy. The rumor was that he rounded up thirty-two men and took the American ship *Yankee* out into the New York harbor. The British were blockading the harbor, and three miles out the *Yankee* was overtaken by the British ship *Beagle*. Mad Jack had visibly stocked the *Yankee* with just the enticements the British would need—fruit, sheep, ducks—and all of it topside. Below were the thirty-two American sailors with their weapons.

It was meant to look like an easy catch, and the thirteen redcoats on the *Beagle* must have been slapping each other on their backs, until the armed Americans jumped out. Outnumbered and outwitted, the British were forced to surrender. Mad Jack towed the *Beagle* to the New York battery to the loud cheers of the American crowds celebrating Independence Day.

The *Times* quoted Percival as saying, "Shucks, we was just having a little fun. We ought to do something to celebrate the Fourth besides listen to a band concert."

"Looks as though you weren't the only Englishman bested by an American recently, Alvanley. What's wrong? Did my wife make you look like a fool last night?"

One of Alvanley's cronies started forward, but the dandy held up a hand. "You're the expert on fools, Dewhurst. But I don't have an American slut spreading her legs for me, making me forget who the real enemy is."

"Bastard." Freddie shot out of his chair, tackling Alvanley and sending them both sprawling into a table of gamblers. The men and cards flew in all directions, but before Freddie could regain his feet, one of Alvanley's thugs caught him and held him as two others took turns pummeling him. Freddie was almost too drunk to feel the full impact of the blows, but he was not so drunk that he didn't look to Alex for assistance.

Ignoring the remonstrations of White's civilized gentlemen, Alex pushed his way past chairs, tables, and glasses, scattering men. Freddie used the diversion to land a blow, and Alex pulled one of the other men off him, landing a hard right square on the man's jaw. Freddie pummeled his opponent in the gut, then looked at Alex and grinned. "I say, well met, Selbourne!"

Alex scowled. "What the devil are you smiling at?"

Freddie didn't have time to respond as Alvanley was bearing down on him. Alvanley swung and Freddie ducked. Alvanley stumbled and clipped the Duke of York, the Prince Regent's brother, in the jaw.

There was a long silence as York shook his head and rose. With an oath, he swung at Alvanley, and then White's erupted into total chaos. Alex grabbed Freddie and hauled him through the mob and into the night. Alex pulled Freddie across the street, and both men collapsed a few doors away.

"What the devil were you thinking, Dewhurst?" Alex demanded. "That was a damned foolish thing to do."

Freddie laughed. "It's not the first, old boy, and it won't be the last I'm afraid."

Alex glanced at him sideways. "You look like hell," he said. Freddie glanced down at his evening clothes, noting his tailcoat was dirty and torn, his cravat had been ripped off, his trousers had a hole in the knee, and his shirt was spattered with blood, probably his own. And for some reason, he couldn't stop grinning.

"All right, let's get you home," Alex said.

Freddie nodded but when he tried to rise, he fell back in a heap against the wall. Alex pulled him up and half carried him around the corner, where he flagged down a hackney and shoved Freddie inside.

"Dashed Americans!" Freddie said when they were underway. "You see what just the mention of one can do? Imagine living with one." He felt the swelling in one of his eyes already and knew it would be black by morning.

Alex smiled ruefully. "I can't say that your appearance in this state will improve matters much."

Freddie drew himself up. "And what state is that, Selbourne?"

"All right, don't call me out, Dewhurst. But you have to admit that women are generally not pleased when their husbands—even men playing the role of husband—arrive home drunk and with all the evidence of having been in a brawl."

Freddie seemed to ponder this a moment. "You're right," he said. "She's going to be mad."

"Mad?" Alex repeated. "I think that might be a slight underestimation." But Freddie ignored him and began pounding on the hackney's roof. "What the devil—" Alex began as the coach slowed.

"I must get her a present. Surprised I haven't done it yet. Take me to Hamlet's!" Dewhurst instructed the jarvey when he opened the hatch. The jarvey exchanged a look with Alex, but Freddie said, "None of that. Take me to Hamlet's."

"One moment," Alex said, and the hatch dropped closed again. "Are you speaking of the play or the jeweler, Dewhurst?" Alex asked with a calm that Freddie could tell did not match his mood.

"The jeweler, of course," Freddie snapped.

"It is past midnight, Dewhurst. They are closed. Now I am going to take you home to your wife, who I am beginning to think has the bad end in all of this, so that I can go home to my own wife. You can get Charlotte a trinket tomorrow."

Freddie shook his head and stopped Selbourne's arm as he raised it to tap the roof of the carriage.

The look in Alex's eye was murderous. "Wait a minute, Selbourne. You are perfectly right. I can't come home with some measly fallalls for Charlotte. Addy said she always wears that emerald necklace from her mother. I need to bring her something special. Get me a flower girl!"

Alex's brow creased. "I don't think Charlotte will—"

"I don't want the girl, just the flowers. We need honeysuckle, Selbourne."

Alex looked ready to mutiny.

Chapter 15

Charlotte wandered about the town house that evening as though it were a tomb. All in all, it was a nice tomb. The servants were more willing to make changes she suggested, Charlotte had eaten a wonderful dinner of dishes native to Charleston, and even Mrs. Pots wasn't acting as sulky as usual.

But to Charlotte the house still felt like a cold, dark vault. Every room she passed, every vase, every knickknack, every damned floorboard reminded her of Freddie. It didn't seem possible, but she was afraid she actually missed him. Without him, London was lonely and dark and senseless. Her real fear was that Charleston, too, might feel empty if he was not there. Her life would be barren without him. She'd grown accustomed to his lectures, the way he tugged the sleeve of his tailcoat when he was irritated, and even his exaggerated concern for the state of his cravat made her smile.

She would miss that in Charleston.

She would miss him.

With a resigned sigh, she started up the grand black and white marble staircase, clutching her skirts in frustration.

She was tired of the incessant little voice in her head pounding away with questions. Where was he? Who was he with? Was he thinking of her? Did he care for her?

Her breath hitched in her throat and she walked more quickly, finally reaching the top of the stairs and starting down the corridor toward his room. She stopped outside, not wanting to enter, unable to resist. Even as she turned the doorknob she knew she was making a mistake. His essence would be strongest here among his most personal possessions, and she was trying to wipe him out of her mind. Wasn't she?

She entered, shutting the door behind her and leaning against it for support as images of Freddie came rushing at her. She shook her head, trying to block them, trying to slow their assault so that she could somehow make sense of them. But it was no use. She was assailed from every vantage point. His voice was in the whisper of her slippers on the rug. His lean, hard body was in the sturdy strength of the bed's foot posts. She parted the velvet drapes, and his smell was in the thick counterpane as she sank into the bed's softness.

She allowed the bed hangings to fall closed again, and in the warm darkness she was enveloped by Freddie's essence. She could almost feel him here beside her, and the longing she felt was exquisite torture. She wanted him—wanted him so much it frightened her. She didn't know how it had happened, but somewhere between that first kiss on the Thames and his defense of her country in the ballroom, she had come to care for him.

She shook her head, the feel of plush counterpane cushioning her cheek. She was falling in love with him, and he saw her as one more annoyance in his life—another annoying female he had to appease. He probably couldn't wait to be rid of her, and it would not be long now before he had his wish.

They were close to finding Cade. Charlotte did not need to be told that. She'd sensed it last night, and she suspected her husband was out searching for information on Cade right that moment. The end was near. For so long she'd yearned to return to Charleston, to the house on Legare Street, and to reclaim her father's shipping business. But suddenly none of that mattered as much. Suddenly home was wherever Freddie was. Home was . . . here.

Not for the first time, Charlotte cursed her nature. In her personality there was no room for the tempering of emotions. She loved violently, wholeheartedly, or not at all. She gave of herself completely and absolutely, and she wanted the same from Freddie Dewhurst.

And she would never have it. She'd had glimpses behind his façade. Last night in the Brighams' library had been the most revealing glimpse yet. But the revelation had not been a welcoming one. Despite his guise as a dandy, he was undeniably a soldier, a warrior. Charlotte knew that type well, knew that even if he felt more for her, he would never surrender to it. Because that's what it would be to him. A surrender. A defeat. A humiliation that would destroy him as utterly as parting from him would destroy her.

The American colonist and the British nobleman. As ever, they were at cross purposes, and this time not even a revolution could put things to right.

Charlotte made her way back to her own room. Addy had disappeared earlier with a pile of clothing, so Charlotte was left with little choice but to don a flimsy white night rail she'd found in the back of the armoire. She was pulling back the covers of her own bed and preparing to extinguish the candles when she heard something shatter.

She ran across the room and flung the door wide. Addy was rushing into the hallway from the servants' wing, and together they peered down the stairs to the ground floor of the house. There was another crash, and Addy clutched Charlotte's arm protectively, then they heard Wilkins fussing and Freddie telling him to "stubble it."

Except that Freddie was barely coherent. Confused, Charlotte tiptoed down the first two steps and stuck her head over the banister.

"Miss Charlotte, you get on upstairs!" Addy whispered loudly. Charlotte waved at her distractedly and took another step. "Miss, Charlotte you is not dressed! Get up here!" Addy tried again, but Charlotte ignored her.

In the foyer was her husband, looking as if he had been dragged behind a carriage through the streets of London, supported on one side by Lord Selbourne and on the other by Wilkins.

"Is he all right?" Charlotte called out. Lord Selbourne and Wilkins glanced up, then both hastily averted their eyes after glimpsing her scant nightgown. She pulled the transparent robe close around her body, for all the good that it did.

"He's fine, Lady Dewhurst," Selbourne answered looking at the wall. "You should retire. We have this under control." Just then Freddie lurched to Wilkins's side, and Wilkins almost lost his hold.

Charlotte frowned. "Is he drunk?"

Selbourne scowled and hauled Freddie up the first few stairs. Charlotte retreated to the landing and Addy. "He has been drinking," Selbourne answered vaguely.

"But what . . . *happened* to him?" She had never even seen Dewhurst's tailcoat wrinkled and now it appeared to be half torn off. And Freddie himself was barely conscious. Selbourne was all but carrying him up the steep steps.

"There was a slight altercation. Really nothing for you to worry about."

They reached the top of the stairs, and Addy disappeared into Charlotte's room, returning with a large shawl. She draped it over Charlotte's shoulders, hiding her from view.

"I suppose you had better put him in my room, Lord Selbourne," Charlotte instructed. "It's the closest, and it appears he will need a nursemaid."

"My lady, I must object," Wilkins, who had followed Selbourne, offered. "I can attend to Lord Dewhurst. I have always done so before."

"Well, Mr. Dewhurst is a married man now!" Addy interjected, hands on her hips. "And Miss Charlotte is going to take care of him. I'll help her if she needs it." Considering Addy had shown little or no interest in her husband before, Charlotte was a bit surprised at her sudden concern. Until she remembered that Addy opposed everything Freddie's valet suggested. And her servant had seemed rather partial to Freddie—right after she'd started wearing her new shawl.

Wilkins glared at Addy, then turned back to Charlotte. "Madam, this *person* fails to understand that tending to Lord Dewhurst is my duty. I would not want you to trouble yourself."

Before Charlotte could reply, Addy retorted, "It be no trouble. And you is going to be in trouble if you don't get yourself out of the way!"

"Is that a threat?" Wilkins screeched. "Did this person just threaten me?"

"Yes, *this person* done threaten you, and she going to do a lot more, too." Addy took a menacing step forward, whereupon Wilkins screamed and darted behind the amused Lord Selbourne.

"All right!" Charlotte finally yelled. "Stop this at once! Lord Dewhurst is hurt, and we must all work together. Lord Selbourne, please put him on my bed. It is through that door. Addy, fetch me water and clean linen. Wilkins, get me a pot of strong coffee."

A few of the other servants were milling about and Charlotte gave them orders as well. Amazingly enough, everyone obeyed without objection.

A chaotic hour later, Charlotte was able to sit down in the cream-colored armchair beside her bed and rest for a moment. The house was finally quiet, and everyone except her had probably gone to sleep. Even Freddie was sleeping. Or comatose.

Strange to see him lying there without all his defenses. No world-weary look in his eyes, no pithy retort on his lips, no bland smile about the corners of his mouth. Just her husband, who in the innocence of sleep resembled her first impression of him perfectly. He was the incarnation of the Archangel Gabriel—strong, golden, beautiful.

Glancing at him, Charlotte shook her head. She was never going to understand the British. He had nothing but criticism when he talked to her of the United States, but before Selbourne left she had managed to get most of the night's story from him. Her fool of a husband had been defending her and started a brawl. Her husband: the defender, the warrior.

Freddie stirred and groaned. Charlotte rose, brushed the light ivory drape aside, and sat on the edge of the bed, mopping his brow with a cool cloth. Wilkins had divested his employer of his clothing and tucked him under Charlotte's silk bedcovers. The servant had then retired reluctantly, and Charlotte and Addy had cleaned Freddie's wounds. Thankfully his injuries were not numerous, and now her only concern was his swollen eye and the bruise forming on his rib cage.

She dabbed the moist cloth around his eye and decided it was looking somewhat better. Addy had gone to the kitchen in search of ingredients for one of the salves she'd always made in Charleston, and Charlotte was alone with Freddie. After a peek at the door, Charlotte lifted the covers slightly to peer at his chest. It felt a little awkward to be sitting on the edge of her bed with a naked man underneath the covers. And here she was lifting those very same covers to examine his body. Not that she had dared look below the bruise high on his rib cage. She *was* tempted, sorely tempted by what she had seen of Freddie's bronze muscular body, contrasting so strongly with her pale virginal sheets. She just hadn't gotten up her courage, until now.

Pulling up the covers ever so slightly, she peeked underneath, feeling exactly as she had when she was five and sneaking a piece of candy. The weak light was just beginning to reveal the hard planes of her husband's stomach when something on the white sheets next to Freddie's elbow caught her eye. Picking it up, she dropped the covers back down, then brought her hand to her mouth as she realized what it was.

Honeysuckle.

He must have been clutching it in his hand when he came home. Had he bought it for her? Oh, why, when she was at her most vulnerable, did he have to do something like *this*?

Charlotte brought the small sprig of flowers to her nose and inhaled deeply. The blossoms still retained a faint hint of fragrance.

"They will never smell as sweet as you," Freddie croaked.

Charlotte's eyes darted to him, and she almost jumped off the bed from the shock of hearing his voice.

"I thought you were asleep," she stammered.

Freddie nodded. "I was, but I think I'm coming around." He took in his surroundings, then tried to sit up.

"No, lie still," Charlotte urged, pushing his shoulder back gently. "You're hurt."

He didn't argue. Instead he put a hand to his forehead and scowled. Finally the pain receded enough that he grumbled, "Where am I?"

"In my room," she answered, feeling her cheeks heat. She was still wearing the flimsy nightgown, and he was naked under the sheet. "It was the closest." Charlotte kept her eyes on the coverlet, trying very hard not to stare at his exposed chest.

"And Wilkins?"

"Everyone has gone to sleep. You should as well. It's late."

Freddie smiled a little crookedly. "Is my condition that bad? I think the last time someone ordered me to go to sleep, I was eight."

"Well, maybe you should listen to someone else for a change. You seem to get into trouble on your own."

Freddie laughed, then held his head again and groaned. "You have no idea, madam."

The laugh was genuine, and Charlotte found herself smiling in response. She liked him without all his armor. Taking the chance that the openness between them would last a bit longer, Charlotte said, "What were you thinking tonight?

Lord Selbourne told me you were defending me and started a fray. Must you always act the part of the warrior?"

With a surprisingly serious look on his face, Freddie reached out and grasped her hand warmly. "You're the true warrior, Charlotte. Not I. Had you been there, half of those men would have wasted no time in pledging their loyalty to you." He brought her fingers to his lips and kissed them tenderly.

Charlotte almost snorted in disbelief, but then his eyes met hers for a long moment. For that moment, she felt like the most stunning woman in the world. But then that was the effect Freddie had on her. And countless other women, too, she supposed.

Still, she couldn't stop her pulse from racing or her heart from filling her eardrums with its familiar pounding. With the heat of his eyes on her, she was on the verge of saying or doing something she knew she would later regard as ridiculous. But he gave her a momentary reprieve as he released her eyes and his gaze traveled to the honeysuckle she still held in her free hand.

"Do you like it?" he asked. "I'm afraid Selbourne may never speak to me again after the effort I put him to in order to acquire it, but I know it's your favorite."

"And how do you know that?"

Freddie put a finger to his lips. "State secret."

"I love it," Charlotte said finally. "But it was not necessary."

"It reminded me of you. Your scent."

She nodded. "Charleston is full of honeysuckle in the spring. It grows all along one wall of my garden."

"You miss your home a great deal, don't you?"

Charlotte looked at him shrewdly. From all appearances, he was quite earnest in all he said, and his sincerity ruffled her more than his usual demeanor. She'd become accustomed to their style of interacting—his bland observations and her angry retorts. But tonight he was different, and suddenly she was nervous. Her heart was hammering incessantly in her ears, and the hand that held the honeysuckle began to tremble. When she looked up, Freddie was watching her with that familiar intensity.

Out of nervousness, Charlotte began talking. To her ears, it sounded like babbling, but she just couldn't seem to shut herself up. "I love honeysuckle. Always have, though the smell can be overwhelming when it's in full bloom."

"Overwhelming, you say?" Freddie murmured.

Charlotte took a quick look at his face—his eyes were moss green and the lids were heavy—then prattled on with growing apprehension. "Y-yes, but honeysuckle is not always overwhelming. Sometimes it takes one quite by surprise. Often I'll be walking along Broad Street and pass a tangle of honeysuckle, but I won't smell it until I've taken three steps past, and then the aroma is so sweet and surprising that I have to turn around and go back to experience it again."

"Yes, I quite understand the impulse." Freddie chuckled. Charlotte paused and finally met his gaze. His fingers caressed her hand lightly, coming to rest on the sensitive skin of her inner wrist where her pulse was thumping wildly. "Although I don't think anyone would ever walk by you without knowing it."

"But I wasn't talking about—" Charlotte protested.

"But I am," Freddie said, rising to a sitting position with surprising agility considering his bruises and the amount of alcohol he'd obviously consumed.

"You should lie down," Charlotte said, not really trying to convince him, her eyes instead drawn to the silk of her sheets as they slid down the bare skin of his chest. "You're injured."

"A flea bite," Freddie murmured. He brought his free hand to her cheek and caressed it as he might a kitten. Charlotte felt the heat flow into her skin as he touched her. Then with an unsteady breath, his right hand tangled in her hair and he pulled her mouth a breath away from his. Charlotte didn't resist, and his fingers cupped her neck possessively. He entwined his left hand with her fingers, pulling her knuckles to his bare chest, where she could feel his heart pounding as hard and fast as her own.

With the barest movement, he brought her mouth to his, nipping the corners of her lips playfully. His touch was light, the kisses whisper-soft, almost tickling her. Then he shifted the kiss to her lower lip and ran his tongue gently along the sensitive flesh there. Charlotte jumped from the flicker of heat that seared through her belly. His hand on the back of her neck stroked lazily, calming her nerves as his lips pressed harder against hers, then withdrew, only to claim her mouth again. He continued stoking the flames of her rising desire, and when Charlotte feared she could not take the waiting anymore, he parted her lips with maddening slowness and skill and twined his tongue with hers.

Charlotte was shocked at her body's rapid-fire response to him. It was only a kiss but already she was squirming to get closer, her body aching, her nipples hard. And Freddie seemed practically unaffected. His control was fortified with steel, while his kisses challenged the limits of her desire. Slow, drugging kisses that pooled heat in her belly and spread it lazily through her limbs; deep, possessive kisses that made her feel weak; hard, insistent kisses that, to her horror, she reacted to by rubbing her aching body against him.

And still he remained maddeningly aloof, and

she was desperate that he feel for her something of the desire she had for him.

Before she lost her nerve, she reached up and ran her free hand along the flank of his body—from the flat of his waist up the muscled rib cage, then skimming across his hard bare chest. His reserve held until she curled her fingers in the smattering of golden hair on his chest. She felt his skin tighten beneath her hand, and then his mouth slanted over hers hungrily.

For a moment she was lost in his need, her own just as great. Then she slid her fingers down his back, and, with a groan, he released the hand he clutched to his heart so that she might have more freedom to explore him. Charlotte eagerly complied, loving the feel of him under her fingertips, loving the way his muscles bunched and tensed as her fingers slowed or she lightened the pressure.

She had no idea she was torturing him, until he repeated her actions in kind. His hands slid under the transparent robe she wore and inched it off her shoulders. He traced the bare skin of her shoulders and arms, with such tantalizing slowness that Charlotte moaned and clutched him tightly. Her fingers dug tightly into his back, but he kept up his gentle assault, only changing his line of attack from his hands to his mouth. Breaking their kiss, he began nuzzling her neck. She arched for him, and he moved one hand to her lower back to angle her for better access.

Charlotte resisted for a heartbeat. She knew well enough what would come next. She tensed, and then surrendered, offering her unconditional capitulation.

Freddie felt her relinquish control and savored the sweet pleasure of her surrender. Already she'd climbed on top of him and was instinctively rocking. Through the flimsy fabric of the nightgown, he could see her hard jutting nipples and forced himself not to run his hand along the pebbled flesh too soon. Instead he laved her neck and made a wet trail to her collarbone, over the ribbons that served as straps for her gown, to the soft skin of her shoulders. His free hand stripped the robe from her body, and he tossed the scrap of silk onto the floor.

Retracing his path, he returned to the top of her gown and the first pink bow of her chemise. One hand still arching her back, he pulled the ribbon loose. It bared the tiniest inch of her creamy skin.

His tongue skimmed over that skin, and he felt her shiver. When his mouth reached the next bow, he pulled that one free with his teeth. Another tiny inch of skin was revealed. Freddie took a deep breath.

Whoever had designed this nightgown had obviously intended to drive husbands and lovers insane. His fingers moved down, and he flicked the next bow. This time as the material parted he was rewarded with a vision of the peaks of her ripe breasts. His fingers caressed the mounds lightly, and Charlotte inhaled sharply.

His gaze flicked to her face, and he saw that she was watching him, her eyes dark and hazy as dusk in London. Locking eyes with her, he untied another bow and then another. His hand skimmed inside the chemise's whispery material, across the curve of one breast, then grazed her swollen nipple. She gasped, biting the sound off as she sank small teeth into her lower lip. But she couldn't stifle the moan that escaped when he rubbed his palm over her hard nub. She drew in breath and held it when he took the engorged nipple between two fingers.

Her breathing became more rapid, more labored, and her breasts rose and fell with her rising passion. Finally, Freddie could resist no longer. He leaned forward and took the rosy nipple into his mouth. Her skin was satiny soft, and she smelled of the honeysuckle he'd brought for her. He brushed his tongue over her, rubbing until she was writhing above him. He could feel her heat searing him through the thin sheet and chemise between them. She was on fire, and he wanted to make her burn even hotter.

And then his calculated seduction went all wrong. She shifted slightly, and then he felt her hands moving on him—down his back, over his hips, and across his thighs. His entire body went rigid when her hands skimmed his upper thighs, and he feared he would explode.

"Charlotte." He grasped her hands, stilling the torment temporarily. "Do you know what you're doing to me?"

Her light fingers had touched him with a tentativeness he was unused to, and that innocent exploration aroused him more than the caresses of the most skilled courtesan. She was looking down at him, her eyes clouded with confusion. But she was still so beautiful that when he looked at her all thought, all semblance of restraint abandoned him. He pulled her to him, cupping the back of her head with his hand and clenching his jaw at the feel of her breasts pressed against his chest.

"Don't you like it?" she whispered. He heard the uncertainty in her voice and knew that if he truly wanted to stop this, now was his chance. One wrong word here, and she would escape him.

He couldn't do it. With a muttered curse, he admitted, "God, yes, I like what you're doing. I like it too much. Slow down or I won't be able to do this properly. I already want you too much."

He felt the jolt of shock race through her, and she drew back to see his face. But Freddie wasn't about to allow those sherry eyes and that sensuous mouth to distract him from his seduction again, and before she could get her bearings he pulled her down beside him, his fingers unlacing the next set of bows and opening her gown to her belly.

For a moment he was riveted in place at the sight of her creamy nakedness in the flickering candlelight. Then he reached down, and although his impulse was to rip the material, he decided against it—he wanted her in this nightgown again—and quickly undid the rest of the bows. He took a deep breath at the sight of her full body bared before him.

His perusal was thorough. He intended to learn every inch of her. Know every one of her hills and valleys, to memorize her planes and curves. After the space of ten heartbeats, Charlotte raised her arms to cover herself, but Freddie caught her wrists and kissed the palms of her hands.

"Shouldn't we blow out the candles?" she said.

Freddie smiled a wolfish grin. "But then I wouldn't be able to see you."

"I suppose that is the point," Charlotte muttered. Freddie kissed her hands again, then came down next to her, the warmth of her body flowing into him.

"You are beautiful," he whispered into her ear, then took her earlobe gently between his teeth.

Charlotte sighed and snuggled closer.

"I want to look at you." His hand skimmed down her breasts to her stomach as his mouth traced her earlobe. He felt her tremble as his hand flattened on her stomach and his fingers splayed, just touching the auburn curls at the juncture of her thighs. "And I want to touch you. All of you." He slid his hand lower and was horrified to note that it was shaking.

"Are you nervous?" Charlotte asked, watching his trembling progress.

He couldn't stop a low chuckle. "I believe I am supposed to ask you that question," he answered.

"Oh," she said. "I didn't mean—"

"Shh," he whispered, pulling her closer and coming up on his elbow to lean over her and kiss the tip of her nose. "I'm not nervous." He ran his hand across her stomach, then over the curve of her hip, and Charlotte inhaled sharply. He silenced her with a long kiss, then drew back and said, "But I am at a loss. I've never done this before."

Charlotte pulled back. "But I thought surely you—"

"That's not what I meant," Freddie answered her, kissing her cheek as his hand slid slowly into the curls below her stomach. Charlotte gasped breathlessly. "I meant I've never been with an innocent."

"I see," Charlotte whispered. He heard her swallow. "So in a way, I'll be your first, too."

He smiled, gazed up at her. "You like that idea, do you?"

She nodded. As Freddie's fingers inched even lower, her eyes rounded. "I do, too."

His fingers flicked over her, and she moaned softly, then thrust against him.

"But we have one small problem, Charlotte," he murmured against her cheek, cupping her where she arched for him.

"Pr-problem?" she gasped.

"Yes," he whispered. "I am going to have to hurt you. I would give you only pleasure if I could, but I'm afraid the first time will not be very enjoyable for you." As he said this, his fingers crept against the lips of her womanhood. Gently he parted them and ran his fingers along her slick folds until he reached her hard nub. There he paused and glided over her, feeling her wetness increase.

Charlotte moaned loudly, apologized in a mortified tone, then went ahead and arched her hips even more as his fingers pressed against her. Clutching the bedsheets, she fought for control—alternately begging him and apologizing for her wantonness. "You must stop," she gasped. "It's not proper and—"

She moaned again as he slid down, spread her legs wider.

From between her legs, Freddie murmured, "Are you certain you want me to stop?" He entered her slick folds with two fingers, testing her readiness for him. Charlotte bit her lip and nodded violently. "If that is what you want, I will stop, but before you issue that order, wouldn't you like to know what you'll be missing?" His fingers slid along her sleek folds again, then he replaced his fingers with his tongue and Charlotte screamed.

Freddie took her response as an affirmative. He slid his tongue over her hard nub, flicking and sucking until Charlotte's breathing was ragged. With his every movement, she was more his, was more swept away by passion.

"Still want me to stop?" he whispered, looking up at her. But she was too far gone to answer.

He rode the tide with her, holding her when it was over and she was breathing deeply. Her head was buried against his shoulder, and she whispered, "I don't know what came over me. I didn't mean to . . . *yell* quite so loudly."

"Ah," Freddie said, rising from his position on the pillow next to her. His arm rested lightly across her stomach and his hand was wrapped around the swell of her hip. "I gathered from your . . . pleas for me to continue, that you agreed with my judgment in the matter?"

"Oh, God," Charlotte moaned and tried to turn away from him, but his hand tightened against her waist and he pulled her back.

"Yes, I think you called me that as well," Freddie teased.

"Oh!" Charlotte tried to pull away again, but he held her so that the small of her back pressed tightly against him. "You are wretched! Let me out of this bed!"

"Not until I make you mine," he murmured, lips grazing the back of her neck. He felt her stiffen, and he understood the reaction. He didn't rightly know where the words came from, but he knew they issued from the depths of his soul.

"This was not part of our agreement."

Freddie moved his hand to fondle her breast, and the nipple hardened at once. "I'm revising the agreement." His hand slid from her breast down the length of her body to her thigh. "I intend to make you mine."

Chapter 16

"You want to make me yours?" Charlotte said, turning to Freddie. "I don't think—" She forgot what she had intended to say next because suddenly she was very aware of his hard member pressing against her belly. She knew enough of men and women to understand what his erection meant, and fear rose in her, overwhelming the earlier feelings of passion.

Freddie had said this act would hurt her. She remembered that much at least from her earlier haze. But as his hand slowly moved to part her thighs, the desire returned, flaring and boiling until she was warm and struggling to catch her breath again. She could not imagine him bringing her body anything but ecstasy. He was doing so again that very moment as his hand stroked her inner thigh.

"We must become one body." His lips kissed her shoulder, then her neck, and his hand on her thigh brushed her auburn curls. "I want to be inside you. Feel it as you climax. Feel the tiny ripples of your orgasm surround me."

His fingers were inside her then, and Charlotte gasped with pleasure. Almost beyond rational thinking, she held on to the thought that no matter what else happened, she wanted this man.

Sinking into the heat of his embrace, she returned the kiss, falling under his spell once again as his mouth and his hands inflamed her. He was not gentle, but she sensed him holding back, and knew that he wanted this to be right for her. In that moment she could have wept with the knowledge that he cared that much for her. Instead she kissed him more deeply, unable to get enough of his lips and mouth and skin.

Then his body was on top of hers, surrounding her like a fortress of flame. His flesh seared hers as he slid every inch of his exposed skin along her raw, sensitive flesh. His chest rubbed against her breasts, and as he kissed her neck, his knee parted her legs. She wrapped her arms around his muscled back and pulled him closer, arching for him when he took her hard nipple between his teeth.

And then he was inside her. He only just entered her, but the feel was different from that of his fingers. Fuller, stretching her slightly. Looking down at his golden head, bent as he laved her nipples, she felt vulnerable and exposed. His hands swept to the sides of her breasts as he cradled her rib cage, and for the first time in her life she knew what it was to be completely in another's power. And she wondered why the realization that she was so completely in his thrall—his in every way now—no longer frightened her. Then she caught the heat of desire in his green eyes and couldn't imagine her life without him.

He rocked inside her gently, not filling her but opening her to him, and she sighed. Holding her gaze, he moved inexorably deeper inside her, and when he rocked again, she felt the first pulses of pleasure thrum through her. He thrust inside her again, and she exclaimed wordlessly, then arched against him. With a determined look in his eye that brought a half smile to her lips, he nestled his head against her neck and locked her legs around his waist.

He moved against her again, and Charlotte gasped at the feeling this new position gave. He was filling her slowly, but she still felt no pain. He thrust again, this time harder, deeper, and Charlotte couldn't staunch a moan of pleasure.

At the same time, Freddie groaned, "Forgive me" and plunged hard and fast into her.

There was a prick of pain, but pleasure overwhelmed her as, finally, he plumbed her depths to the hilt—filling her body and her soul. Matching his driving rhythm, she held on, gripping him with all her strength when she found fulfillment. Only this time it was he, not she, who cried out.

Freddie waited until Charlotte had drifted off to sleep before he left her bed. Without the cushion of desire, the aches and soreness of his earlier battle were beginning to make themselves felt. But he knew if he stayed with Charlotte, he would not be able to resist having her again. She was too tempting, and although he had given her more pleasure than pain, she would feel the effects of her deflowering in the morning.

He'd tried to be gentle, but he'd felt her stiffen when he broke the barrier of her maidenhead. There had been no thrill in that act, only the fear that he had caused her pain and then a wash of pleasure so intense, he was no longer capable of thought. Perhaps that was why men prized virgins so highly. As careful as he tried to be, she was so small and tight that it drove him to the limits of his passion. He *needed* to have her again.

She had been a virgin. He had been her first, and the thought pleased him. The noble Cade Pettigru, who held an undeserved mysterious power over her affections, had not had her. She had spoken the truth about that, at least.

He opened the dressing room door connecting their rooms and tried to quell the pang of regret he felt at leaving her. She looked exactly as he'd pictured her when, for so many nights, he'd stood on his side of that door, head leaned against the wood, torturing himself with erotic visions. And there she was in the flesh—thick cherry hair splayed against the white pillow in glossy curls, one arm thrown over her head, hand tangled in her hair, the other resting lightly on her stomach, which rose and fell rhythmically. Her eyes were closed, and her tawny lashes made a pale shadow beneath the lids. Her lips were slightly parted, pink, and swollen. His eyes traveled down the length of her body—half covered by the white sheet, pale and colorless against the rich peach of her skin.

She was perfect—large breasts that overflowed in his hands, a curve at her stomach, then a lush swell at her hips. Her legs were not overly long but rounded and well shaped. He groaned silently, thinking how much he wanted them wrapped around him again.

Forcing himself through the door, he left his wife.

His wife.

Not yet, but he would remedy that soon enough. He'd taken her maidenhead, and in his mind that meant he was already bound to her. But he would move quickly to make it law. He would not allow the captivating creature in the next room to be anyone's but his.

He had been right in thinking her dangerous.

He could see now that having her once would never be enough. With each caress, each touch, she left him wanting more.

Freddie poured himself a brandy and paced his room, trying to ignore the soreness in his ribs and jaw from the night's brawling. The irrational part of his mind told him to avoid her. He already felt too much for her. Why, just look at the way she had muddled his perfectly structured life. His mother and sisters were barely speaking to him, the betting book at White's was full of wagers as to how long his marriage would last, and Alvanley was probably plotting revenge. At home, Freddie seemed unable to make it through one uneventful dinner with Charlotte, Wilkins was continually in a pet, and, horror of horrors, at breakfast he had seen his name on the gossip page of the *Morning Post,* not once but twice this month.

And he couldn't care less. It didn't even matter anymore that she was an unfashionable American. Absolutely appalling how little he thought of fashion lately. Despite his precautions, somehow she had managed to find her way through his defenses. Beneath his mask and into his heart—a place no woman had ever occupied before. A place he was not even certain he wanted occupied.

The rational part of his brain argued that when

she was his wife, he wouldn't be able to keep her at bay. It might have been overindulgence in drink or an earlier blow to his head, but the notion of sharing his life with her, sharing his future, sharing a family no longer made him shudder. In fact, he could no longer imagine life *without* Charlotte.

He could count on her to be loyal and faithful—two traits in scarce supply among ladies of the *ton*. But could he win her affection? Could he show her there was more to him than the money she thought she needed so desperately? Could she see past that, past all the starch and lace to the man he really was?

Perhaps in time he would earn her love, but at least until that point he'd have her commitment. In this one arena, marrying a colonist was not such a bad thing. He might not appreciate her primitive notions of fashion and deportment, but he was as old-fashioned as any colonist on the subject of morals. When he married, he married for life, for fidelity, and—dare he even think it?—for love. Yes, there it was. He was half in love with Charlotte, would be mad for her once she was safely his.

Freddie leaned back in his chair and stared at the dying fire in his hearth. She was almost his, and now nothing would stand in his way.

* * *

Charlotte woke earlier than usual. Without even opening her eyes, she knew the sun was barely peeking over the horizon. She also knew she was alone.

Rolling over, she stared at the empty space beside her. She might have thought the night a dream if not for the telling soreness. A small pain gripped her heart before she pushed it away. Freddie probably did not want to infringe on her privacy. Yes, that was why he'd abandoned her. It had to be the reason, because nothing would ruin her good mood this morning.

For the first time in months, she hadn't thought of Thomas and her father's death immediately upon waking. And for the first time in five years, she felt as if the world might hold something more for her than debt and worry. How long had it been since she'd even allowed the idea of a husband and family to flit through her thoughts? But would Freddie want that? And could she stay if he did not care for her as she did for him?

She must have dozed off again because the next time she woke, Addy was banging about her room, looking pointedly at the nightgown and robe scattered across the rug. Her maid was adding lavender oil to steaming water in the copper tub, and the sight of the washbasin in her room made Charlotte blush.

Charlotte took her baths in the evening, Freddie in the morning. Charlotte doubted Freddie was even aware of the arrangement that had established a modicum of peace between Addy and Wilkins. But if the tub was in her room this morning, Addy must have guessed what had happened last night and assumed her mistress would want a bath.

Charlotte groaned. Probably the whole household already knew. At the sound, Addy turned to her. "So you is awake. Hmpf. Finally."

Charlotte pulled the sheet over her head and mumbled a good morning.

"No need to hide under there, Miss Charlotte. You don't have to answer to old Addy 'bout all your goings-on. Lord knows, you is a grown woman."

Charlotte peeked out from under the sheet, uncertain as to whether Addy was being sincere or not.

"Course you ain't a *married* woman," Addy went on, and Charlotte pulled the covers up again, "but you is old enough to know what's right and what's wrong. You don't need Addy here to tell you."

From under the covers, Charlotte mumbled, "Can I have a few moments alone? I'll call you when I'm done with my bath."

"You do that," Addy said, her voice a fraction softer. "But you'd best not tarry too long. That fool girl Hester going to be in here soon to straighten up, and you know she nosier than a cat."

Because Hester probably would be in to straighten the room soon, Charlotte ripped the sheets off the bed and stuffed them in the back of the armoire. The last thing she needed was the household speculating about the blood on those sheets. Then she hurried through her bath and was just pulling her chemise over her lace-frilled drawers when there was a rap on her door, and it was pushed open.

Not bothering to look, Charlotte said, "Will you shake the wrinkles out of my light blue muslin, Hester? I think I shall wear that today."

"Not if I have anything to say about it," an authoritative feminine voice barked. Charlotte almost pinched a nerve in her neck, she whipped it around so quickly.

Dewhurst's mother looked exactly as Charlotte remembered—be-feathered, be-ruffled, be-ringed. She thumped her walking stick on the floor and took in Charlotte's room with one shrewd glance.

Charlotte searched for her voice, hoping to distract Lady Dewhurst from the absent bedsheets and the flimsy nightclothes on the floor. "Lady Dewhurst!" she finally choked out. "How good to see you. But what are you doing here so early?"

"Early? It's nigh eleven in the morning, and if you do not hurry you will not be ready when your callers arrive. Mark my words, there will be a line at precisely three, and as I understand it, Madam

Vivienne is on her way with the rest of your wardrobe."

"Callers?"

Dewhurst's mother gave her an exasperated look. "Yes. Word is out that you've been invited to the Winterbournes' ball, and the curious will come to gawk."

Opening the walnut and sandalwood armoire, Lady Dewhurst rifled through Charlotte's dresses, then shut the cabinet just as quickly. "Appalling. Thank God I had the foresight to send my maid to collect a few of your dresses from Madam Vivienne this morning and bring them along. Here," she said, indicating a pile of fabric she'd set down next to the armoire. She sorted through it and pulled out a pretty white muslin morning dress with small lavender flowers. "Wear this."

Charlotte didn't dare argue, and when she'd have called Addy to help her dress, Lady Dewhurst waved the notion away and insisted on lacing Charlotte's light demi-corset herself. Moving as efficiently as Addy, the woman then began securing the small buttons of the gown.

For a moment Charlotte wondered if this was what it would have been like had her own mother been alive. Sometimes Charlotte had the vague feeling that she was missing some vital connection in her life, some aspect of female bonding. Strange that she should think of her mother now, when she was so far from home and almost all that reminded her of Katherine Burton. But, then again, perhaps here in London she was closer to her mother than she had ever been. Charlotte found herself wondering how Katie Burton felt after her first night with Charlotte's father. Had she longed for someone to confide in? Had she wished she could share her experiences with her own mother back in England?

Charlotte couldn't really imagine anyone wanting to confide in Lady Dewhurst. Then, almost as if she read Charlotte's thoughts, Lady Dewhurst finished her task and remarked, "As I suspected, this looks well enough. But where is my son?" She gestured to the disheveled room. "He's keeping you occupied, I see. Are you breeding yet?"

Charlotte choked on the pat answer she had had ready on her tongue.

"Too soon to know, of course," her mother-in-law filled in. "But if I know my son, it won't be long. Oh good Lord, girl, stop blushing. We don't have to discuss it if you don't want to."

"And how have you and Lydia been?" Charlotte quickly changed the subject. Perhaps she did not really want anyone to confide in after all. "You seem well," she added.

"I am quite well, and Lydia . . . hmm, we shall see tonight how things go with Lydia."

Charlotte slanted a curious glance at Lady Dewhurst, then crossed the room and sat down at her small ebony dressing table. With its Sèvres porcelain plaques in various floral designs and the delicate ormolu mounts, the table was easily Charlotte's favorite piece of furniture in the room. Sometimes she would sit at it for hours and trace the designs on the plaques of the table and the mirror. Now she adjusted the graceful black and gilt curule chair, feeling just like one of those ancient Roman senators who had once presided in similar chairs.

"Are you speaking of the ball tonight?" Charlotte asked, pinning up her damp hair and threading a white silk ribbon through it.

"We expect Lord Westman to make Lydia a proposal," Lady Dewhurst said, eyes trained on Charlotte's progress. A slight twist of her mouth or a raise of an eyebrow guided Charlotte's actions. Charlotte might not always agree with her mother-in-law, but the peacock did know her coiffures.

"I assume Lydia will accept."

"Mmm," Lady Dewhurst said noncommittally. Charlotte craned her head to the side to see the baroness, but with a swish of her plum skirt, the older woman moved quickly out of sight. Before Charlotte could press any further, there was a hesitant tap on her door.

"Come," Lady Dewhurst answered for her.

It was Hester. "Your Ladyship, pardon me, but would you like me to straighten up now and gather your washing, or should I come back later?" The plump maid bobbed her head up and down as she spoke.

"You may begin your duties now," Freddie's mother commanded before Charlotte could even open her mouth.

Hester bobbed her head and addressed Charlotte again. "I don't want to be in the way, my lady."

Charlotte smiled. She was really beginning to like Hester. "You won't be in our way, Hester. We are going down to breakfast just now anyway."

Once in the dining room, she and Lady Dewhurst gathered a few morsels from the sideboard and seated themselves. Mrs. Pots bustled about fetching various items for Freddie's mother before the housekeeper took her leave. As she exited through the butler's pantry, she paused and said to Charlotte, "I left copies of the menus for today and tomorrow on the desk in the morning room, my lady. If you have a free moment, please look it over and instruct me as to any changes you would like made. I am, of course, always ready to serve." And then she smiled.

Charlotte gasped. Never—*never*—had she seen Mrs. Pots smile. The woman's mouth was as immobile as a slab of granite. And always ready to serve? When had that ever been the case? And when had Charlotte ever seen a copy of the menu, despite asking for one every day?

Charlotte shook her head and blinked. Something was definitely different this morning, and it was more than just her relationship with her husband.

As an afterthought, Charlotte called out, "Mrs. Pots!" She didn't really expect the housekeeper to return—she'd never responded to any of Charlotte's summonses before—but the housekeeper opened the servants' door almost immediately.

"Yes, my lady?"

Charlotte stared, then mumbled, "Addy. Have you seen her this morning?"

"Of course, madam. She's in the kitchen with Monsieur Julian. When you look at the menu, you will see that we plan to make sweet potatoes and cornbread again tomorrow night, and this time Monsieur wants them to be perfect."

"He *does*?"

"Of course, madam. That is why he has requested Mrs. Addy's help and advice. Would you like me to fetch her for you?"

"No. No, that will not be necessary," Charlotte answered, her head spinning. "I was just . . . wondering."

Charlotte's eyes flicked to her mother-in-law, who was contentedly sipping her coffee and staring out the window behind Charlotte. She didn't really want to ask this question, and especially not in front of Freddie's mother, but she had to know.

"There is just one more thing, Mrs. Pots." She

hadn't even asked yet, and Charlotte could already feel her cheeks burning and a small trickle of sweat running from the neck of her gown to edge of her stays. "Is Lord Dewhurst at home?"

Lady Dewhurst's head snapped to regard her, but Mrs. Pots seemed nonplussed. "No, madam. He left quite early this morning."

"Thank you, Mrs. Pots," Charlotte said quickly. The housekeeper had looked as though she wanted to give more information, but there was no need for everyone—Freddie's mother, rather—to understand how little Charlotte was involved in the life of her husband.

Mrs. Pots smiled again—again!—and disappeared behind the door.

Charlotte dared not move lest she awaken from what must be a dream of the perfect household staff, and it was only Lady Dewhurst's raised voice that finally got her attention.

"Did you hear me, Charlotte?"

"No, I'm sorry. I beg your pardon." She tore her gaze from the servants' door and gave it to the woman seated across the mahogany table.

"I said that you have done a wonderful job with your servants. I was worried that they might not respect you at first, being that you are an American and that they had little time to adjust to the idea of my son taking you as a bride, but I see now that I should never have worried. You obviously know what you are about." With a delicate gesture, Lady Dewhurst placed a piece of apple tart into her mouth.

After breakfast Charlotte and Freddie's mother retired to the drawing room. Madam Vivienne arrived on time, and Charlotte was soon wrapped up in choices of lace and fabrics. To her surprise, the gowns that had been ordered suited her perfectly. The colors and the styles and the fit complimented her in every way. Swirling around in a copper satin ball gown, she felt as light as spun glass. "I don't remember discussing this gown," she said. "It's lovely."

"Ah, but of course!" Madam Vivienne replied. "Monseigneur Dewhurst has the best taste, and his selections are always *recherché. N'est-ce pas?"*

"Dewhurst—I mean, my husband gave instructions for this gown? But I don't remember—"

Madam Vivienne shrugged in that delicate, neat French way. "He stopped by my shop and suggested a few additions."

Charlotte blinked away her surprise. "But how did you finish the gowns so quickly?"

"Mon chérie, you are wed to a *raffiné* of the *ton! Tout le monde* is at your feet. You shall never wait for anything again, *n'est-ce pas*?"

But Charlotte did wait an eternity for the brass and ebony drawing room clock to strike five.

For once she rejoiced that she had very few people in England whom she could call friends. Etiquette demanded that mere acquaintances call no later than five, the hour from five to six being reserved for good friends and relatives like her new sisters-in-law. But Charlotte did not expect to see them, so at precisely five, Lady Dewhurst departed and Charlotte stretched out, exhausted, on the mint green chaise longue.

"What a commotion!" Addy clucked as she hurried into the drawing room. "How's my sugar? You not too tired, are you?"

Charlotte smiled, glad to have the old Addy back again. "No. I've survived another day in Society, and, of course, I suppose I shall have to return all of these calls, but right now I'm content to lie here."

"You hungry, sugar? I can get Monsieur Julian to fix you something real good."

Charlotte raised an eyebrow and sat up on her elbow. "And what is this sudden closeness between you and the cook? Come to think of it, what is going on with everyone today? Hester was positively *polite*. Mrs. Pots *smiled* at me, and I haven't heard Wilkins fuss once today. Is there something I should know?"

"Oh, Miss Charlotte, these here servants is finally showing real respect after they seen how you took care of Mr. Dewhurst last night. You didn't tolerate no dawdling or silliness. They's never seen you take control like that. I imagine that's what did it."

Charlotte flopped back on the plush bolster pillow and contemplated Addy's words. Perhaps that was it. She had never considered how much the servants must esteem Freddie, but then her own servants in Charleston had loved her as well. And why shouldn't Freddie's servants respect him? He was generous and fair as far as she'd seen.

Another tap at the drawing room door, and Charlotte sat up, half hoping to see her husband in the flesh. Instead she was greeted by Dawson. The butler had been dutifully showing her callers in all day.

"The Countess of Selbourne has just arrived. Is my lady still receiving?"

Charlotte shot up and straightened her gown. "Of course! Show her in immediately, Dawson."

The butler nodded, and a moment later a smiling, beautiful Lucia crossed the room and clasped Charlotte's hands in warm welcome. "I only have a few moments. Lord Selbourne is to collect me at half past five, but I will see you tonight at my sister's ball?"

Charlotte nodded, and Lucia seated herself comfortably next to Charlotte on the chaise. "How have you been, Charlotte? You are positively glowing. Matrimony agrees with you."

Charlotte laughed. "I should ask how you've been. You're the one who's glowing."

"She ought to be," a familiar voice rumbled from the doorway. "She's finally going to make me an uncle—well, in a manner of speaking."

Freddie smiled warmly at Lucia before his gaze flicked to Charlotte. His eyes were on her for barely an instant, but Charlotte's pulse began to rush. All the intimacies of the night before came flooding back to her.

"How could he!" Lucia demanded. "It was supposed to be a secret!"

Lord Selbourne appeared behind Freddie in the doorway, and Charlotte was stunned to see him smile contritely. "Sorry," he mumbled. "But Dewhurst figured it out."

"Figured it out!" Lucia rose and stood before her husband with her hands on her hips. Wisely, Freddie moved aside. "How, precisely, did he figure it out?"

"Can't remember exactly."

"I think I began to suspect," Freddie interrupted, eyes twinkling with mischief, "when Selbourne strode into Brooks's and bellowed, 'I'm going to be a father!' at the top of his lungs."

Charlotte giggled, and Freddie waggled his eyebrows.

Lucia leveled a scathing glance first at Freddie, then at her husband. "Alex, how could you! That was not part of our plan, and you know it."

"Ah, yes, The Plan," Selbourne said in a tone that intimated he'd had vast experience with his wife and her plans.

Lucia raised an eyebrow. "I see. Well, I suppose you know what this means, don't you?"

"I do, do I?" Selbourne said smugly.

"Yes. It means that we must call on my mother and tell her the news. She will never forgive us if she's last to know."

Alex's smug expression cracked and splintered. "Your mother?"

"Come on," Lucia said tugging on his arm. "We'd better go before it's too late. Mamma will be dressing for the ball this evening."

Charlotte rose as Lucia ushered her reluctant husband through the drawing room door. When he had trudged through, she turned back around and hugged Charlotte with fervor.

"I am so happy for you," Charlotte whispered.

"Thank you," Lucia said, leaning back. Tears were sparkling on her eyelashes. "Soon it will be you as well!" She threw a glance at Freddie, who was leaning on the marble mantel, and squeezed Charlotte's arms. "I'll see you tonight!"

Then she was gone, and Charlotte and Freddie were left alone.

Chapter 17

Freddie drank in the sight of Charlotte as though it had been an epoch rather than a few hours since he'd last seen her. He traced the slope of her collarbone framed by the border of lace on the scooped neck of her gown, then admired the roundness of her arms where they peeked out of the long flimsy sleeves and the tumble of cerise curls that had escaped the silk ribbon binding that tumultuous mane and now skimmed the arch of her shoulder.

And again he was awed by the fact that this radiant woman was his wife. Or would be soon. What had he ever done to deserve such perfection? He really did not think she realized her own allure and sensuality. And he had been entrusted with her; he would be the one to awaken her senses, show her the pleasures of the body, and perhaps one day the one to possess her love.

There was a blush flaming her cheeks, and Freddie realized he'd been staring too long. This drift in his thoughts needed to be staunched until he possessed her more definitely. Until Pettigru was safely locked away—out of commission and out of Charlotte's heart—Freddie had to check his reaction to her. What if he lost all control of his emotions and began blubbering about how much he cared for her? What if she did not feel the same? He could not risk it.

He threw a shield over his heart and a mask over his features, then executed a flawless bow. "Lady Dewhurst. Forgive my impertinence, but your loveliness, as always, enthralls me."

Charlotte blinked, and when he held out a hand, she took two halting steps toward him, then paused and cocked her head, eyes regarding him coolly. Freddie made no move to close the gap. She would have to come to him.

"You must have left very early this morning," she said finally, and the sound of her voice almost unraveled his resolve. Instead he resisted the urge to grab her and claim her impertinent, honeyed mouth with his own.

He said in a blasé tone, "Indeed." Still leaning against the mantel, he traced the pattern of the white marble shot with peach, his fingers slow and impassive in their movements, his gaze fixed on her under lowered lashes but with the intensity of a cat watching a sparrow.

Charlotte glanced at the Brussels carpet, shuffled, and murmured, "You did not have to go . . . last night . . . to your own room, that is."

Freddie started, covering his shock by taking great care to adjust the sleeve of his coat. If she had been his mistress, he would have teased her with words of innuendo and promise. But he'd never cared for a mistress as he cared for Charlotte.

Charlotte was . . . different.

"I did not wish to disturb your sleep," he said. "And, of course, I am used to my own bed."

Charlotte flicked her eyes to his face, and he thought he saw a flash of pain. Before he could smooth it over, she said, "Where have you been all day?"

Freddie tensed. So the chit was not content with possession of his heart. She wanted his freedom as well. Dashed colonists.

Freddie yawned and waved his hand dismissively. "At my club. Out and about. Customarily, a wife does not query her husband about such matters, madam."

The hurt look on her face deepened, and she reached out to clutch the back of an armchair upholstered in cream and light green. Through clenched teeth, she said, "Perhaps that is because husbands customarily inform their wives of their plans for the day. I had to ask Mrs. Pots if you were at home this morning."

Freddie shrugged. "What else are servants for?"

Charlotte huffed. "It's embarrassing and counterproductive to our purposes, that I should not know the whereabouts of the man who is supposed to be my devoted husband. The hired help know more about you than I."

Freddie pulled out his gold pocket watch, flicked the warm metal cover open, and considered the time. "Would you prefer I left a detailed schedule each day before I disembark?" With studied elegance, he snapped the watch shut and repocketed it.

Charlotte threw her hands in the air resignedly. "Oh, never mind! You are absolutely impossible. I do not even know why I attempt conversation with you. Obviously I am just an annoyance in your life. An interruption."

Freddie smiled and raised a golden eyebrow. "A pleasant interruption, madam."

Charlotte's jaw dropped, and Freddie realized he'd taken the studied indifference too far.

"Is that all last night was to you?" Charlotte said, voice low and ominous. "A *pleasant interruption*?" She was almost shaking with fury, and he ached to gather her close. He took a stilted step toward her, reached out, but Charlotte shrank back.

Recovering himself quickly, he said, "What do you want me to say, madam?"

Charlotte turned away from him and began to pace the floor. "What do I want you to say? I don't even know where to begin!" She turned on her heel and faced him. "I want you to use my *name*. I'm Charlotte, not 'madam.'" She paced away from him again and paused in front of a giltwood and ormolu side table on which stood a large Greek alabaster vase. Tracing the smooth dancing figures carved on the antique, she spoke, almost inaudibly, so that Freddie had to strain at every word. "I want you to wonder about me when you are not here. I want you to miss me. I want you to . . ." She paused and glanced over her shoulder at him.

Freddie clenched the cool marble tenaciously to stop himself from going to her, taking her in his arms, and kissing her into reassurance. But he would not. He had no doubt touching her would be his undoing. He would not show her how vulnerable he was to her. How much control she'd already wrested away from him.

He straightened and stepped away.

Charlotte was watching and shook her head. "It's hopeless, isn't it?" Turning, she opened the large white paneled door of the drawing room.

Freddie could not stop her name from escaping his lips, and he was mortified when she looked back at him, eyes hopeful.

He would *not* allow her to control his emotions. He would rein them in. He would temper his reaction to her. He made a show of flicking the pleated cuff of his lawn shirt, then said almost as an afterthought, "Be ready for the Winterbournes' ball at nine. I see that Madam Vivienne has delivered your wardrobe. Wear the russet gown tonight."

Charlotte gave him a scathing look, and said, "It's a comfort to know you never forget what is truly important."

The carriage ride to the Winterbournes' mansion in Grosvenor Square was so silent Charlotte could hear her blood pumping through her heart. She swore she could hear the coachman's heart beating and the horses' as well. But she could not hear Freddie's heart, though her husband was seated beside her. Dewhurst, she decided, had no heart.

Although Freddie hadn't said a word about her gown, she knew he was not pleased she had so deliberately disregarded his wishes. But by the time Charlotte tripped lightly down the marble steps in Dewhurst's foyer to where Freddie awaited her, the late hour rendered any protest or argument on his part futile. Freddie had simply nodded at her, and with his usual élan, escorted her to the carriage.

Where he proceeded to ignore her completely.

Charlotte did a passable job of ignoring him as

well. She stared out the window and hardly ever gave him a sideways glance. Her husband might hate her and be ready to finally rid himself of her, but at least she had the servants on her side. Dawson had smiled at her, Mrs. Pots whispered that she looked lovely, and even Wilkins had nodded with something in his face that resembled approval. Not everyone hated her.

A ridiculous hour later—ridiculous considering Freddie's town house was only a few blocks from Grosvenor Square—Freddie and Charlotte, the Baron and Baroness Dewhurst, arrived at the Winterbournes' ball. They were more than fashionably late, and the dancing had already begun.

Charlotte thought the town house was overwhelming and the marquis and marchioness even more so. She clutched Freddie's arm when she stepped into the huge marble-tiled entry and glimpsed the gleaming massive white marble staircase before her. She half expected Freddie to admonish her for wrinkling his tailcoat, but he said nothing, merely led her to the marquis.

Charlotte hesitated when she saw him. Not only were his height, his broad shoulders, and his granite expression imposing, he looked so much like his half brother, the Earl of Selbourne, that for a moment Charlotte wondered why Lucia was not on his arm. But then she remembered that the petite, dark-haired woman next to him was Lucia's older sister, Francesca. The sisters bore little resemblance to each other, sharing only the same engaging smile.

"Dewhurst," Lord Winterbourne said stiffly. "Glad you could make it."

Charlotte smiled behind her gloved hand. The marquis barely moved his mouth or the muscles of his face.

"How are you, old boy?" Freddie said with a flash of the lace at his sleeve. "I wouldn't miss your do for the world."

Winterbourne twisted his mouth in a sort of half smile, half grimace, and Freddie gestured to her. "This is my wife. Charlotte, the Marquis of Winterbourne."

"Lady Dewhurst," Lord Winterbourne said in a low voice and bent over to kiss her hand. "Welcome. Please meet Lady Winterbourne, my wife. Francesca, this is Lady Dewhurst."

Freddie and Charlotte took a step to the right and Charlotte curtsied to Lady Winterbourne. The marchioness was as genuine and sweet as her sister, Lucia. "How good to finally meet you, Lady Dewhurst. You're perfectly lovely as promised."

"Thank you."

The marchioness turned her laughing, chocolate brown eyes on Freddie. "It's about time you married! Lucia and I despaired of you ever settling down." She winked at Charlotte. "He's been quite the libertine these last few years, my lady. A horrendously bad example!"

Freddie smiled lazily. "I hardly think your own husband ever needed me to serve as instigator. In fact, I rather believe the boot is quite on the other leg."

"Not anymore," the marquis said, wrapping an arm about his wife's tiny waist. "Now we're both leg-shackled, and we'll have to leave the carousing to the bachelors."

Freddie smiled, but his attention was elsewhere. "Excuse me, my lord." He nodded. "Ladies. I see my cousin, and I've been meaning to speak to him." He gestured to Sir Sebastian, loitering nearby in the dining room, and with an overdone bow, he took his leave.

"Now, my lady, you must come with me," the marchioness said. "My sister has been asking for you."

Lucia was indeed craning her head over the crush of people waiting in the hallway to enter the ballroom. Charlotte could hear the strains of the orchestra playing a minuet. Somehow Lucia made her way through the throng, and a moment later, Lucia reached them and embraced Charlotte warmly. "Isn't she beautiful, Francesca? I adore that gown, Charlotte. The color was made for you."

Lucia and Charlotte left Francesca to do her duties as hostess and moved toward the ballroom. Charlotte shivered under the scrutiny of the *ton*. It felt as though everyone she passed took a moment to assess her appearance. Some of the men even had the audacity to raise their quizzing glasses. Women as well!

Charlotte knew that Lucia could not be oblivious to the inspection, but she never appeared to notice it or allow the stares to bother her. She chatted amiably, and Charlotte realized that she was not safe from scrutiny, but in the presence of the powerful, striking Countess of Selbourne, she was at least protected from scathing remarks. Charlotte took a glass of champagne, sipped it, and began to relax.

That was, until she entered the ballroom, and Lucia remarked, "I do not know how long I shall have you to myself. Undoubtedly every man here will want to claim you for a dance."

Charlotte laughed derisively. "Not likely." But the idea of having to chat with a strange man as he twirled her about was unsettling. She wanted to be free to look for Cade, not forced to focus on etiquette and social niceties.

As the music swelled to an end, Lucia waved at Freddie's cousin Middleton, who strode blithely through the door. "Sir Sebastian!" she called.

Charlotte looked up to see the handsome, fair-haired lover saunter their way. "Ah, my mistresses Selbourne and Dewhurst, 'which of you all will now deny to dance.' " He twirled his quizzing glass expertly so that the light glinted off it.

"You may dance with Lady Dewhurst, sir," Lucia ordered him. "Quick! Claim her before the crowds descend!"

Ever gracious, Sebastian bowed again and turned to Charlotte. "Will you do me the honor, madam?"

Charlotte smiled. Ever more she was beginning to appreciate Lucia. The countess made graciousness seem effortless. By soliciting Freddie's cousin as Charlotte's partner, she'd effectively made Charlotte's evening much easier. Not only because Charlotte could now watch for Cade—a consequence Lucia could obviously not anticipate—but also because, unlike some of the other men of the *ton*, Charlotte would be "safe" dancing with Freddie's cousin. In fact, looking at his orange coat and breeches and mauve waistcoat, she imagined she was in more danger from suffering color blindness than a sudden onslaught of passionate overtures. She almost wished he would don his old-fashioned Elizabethan clothing again.

As Middleton led Charlotte to the dance floor, she realized she would miss Lucia back in Charleston. Charlotte had begun to think of the woman as her friend.

Like Freddie, Middleton was an excellent dancer. As he turned her about, he explained that the forms of any dance should be looked on as one more opportunity to quote poetry to the ladies, and he recited a litany. But Middleton did not forgo all conversation either, and Charlotte soon found that she was enjoying herself immensely.

"I hope I am not keeping you from any particular young lady, Sir Sebastian." Charlotte's eyes twinkled, and she raised a coy eyebrow. At one time she had been an excellent flirt, and she was interested to see if she'd retained any of her charms.

"Good God, no!" Sebastian leveled a contemptuous glance at the room, and Charlotte followed it. "Rather, you've saved me from the matchmakers temporarily. Wouldn't have even left the card room if Dewhurst hadn't sent me."

Charlotte's head snapped to attention. "Freddie? But what does he have to do with anything?"

"Thunder an' turf! I probably shouldn't have mentioned it."

"Perhaps not, but you did," Charlotte pressed.

They separated for the next form of the dance, and when they came together again, Middleton said in a low voice, "Dewhurst asked me to play escort for you tonight."

Escort? Charlotte shook her head angrily. "Are you spying on *me* now? I am certain the War Office could find better things for you to do with your time."

"Shh! Tare an' hounds! I was *not* spying on you," he hissed, glancing about nervously. "If I wanted half of the beau monde to know I worked for the Foreign Office, I'd take out an ad in the *Morning Post*."

They separated for the next form, and by the time she placed her hand on Sebastian's arm again, her thoughts had jumped ahead. "Sir Sebastian, is there a particular reason my husband asked you to sp— ah, escort me? Is"—she glanced about quickly—"Cade Pettigru here?"

Middleton looked like a trapped insect. He squirmed, wriggled, and finally murmured, "Do not even say his name. Yes, there is a possibility our friend is here tonight. Do you remember what to do if approached?"

For a moment Charlotte had no idea, then slowly she nodded. She knew Freddie and his cousin wanted her to lead them to Cade. Innocent or guilty, she did not care. She would never betray Cade. If he were present tonight, she'd have to slip away from Sir Sebastian and warn Cade. She'd tell him to run as far and as fast as possible.

The dance ended and Middleton led her off the dance floor. Charlotte was trying to think of a suitable excuse to escape Freddie's cousin when Lord Alvanley approached.

"Sir Sebastian, Lady Dewhurst." The dandy bowed with a flourish, but Charlotte looked past him to where Lucia stood conversing with Lady Jersey—or rather nodding—as the esteemed patroness of Almack's, nicknamed "Silence," prattled on endlessly.

"Good to see you again, old boy. Still looking for a Chinese snuffbox?" Middleton inquired.

"I might be. Depends who's selling." Alvanley turned to her. "And how are you enjoying the evening, my lady?"

"It's splendid." She began inching away. "Oh, dear, I think I see Lady Selbourne waving at me."

Alvanley didn't bother to look. "Oh, she'll be engaged with Silence half the night. If you are not already spoken for, might I partner you in the next dance?"

"Oh, but I—" Charlotte began.

"Perhaps later," Middleton said.

Alvanley frowned. "Rubbish." He took Charlotte's arm and began leading her to the dance floor.

"What are you thinking about, Freddie?" Lucia asked, coming up behind him. He did not look at her, did not alter his focus from his wife, now being led to the dance floor by Lord Alvanley.

"I made a mistake," he muttered.

"Have you?" Lucia's eyes widened. "I daresay, I've not heard you admit that before. I thought admitting fallibility made men too mortal. Gods, after all, don't blunder."

"I'm not a god." Freddie craned his head slightly to follow Charlotte and Alvanley's progress. "I'm a dashed fool."

"Of course you are. What have you done this time?"

"The bronze satin. It's stunning. The russet sarcenet would never have been as charming."

"Freddie!" Lucia cried, and he tossed her a smirk.

"But," he continued, "I shall not make another mistake and allow her to dance with Alvanley."

"Oh, he's harmless."

Freddie didn't answer, and Lucia looked away from the dance, a waltz, which was just commencing, and sliced a glance at him with her sapphire eyes. "Freddie, you cannot think to cut in."

"Excellent suggestion, madam. If you will excuse me?"

"But I was not—! Oh, dear."

Lucia's jaw dropped as did those of the rest of the guests as Freddie carved through them and arrested his wife on the dance floor.

"You're dancing with my wife, Alvanley."

Charlotte let out a small squeak of astonishment, but Alvanley did not falter. He turned Charlotte away and said, "So I am, Dewhurst. And you're interrupting. Go 'way."

Freddie felt his face heat and clenched his fist to quell the urge to smack Alvanley so hard the man's head spun around. Freddie caught a glimpse of Charlotte, her sherry-colored eyes wide and concerned. Alvanley turned her again, and Freddie caught her arm, tugging her out of Alvanley's embrace and hauling her into his own.

"As a matter of fact, you are the one interrupting. From now on, no one dances with my wife but me. Madam?" he inquired, but did not wait for her response before sweeping her back into the dance. Pulling her close, he turned and swirled her until he knew she was so dizzy, she was no longer thinking of Alvanley or Pettigru or any other man, only of how to keep up with him.

Freddie's thoughts, however, were of a more earthy nature. He loved the way she felt in his arms—the light press of her hand in his, the warmth of her body when he pulled her close. Heady with lust, he lowered his hand on her back slightly so that his fingers just grazed her derriere.

Charlotte trembled. "Sir, we are much too close."

Freddie smiled. "I like you close. I want you closer."

Her eyes flicked to his mouth, and he knew what she was thinking.

He leaned closer. "If you continue to devour me with your eyes in that manner, I might be forced to take you right here."

She shivered, and he felt the tremor through to his own bones. "That might cause quite a scandal," she murmured a moment later.

Freddie chuckled. "At this point I imagine the whole room is so scandalized that nothing we do will produce any greater effect."

"Well, it is not every day that their paragon of etiquette breaks a rule, my lord."

Freddie pulled her nearer, so near that his mouth was mere inches from hers. "Don't do that, Charlotte." He heard her catch her breath and swore he could hear the pounding of her heart.

Her dark eyes collided with his. "Do what?" she breathed.

"Call me lord. It's not you." Rapidly he spun her around the floor until she was breathless and laughing. "*This* is you." He pulled her flush against him again, and warmed at the desire and promise he saw in her face.

"And do not presume to know everything about me, my little Yankee. I rather enjoy breaking the rules for you. Are you suitably shocked?"

"Scandalized."

"Good. Then let me scandalize you further." Taking her hand, he marched off the dance floor, pulling her behind him.

Chapter 18

Charlotte resisted Freddie only until she realized that doing so would cause a spectacle, and then she merely sent a fleeting look to Lucia. Lucia gave her a sympathetic wave, and then her friend's blond hair was out of sight as Freddie tugged Charlotte through the ballroom door.

Charlotte turned, eager for a last glimpse of the room and possibly Cade, but she saw no one who looked like him.

It was only a few feet to the stairs and twenty-some steps to the next level of the house, but the distance felt farther than Charleston to China. They must have passed fifty or more guests, and each one turned to stare at them incredulously. Charlotte stared back. For a moment she was certain one of the dark-haired men was Cade, but when he turned his head, he had dark eyes, not Cade's vibrant blue.

Despite the stares and Charlotte's resistance, Freddie continued to drag her in his wake. They passed a gilded mirror in the hallway, and Charlotte noted that the color of her face matched her hair. She felt a bead of sweat trickle down her back, and the dress that had seemed so light and frothy now felt like a suit of armor.

Finally they reached the landing, and Freddie threw open a door, pulling Charlotte in behind him. He slammed the door shut, and the small parlor immediately took on an intimate feel. A brace of candles burned near a small gold upholstered chaise longue in the center of the room; otherwise, all was darkness and shadows. How was she ever to find Cade when her husband had her locked away like this?

Freddie rested the palms of his hands on either side of her shoulders and leaned against the closed door.

"What are you doing?" Charlotte wiggled in the confined space and tried to tug on the doorknob. "Surely this is improper."

"Shockingly so. We are hopelessly unfashionable now, my little Yankee."

"I'm a Southerner, not a Yankee, and since I have never been fashionable, I couldn't care less. But you"—she ran her gaze over him, then raised a brow—"you have your reputation to worry about."

"I shall take the risk, I think." He smiled down at her, then removed one arm from the door and pulled at his cravat. It fell in a snowy white tumble down the dark blue of his tailcoat. Leaning forward, he cupped her cheek, and kissed her.

When they parted, she said breathlessly, "Are you mad? You can't possibly think to—to—"

"Make love to you?" He took one of her curls in his hand and seemed to test its weight. Mesmerized by the elegance of his long, aristocratic fingers, Charlotte forgot what they had been discussing. But when he moved to kiss her again, she abruptly sidestepped.

"Not here!"

"You prefer another room then?" Bringing the curl to his nose, he inhaled deeply.

"I prefer—" Charlotte had to tear her eyes from his molten gaze. Cade. She had to remember Cade. "I prefer that we return to the ball immediately. Sir Sebastian mentioned that Cade might be in attendance this evening." Charlotte ducked under Freddie's shoulder and scooted away.

"I see." Freddie crossed his arms and leaned against the door. "And you hope to see him."

"Of course. Isn't that what I'm here for?"

His warm green eyes turned steely gray, and he said, "Yes. How could I forget your lover or the one thousand pounds I owe for your services?"

He reached up and viciously yanked at the top button of his white lawn shirt.

"Stop calling Cade my lover. You know that's not true. And as for the money, I—I don't care about that."

Freddie's hands stilled and he eyed her narrowly. "Not at all?"

It was true, but she didn't want to contemplate that right now. Instead she said, "Cade was—is my friend. I have to help him or else he'll be—"

"Drawn and quartered most likely." What looked like anger flitted across Freddie's face. "Treason is a serious matter." Freddie tugged another button open.

"Treason!" Charlotte felt her heart lurch into her throat. How could Dewhurst speak of capital punishment and torture so lightly? "But Cade's an American. If he's a spy, it's not treason but an act of patriotism."

"Patriotism?" Freddie barked out a laugh. "If we excused every spy who argued patriotism, Napoleon, not Prinny, would be redesigning Carlton House right now."

"And perhaps that wouldn't be such a bad turn of events. You English would do well to be brought down a notch or two."

Freddie's eyes slitted. "You hate us that much, do you?"

Charlotte opened her mouth to speak, to give her usual rejoinder. Her hatred of all things

British had become almost a mantra to her. But for the first time, it brought her no peace. "No. I don't hate all of you." Finally she looked into her husband's eyes—rather, the man who'd played the role of her husband, for better or worse—and said, "Not all of you."

Her words hung in the heavy air between them, and then she was pressing herself into his embrace. His arms around her felt strong and safe and . . . almost like home. He held her so tightly, so tenderly that it made her want to weep. She didn't want to leave him, didn't want to have her father's business, didn't want Charleston back without Freddie. But did he feel the same, and was it enough to make her happy here in England?

"Charlotte," he whispered. "Don't cry. This will all be over soon."

She stiffened at his words but held on to a fragile slice of hope that what was burgeoning between them would survive whatever happened when they found Cade. Would Freddie want her to stay with him? Make her his wife in truth?

Cupping her face in his hands, he leaned down and kissed her slowly, teasing her lips apart. She wanted to resist, tell him all her fears, but she couldn't muster the willpower. Before she realized what had happened, she was relishing once again the taste of him, the feel of his lips on hers, the growl in the back of his throat when she ventured to run her tongue lightly over his lower lip.

She felt his control shatter. It smashed into a thousand pieces and then his mouth claimed hers in a bruising kiss that he deepened until she responded hungrily. She moaned when he ran his hands along the slope of her neck to the arches of her shoulders. She cried when, with the pads of his fingers, he traced the sensitive skin, teasing and cajoling each sleeve down her arm. Gently breaking the kiss, he bent down and curved his mouth over one shoulder, his hands moving to caress her hips and pull her intimately against him.

Charlotte felt the proof of his arousal, and reason made one last bid for attention. "We must stop." She tore herself from Freddie's tantalizing kisses, straightened the sleeves of her gown, then pressed her palms against the heated flesh of her cheeks. "If we're found, what will people say?"

"Yes, what will they say?" Freddie drawled, reaching out to slip her sleeve down again. "I can see the papers now. 'Lord D——is besotted with his Yankee bride.' "

Charlotte grimaced and tugged the sleeve back in place. "Well, I certainly hope that's not the headline. I keep telling you that I am a *Southerner*, not a Yankee. Neither you nor your press seems to understand the difference."

"Well, my darling Yankee," he said, caressing her cheek, "you may have to get used to the title."

"But I just told you—"

"And I am a lord not a mister, and you have yet

to get that right, except, I suspect, when you feel like it."

Charlotte gave him a withering look, but Freddie only smiled and undid another button on his expensive shirt. Charlotte blinked. How had so much of his enticing flesh been revealed? The shirt was positively gaping, the contours of his firm muscles played on by the flicker of candlelight.

"We *must* return to the ball." Her voice was pleading, but her eyes were riveted to that expanse of bronze skin.

"We will." Freddie took a step toward her. Reaching out, he lightly touched her arm. "In a moment."

Charlotte retreated and stumbled over the back of the plush azure chaise longue behind her. "Freddie, if we don't leave now everyone will be talking about us."

Freddie took another step forward and wrapped his hand around a thick curl that had come loose from her coiffure. "They already are."

"But Lucia is probably looking for us."

"Doubtful." He tugged the hair lightly, and Charlotte had no choice but to follow where he led. He guided her into his arms.

"What if someone comes in?" She was breathing slightly faster now because she could feel the heat pulsing from his body. And—dare she admit it?—there was something exciting about being intimate with Freddie when they might be caught at any moment.

"I locked the door."

He sank his hand into the depths of her hair and dragged her hard against him. Charlotte tried to resist, but she felt exhilarated and wicked. Even when his mouth locked with hers again and his tongue delved into her mouth, infusing her with a heat so searing it made her knees weak, she tried to defy her attraction. But her yearning was too much. He would never be hers. Soon she'd be back in Charleston—alone and struggling with no time for thoughts of passion. If Cade were here, tonight might be her last with Freddie.

And suddenly she ceased the struggle and melted against him. Melted into him. He groaned deep in his throat and combed his fingers through her hair, loosening the pins and ribbons woven into it as he did so. She felt the weight of it lessen and disperse as it fell in sections down her back. Freddie's hands followed, and soon his palms spanned the curve of her waist.

Then it was Charlotte's turn to touch and explore. She glided her hands across his chest, unfastening his waistcoat and spreading the V of his shirt wider. He kissed her more ravenously with each stroke of her fingers, and somehow she found the strength to pull away. But only for a moment and only to press her mouth against the rapid pulse at his throat. He groaned as she slid her tongue down his hot, sweet skin, kissing a trail down his chest.

"God, I want you," he said hoarsely, and his hands were as rough as his voice when he trailed them over her hips and grasped her buttocks. In one fluid motion, he lifted her and pressed his throbbing arousal against her. Somehow he moved, and before she knew what had happened, she was on the chaise, her legs open and Freddie moving against her.

Charlotte knew she should fight this. But she was breathless with need. She threw her head back and cried out when his fingers grazed her intimately. The rush of sensation restored her senses for a heartbeat, and she was able to push ineffectively against him. "Freddie. We *can't*."

He drew back, his eyes moss green with desire and his face shadowed. "Are you still sore from last night?" he murmured. "Have I hurt you?"

Charlotte averted her eyes. "No, it's not that. We just *shouldn't*. Not here."

" 'Wilt thou leave me so unsatisfied?' "

Charlotte took a shaky breath. "Not you as well. Your cousin already has claim to *Romeo and Juliet*."

"You wound me, madam, but I might be persuaded to forgive you." He leaned down to kiss her, but she wiggled away.

"Freddie!"

"I want you, Charlotte." Freddie's voice was

husky, and when she met his eyes they smoldered. "Now. Here."

He pushed provocatively against her again, and the sudden pleasure was so great that Charlotte nearly forgot her objections. She knew now that, given half a chance, Freddie could double, no treble, that sensation.

Perhaps if she just gave in for one small moment.

Charlotte felt the chaise's silk upholstery on the backs of her stocking-clad thighs where her dress was hiked up. The disparity between the cool silk and her husband's hot caresses made her shiver, and never more so than when he knelt in front of her and opened her legs. He never ceased kissing her, but his hands came alive—palms making lazy circles on her knees, fingers tripping up her thighs to her garters and back down again. The material of his coat was soft against her skin, but Charlotte wanted to feel him—feel his flesh on hers. She reached forward and pushed the coat half off his shoulders. The fit, of course, was tight, and Freddie merely gave her a half smile as he shrugged out of the garment.

He bent to kiss her again, but Charlotte stopped him with two fingers on his chest. "The waistcoat, too."

Freddie raised an eyebrow but complied, unbuttoning then tossing the white silk over the back of the chaise longue.

"Any other requests, madam?" His fingers

played on her knees again, this time reaching down to learn the contours of her calves.

"The shirt," Charlotte choked out, breathless from the sensations caused by Freddie's fingers and incredulous at her own audacity in ordering him to undress.

Freddie removed one dainty bronze ribbon slipper from her foot and placed his hands again on her thighs. "Be my guest." In his smile there was a challenge, and in his eyes a tempered passion. Charlotte wanted to see his eyes heat and burn for her.

Roughly pulling off one white glove, then the next, Charlotte threw them aside and reached up to caress Freddie's neck with her fingertips. He watched her every movement, clenching his hands on her thighs slightly when her fingers first touched him. Meeting his eyes, which were now beginning to smolder, she slid her fingers down the open V of his shirt. Then she withdrew and her fingers skimmed down the fabric, feeling the hard planes of his chest beneath, until she reached his waistband. With a jerk, the fine lawn was free and she pulled it over his head, exposing his chest to her eager gaze.

Slowly, ever so slowly, she returned and allowed her fingers to brush against the flesh at his throat, then the broad expanse of his chest. She paused, glanced up at him, and moved lower. Freddie's grip on her thighs tightened, and she traced a bold path of hard strokes across his ribs and over the hard muscles of his back. With a jerk, she pulled him to her and closed her legs against his smooth flesh. His skin was deliciously hot along her inner thighs, where her stockings did not reach.

"You're so *warm*," she whispered against his throat, kissing the line of his jaw and rubbing her lips against the brassy stubble she felt there.

"I'm burning up." His breath tickled her temple lightly. "But you're not shivering . . . yet."

"Hmm?" Charlotte murmured, tracing his earlobe with her teeth. Freddie's fingers clenched her thighs more tightly. She tilted her gaze up at him. "Why would I shiver?"

Freddie ran his hands up her legs, pausing at the juncture between them, the pressure from his fingers so light that she could barely feel it. But she knew he was there, felt the slightest caress, and almost jumped as he grazed the sensitive skin. "Ah, now you're shivering."

Charlotte glanced down. The folds of her skirt blocked the movement of his fingers but not the sensation. He cupped her gently, then inserted one finger, sliding it against her, repeating the motion until she couldn't stop herself from arching and crying out.

At the sound of her voice, Charlotte flushed. "Stop, Freddie. Someone will—oh!"

Freddie's fingers rasped against her slick, swollen folds mercilessly and she was lost again momentarily. "You . . . must . . . stop," she finally managed.

"Very well." His movements ceased and he withdrew his hand, leaving it resting gently on her thigh. Charlotte blinked once. She hadn't really expected him to stop. Hadn't really wanted him to, but she couldn't very well ask him to start again when he was only doing what she asked. And it *was* for the best.

Resigned, Charlotte reached down to straighten the material of her skirt, but Freddie moved quickly and caught her hands. "Lie back."

Charlotte met his eyes. Oh, George Washington. He didn't really intend to stop after all. She bit her lip in frustration and indecision. "I don't think that's a good idea."

A ghost of a smile curved at his lips. "I'll stop anytime you say." She narrowed her eyes, and he added, "Give me one moment." Charlotte pressed her lips together, and Freddie whispered, "Lie back."

She did. The chaise longue must have been at least six feet in length because Charlotte didn't even reach the head. She sank into the padding, her feet dangling at the knee from the bottom.

Suddenly Freddie grasped her legs and pulled her forward so that she was pressed intimately against his bare chest. Before she could respond, he rubbed against her, the light dusting of hair on his chest stroking her. Charlotte didn't know whether to protest or wriggle against him. He repeated the provocative motion, then flipped up her skirt in one quick movement.

The forbidden feel of the air on her tender flesh combined with the heat from Freddie's chest pressed against her was exquisite. Charlotte closed her eyes, deciding she would stop him. Just one more minute. And then, unexpectedly, he moved away. Charlotte opened her eyes in time to see Freddie bend down and kiss her lower abdomen. She trembled as his tongue laved a path from her belly to her auburn curls.

Freddie moved lower, and a jolt of pure pleasure shot through her. With a vague memory of what he'd done the night before, and a keen sense of embarrassment at having allowed it, Charlotte levered herself on her elbows. "No—don't—*what* are you doing?"

Freddie peered up at her. "Making you ache." He bent again, touching his tongue to her. "And burn."

"Yes!" Charlotte cried out before remembering herself. "I mean, no! You—oh!" She fell back on the chaise as Freddie parted her thighs and pressed his mouth against her once more.

And then nothing mattered but the feel of his tongue swirling against her. She was acutely aware of everything—the pressure of his thumbs against the skin of her thighs, the tickle of his cheek when he turned it, the rush of blood in her head and the thumping of her heart. She no longer heard the distant drone of the orchestra music or the rise and fall of people's voices. There were only Freddie and she: her breathing in tune with his every movement, his knowing response to her slightest tremor. Vaguely she wondered how such a complicated man managed to make everything so simple.

And it was simple: she was meant to be with him. Charlotte knew it intuitively, knew it physically, and now knew it consciously. She would never have permitted anyone else to touch her this way. Couldn't imagine why she allowed Freddie, except that she trusted him. When she needed help, he was there to offer it. When she needed to laugh, he could be counted on to supply the humor. When she needed passion, he proved more than equal to the task.

Of course, he was a warrior, whose shields and bastions would be difficult to breach, but she loved him in spite of it.

She loved him.

And with that undeniable realization, Charlotte gripped the arms of the chaise. Freddie stroked her expertly once more, withdrew to discard his clothing, and plunged into her. With a cry, Charlotte came apart.

Chapter 19

As an immaculately dressed Lord Dewhurst led Lady Dewhurst through the crowds on the stairs a few minutes later, Charlotte was absolutely positive that everyone at the ball knew what Freddie had just done to her. She felt that it must be written all over her face. And, catching a glimpse of her features in one of the foyer's mirrors as Freddie ordered their carriage, Charlotte almost groaned.

She looked completely debauched. Her hair was down, her dress wrinkled, her cheeks glowing. Not to mention that it was much too early for them to leave the ball. Then Freddie was behind her in the round gilded mirror, smiling. "Wait until I get you in the carriage," he promised.

"The carriage?" Charlotte couldn't keep a

tremor of her excitement from seeping into her voice.

"Oh, yes. We have unfinished business, Madam Yankee."

Charlotte grimaced at the nickname, then laughed anyway because Freddie was beside her, and he wanted her, and nothing else mattered.

"Speaking of unfinished business," Lord Winterbourne said, coming into the foyer from the dining room. "May I steal your husband for one moment, Lady Dewhurst? Lord Selbourne and I need a private word."

"Of course," Charlotte said, and all the delicious warmth of a few moments before dissipated. Cade. They would be talking of Cade, and if she and Dewhurst left the ball now, how would she warn Cade? Freddie gave her a look rife with promise, then turned and followed Winterbourne.

She watched her husband go, the thrum of him inside her still a lingering feeling. Perhaps Cade wasn't here at all. He'd managed thus far on his own. Surely he could smell a trap when one was baited for him.

Silently she prayed Cade was safe and far, far away. Then she prayed Freddie would return to her soon. Prayed he would make good on the promise that had been in his eyes. Feeling a bit too warm and too dreamy for conversation, she stepped outside and meandered down the drive.

A flurry of footmen and grooms along with a smattering of guests alighting from carriages swirled around her, but she paid no notice. She saw the dark man extricate himself from the tight cluster of footmen as she passed, but her gaze drifted by him without pausing. She continued strolling, the feel of the cool English breeze pleasant on her warm flesh.

She saw the hand move behind her before she felt its weight on her shoulder. "So it's true. You've turned traitor."

Her lungs seized up and her heart thumped wildly against her ribs as Charlotte turned sharply toward the low male voice with the familiar drawl. She almost tripped, but Cade caught her. Before she could speak, he tugged at her elbow, leading her into a dark patch of shrubbery. When their figures were obscured from any onlookers, Charlotte hissed, "Cade! Oh, George, but I prayed you'd be far away from here."

He gave a short bark of laughter. "Why? Are your own countrymen so repulsive to you now? Lottie, how could you marry that filthy spy? If your father knew, he'd roll over in his grave."

Charlotte shook her head, her fingers gripping Cade's sleeve desperately. "No, Cade. You don't understand. I'm not really married to Freddie. It's all a ruse to get to you."

Cade's eyes darkened. "I see."

"No, no, you don't see," Charlotte said. "I had no choice. After you abandoned me, I had to do what they said."

"I told you I'd come for you. If you had just waited—"

"Waited? How was I to know what those men intended? I did what I had to do to survive. What I had to do to protect you."

"Protect me?" Cade sneered. "How can spreading your legs for an English bastard protect me?"

Charlotte flinched back. She'd never heard this tone in Cade's voice before. He was just scared, pressured, and desperate. She would be, too, in his place. "Cade," she said in her most soothing tone. "I've only played the part of Freddie's wife so that I could protect you. The English government knows that you're a spy. They want to capture you and try you for treason. I thought I could warn you, help you get to safety, and Freddie said that innocent or guilty he'd pay me one thousand dollars to play the part of his wife."

"He's paying you?"

"Yes. Don't you see? The British have taken so much from me. I thought this time I could take from them, buy back Burton & Son Shipping, make everything like it was."

But Cade was shaking his head. "Oh, Lottie. How did you ever become involved in this?" His voice was that comforting, older-brother tone she remembered.

"But I told you—"

He placed a finger over her lips and shushed her. "Do you trust me? We haven't much time."

"Of course."

"Good, then let's go."

"But . . ." Charlotte glanced back at the Winterbourne mansion. There was no sign of her husband on the walk or in the doorway.

"Charlotte, quickly. Come with me."

She was torn. She did not want to leave Freddie, but she had known Cade all her life, and he needed her. She would find Freddie later and explain. She would ask him to forgive her for helping Cade escape.

"Very well," she said to Cade. "Let's go."

He had a carriage waiting and instructed the driver to take them to Freddie's town house to retrieve Addy and then to the docks. Charlotte gave the driver the directions, and when the carriage was under way, Cade sat back and gave her a hard look. "I must be frank with you, Charlotte, and I can tell this is not information you will welcome."

"What is it?"

"It concerns your—Dewhurst."

She nodded, encouraging Cade to continue.

"He was right. I am a spy, and at this moment I'm in possession of a file of codes which could turn the tide of world events."

"What do you mean?" Charlotte gaped at him. "Which codes?"

"The codes the British generals are using to cipher their missives to one another. With this information, the French can decode the British army's secrets. The French generals will know troop movements, supply lists, battle plans." Cade smiled triumphantly. "Our friends the British are doomed. And therein lies American victory. But first we have to deliver the ciphers, and we must sail for France tonight."

"But—" Charlotte did not continue. She could not. Her throat had constricted, closing her airway tight. Though she had no loyalty to England, there was something patently unfair about this strategy. It seemed like cheating to steal the Brits' own codes and use them against them.

If Cade succeeded in delivering the codes, would that guarantee France victory? What would that mean for Lucia and Lord Selbourne, Sebastian, Lydia, poor Wilkins, even Mrs. Pots? And what would it mean for Freddie? How could she be part of something that might destroy the lives of so many people she cared about and the man she loved? But how could she choose between her enemy and her friend?

"I know you want to return to Charleston, and we will," Cade was saying. "First I must deliver these documents, and then I'll take you and Addy home again. Ah"—he peered out the windows of the carriage—"we've arrived."

Charlotte looked out the window as Dewhurst's

town house came into view. How could she tell Cade that she was already home? How could she let him go, knowing that those codes might hurt the people she'd come to love?

"Dewhurst isn't exactly a pauper, is he?" Cade said, staring at the house. "Does he keep banknotes lying about?"

"I—I don't know," Charlotte stammered, sickened at the idea of taking Freddie's money.

"What about jewelry? Something we can sell for a quick profit?"

Charlotte bit her lip. "I don't feel right taking his money, Cade."

"But you told me he promised you a thousand dollars. He owes you a bauble of some sort at the very least."

"No," she whispered, shaking her head. "I couldn't take that. Not now."

The carriage slowed, and when it stopped Cade fixed her with a hard look. "Why not? What's happened to change your mind?"

"I just"—Charlotte twisted her fingers in the satin of her gown—"I don't think it's right."

"Is that so?" Cade's face contorted into a rictus of rage that she didn't recognize. She realized he frightened her now. "Charlotte, I don't have the time or leisure to play the sympathetic friend. These codes"—he patted his breast pocket—"won't wait for your lust for Dewhurst to run its course."

"Cade!" Charlotte shrank back from the ice in his tone. What had happened to the man she'd known in Charleston? The sweet-natured, brotherly friend?

"I saw you dancing with him, Lottie. And I saw him drag you from the ballroom. You followed like a bitch in heat. If you want to spread your legs for a British bastard, that's not my affair, but for God's sake, at least take the money you're owed for it."

Without thinking, Charlotte slapped him. Hard. She was immediately shocked at her action, then regretted not hitting Cade harder when he only laughed. He grasped her elbow and pushed her out of the coach. "Slap me all you like, Lottie, when we're in Paris. Right now, you've ten minutes to collect your maid and money."

"Stop it, Cade." Charlotte struggled to free herself, but Cade marched resolutely up the walk. "I'm not going with you. I'm not going to Paris, or Charleston, or anywhere with you!"

"Oh, yes, you are." They reached Freddie's door, and Cade hauled her up against him. "You know I have the codes. Do you think I can leave you here alive with that information? You'll come with me because if you don't, I'll have to kill you."

Charlotte made a strangled gurgle of surprise.

Cade put a hand on the back of her neck. "Now, don't make a scene. Get Addy, get the money, and we get out. No one will be hurt, unless you decide to play the heroine."

Charlotte looked into his face and knew he was capable of inflicting the pain he promised. Who was this man? Certainly not the same boy who'd rescued her kitten from a tree when she was five or danced with the wallflowers at balls. Something in Cade had changed, hardened him. Whatever it was, she was obligated to protect the innocent bystanders. She couldn't allow Mrs. Pots, Wilkins, even Hester to get in Cade's way. Thankfully, Freddie had given most of the staff the night off.

With a last look at Cade, Charlotte opened the door and peered into the foyer. It was empty and only dimly lit. The staff had not anticipated their master and mistress would return so early and would probably not think to light the chandelier for several more hours.

Charlotte motioned to Cade to follow her across the foyer and up the stairs. She prayed none of the staff would be curious enough to venture out of the servants' quarters to investigate who was home, and she was thankful Cade was silent and moving as stealthily as she. They climbed the stairs, and Charlotte led Cade to her own bedroom. Addy sometimes sat in the rocking chair by the window and sewed when Charlotte was away. Her maid didn't feel easy around the other servants and valued any time alone.

When Charlotte opened her door, she breathed a sigh of relief to see Addy was indeed inside. Her maid turned to see who had entered, and Charlotte had to shush her with a finger to her lips. Only when Cade was inside and she'd closed the door did Charlotte speak. "Addy, quick, get our things together. We're leaving."

Addy rose, her dark eyes bright with surprise. "We is leaving, Miss Charlotte? Tonight? We is going home?"

"Yes, Miss Addy," Cade said. "After a brief stop in Paris."

Addy looked from Charlotte to Cade, then back again. Charlotte knew her friend could see the fear on her face, but Addy remained as composed as ever. "I s'pose one more trial on this here long journey won't kill me."

She opened Charlotte's armoire and began pulling out dresses and hats, but Charlotte said, "No, Addy, leave all that. We'll only take what we came with."

Addy set the dresses back and gave Charlotte a slow appraisal. "And where is that Mr. Dewhurst?" she asked. "Isn't he coming?"

Charlotte shook her head. "No, of course not." She tried to affect humor and lightness. "Freddie wouldn't deign to allow his name to be spoken in such an unfashionable place as Charleston."

"But he know you're going?"

Charlotte shifted. Why was Addy drilling her

now? What did she care for Dewhurst? "No, Addy. He doesn't know, but I'm certain he'll have a dinner party to celebrate when he learns that I'm gone."

Addy gave her a curious look. "I wouldn't have taken you for the type to run away, Miss Charlotte. Leave and not even say good-bye. I never took you for no yellow belly."

"Oh, good God, Addy," Cade said. "Can you save the lecture until we're under way?"

"Addy," Charlotte said, crossing to her and attempting to soften Cade's harsh rebuke, "it's better this way. Trust me. I'm an inconvenience to Freddie. An inconvenience he's grown fond of, but an inconvenience nonetheless. He'll be glad that I left this way. It's easier for everyone."

"It's easier for you," Addy said. "You ain't got no choice to make this way."

"Choice?" Cade said. "What choice is there? Would you rather she stay here as his whore than return home where she can rebuild her life?"

"Hmpf," Addy said, crossing her arms. "You don't know everything, Cade Pettigru. That Mr. Dewhurst was goin' to marry my sugar."

Cade laughed. "Is that what he told you to lure you into his bed?"

Charlotte's face flushed, and she felt the tears spring to her eyes. "Addy, I want to go home," she whispered.

"And you sure 'bout that?" Addy asked.

"Yes!" Charlotte answered, exasperated. "There is no way Freddie would want me to stay. No way. Unless—" She broke off as a figure stepped into the room behind Cade and silently closed the dressing room door behind him. "Unless—"

"Unless he loved you," Freddie said and raised his pistol.

Freddie watched the blood drain from his wife's beautiful face. No, she wasn't his wife, he amended. She was a woman playing his wife, a woman he had made love to, and when he'd left her alone for five minutes, she'd run off with another man. Freddie pointed his pistol at that man: Cade Pettigru. Finally the spy was before him, and undoubtedly on his way out of the country with the new British codes.

If Freddie had emerged from Winterbourne's house three seconds later, the codes might well be on their way into enemy hands tonight. How many men would have died when secret English orders and plans were deciphered if he had not seen Charlotte climb into the carriage with a man? This man. This *traitor.*

"Freddie!" Charlotte gasped.

"Ah, I see you remember my name after all, madam. Please don't tell me you were going to leave without saying good-bye." His tone was light and mocking, but he kept his gaze hard and steady on Pettigru. When the spy shifted slightly,

Freddie stepped forward. "Go ahead. Reach for your gun, Pettigru. I want to shoot you."

Pettigru sneered. "Pampered English aristocrat. Is your aim as weak as your ale?"

"Cade, no," Charlotte said, and the concern in her voice cut Freddie more than the sharpest rapier to his heart. "Freddie, please. Don't hurt him," she begged.

He gave her a hard look. "Was it all a lie, Charlotte? Was it just a fabrication in the name of money and patriotism, or was there some truth in what we shared?"

Charlotte gaped at him. She opened her mouth to speak, but he couldn't give her the chance. His reflexes took over and he fired, the bullet deadly and accurate, hitting Cade Pettigru in the heart.

Chapter 20

Charlotte couldn't believe what she'd seen. One moment Cade had been standing beside her. Freddie and she had been talking. And the next moment, there was a loud bang and blood was soaking the carpet beneath Cade's chest as he lay on the floor and labored to suck in air. Charlotte knelt beside him, cradling the head of the man who truly represented the last of her family. His breath rattled in his chest once more, and then he was silent.

She was alone.

"Miss Charlotte," Addy said, putting a hand on her shoulder. "You come away from there. There ain't nothing else you can do."

She knew Addy was right, and yet a fury she had stored over the years, an impotent, festering thing, boiled up inside her. "*You*," she spat at Freddie, rising to her feet and pointing a blood-stained hand at him. "You killed him."

Freddie looked nonplussed. "It was him or me," he said, indicating Cade's limp fingers, which were clutching the butt of a pistol she hadn't noticed. "And while I'm certain the outcome was not to your liking," Freddie went on, "I really had little choice." He reached down, flicked open Cade's tailcoat, and removed an envelope stained with blood. "The codes," he said, holding it up. "Your friend would have sold them to the French, and ensured the deaths of thousands of my countrymen. I daresay, in my position, madam, you would have done the same."

"No," Charlotte said, though she knew he was right. "No, I wouldn't have killed Cade. I could never—"

"Then you would have preferred I die?" Freddie said, his voice raw with anger. He crossed to her and grabbed her sleeve. Behind Charlotte, Addy made a low moan. "Have I killed your lover, Charlotte? Have I been an even bigger fool than I thought for believing even for one instant that you could have ever loved me?"

She stared at him. Had he known how she felt? Had he known all along?

"I—I did—I *do* love you," she said, her lips numb and clumsy. She paused, waiting, hoping, pleading for him to tell her he loved her, too. If he loved her, she'd do anything for him. She waited, and the silence dragged on. She would not beg him to love her back.

Finally he gave her a rueful smile. "Do you, Charlotte? Do you love me? Or was it all a ploy to save Pettigru? Or perhaps it's my money you love."

"Stop it," she said, tears blurring her vision. "You're angry right now. You're not seeing clearly."

"I see quite clearly." He reached into his pocket and withdrew several notes. "Here's a hundred pounds. Tomorrow I'll go to my solicitor and arrange for the remainder of the thousand pounds I promised you. Maybe the blunt will fill the hole in your cold heart." He stepped past her and opened the bedroom door. Charlotte could see several of the servants were standing outside, undoubtedly alerted by the sound of the gunshot. "Go call for a Bow Street Runner," Freddie said to one of the footmen. "Tell him I've shot an intruder."

Charlotte dropped the money on the floor and wanted to follow it down. She wanted to sink to the floor, curl up, and die with Cade, but Addy came up behind her and whispered, "Stand strong, sugar."

Charlotte listened. She would be strong, and she would not stand for Dewhurst's accusations.

Later Charlotte would marvel at how easily

they had slipped away. Not that Addy had made things easy with all her arguing and protesting, but with the house drowning in investigators, surgeons, and Freddie's colleagues from the Foreign Office, no one had even noticed when she dragged Addy to the front door, calmly opened it, and walked out.

No one had told them to stop or ordered them to turn around when they flagged down the hackney and directed the jarvey to the docks. No one had blinked when Charlotte bought the tickets for passage back to Charleston via a change of vessels in the Caribbean islands, and no one blocked her way when she boarded the ship. A few hours later, they were under way, and as the gray light of dawn peeked over the water, Charlotte said goodbye to England and Freddie Dewhurst.

It was the hardest farewell yet. Her mother, her father, her brother—those partings had battered her heart, but leaving Freddie was tearing it in two. But could she really have stayed? Could she have lived with a man—lived with herself—if she'd stayed and he didn't love her? She waited and prayed, but Dewhurst hadn't confessed his love to her. The simple fact was, he didn't love her. He wanted her. He desired her, but he didn't love her.

She leaned against the ship's rail and stared at the miles of sea between her and home. Yes, Freddie had killed Cade. He'd also defended her country to a group of his acquaintances and paid the price. But that wasn't love. That wasn't sacrifice. How could she give up her home, the life she'd fought so hard to rebuild, for a man who didn't love her enough to make the same sacrifice he expected of her? She closed her eyes until she heard Addy come up beside her.

"Now, Miss Charlotte, it's getting cold. You come down below and have some hot tea."

Charlotte glanced down at the black mourning dress she'd donned before leaving London. She hadn't thought to bring a wrap, and she was cold and her skin was stinging from the harsh wind, but she was not ready to go down. She needed the numbness the cold brought. "No, thank you. I need the air right now."

Addy frowned but didn't argue. She turned to go, but Charlotte caught her arm.

"Addy, do you think I made the right decision? Do you think it's right for me to go home? With—without him?"

Addy gave her a sad smile. "Sugar, I known you from the first second you was born, and this is the first time I ever heard you ask such a question. You ain't one to question. Right or wrong, you always know your own mind, and I'm not goin' presume to tell it to you now."

"That doesn't help me, Addy."

Addy smiled. "You too old for my help now, sugar. You don't need me anymore."

"Yes, I do," Charlotte protested. "You're not going to abandon me when we get back to Charleston, are you? I don't know what I'd do without you."

Suddenly there was a commotion and several sailors rushed aft. Charlotte and Addy were midship, starboard side, and with a curious exchange of glances, they made their way aft with the rest of the passengers.

Several sailors were passing a spyglass among them and gesturing to something in the distance.

"What is it?" Charlotte asked.

"Another ship, ma'am," one of the sailors answered.

Charlotte tensed. Though she'd booked passage on a merchant ship headed for the Caribbean, there was a war on. If the French or the Americans ran across the British ship and captured her, they could all be taken prisoner.

"Who is it?" Charlotte asked.

"Not sure," the sailor, a young freckle-faced boy, answered. "She's hoisting her flag right now."

The ship was too far away for Charlotte to make out anyone on board, but when she squinted, she could just make out the flag unfurling in the wind. The ship was British. Charlotte sighed along with the rest of the passengers. There would be a hundred near misses like this in the days to come, and Charlotte hoped her nerves could withstand the tension.

The freckle-faced sailor was smiling and relaxed now. "One of ours, probably hoping to sail with us for a bit. It's a small ship, not made for the open sea like this. Would you like to take a look, ma'am?" He offered the spyglass to Charlotte.

"Thank you," she said, exchanging an excited look with Addy. Charlotte raised the glass and peered out over the ocean. At first there was only a blur of flat blue water, then sky, but gradually as she gained control of the glass, she focused on the ship. It was indeed a small yacht, one she would not expect to see this far from land. It looked familiar for some reason, but she could not place it. In any case, it was moving at a fast clip and would soon overtake them. She studied its sleek lines, noting very few sailors on deck. She scanned past one, then trained her glass back. The poor man looked to be violently seasick. His head was hanging over the side of the ship, his blond hair dangling in his eyes, and the ends of his cravat dancing in the wind.

Charlotte let out a shriek and stared harder. No wonder she recognized the ship. She'd sailed the Thames on it. With Freddie—the man hanging his head overboard.

Beside her there was another commotion, and she turned again to the freckled sailor. He indicated the flag the yacht had just raised. "They've just signaled to us that they want to pull alongside, and the captain's allowing it." The boy shook his head. "I don't know who's on that vessel, but he's mighty important. Our captain doesn't pause for no man."

But the whole world seemed to stop when Freddie Dewhurst said the word. George knew, he'd turned her entire existence upside down. But could it really be he? And if it was, what did he want? Did he intend to drag her back to England? Try her for treason? She shivered, thinking of the cold look in his eyes when she'd pleaded for Cade's life.

She could not bear to see him look at her so coldly again. She'd rather be drawn and quartered. It wouldn't hurt half as much as the loss of Freddie's love.

Freddie had been furious when he'd discovered she was gone. Dash it if the woman wasn't slippery as an eel. He turned his back for one moment!

And perhaps he was well rid of her. A woman who left after all they'd shared, after he'd opened his heart to her—well, perhaps he hadn't exactly opened his heart. He'd wanted to, but in that moment, while she knelt beside Pettigru and begged Freddie with her eyes to love her back, he could not say the words.

He could not give up those last vestiges of control to her. And so he'd lost her—and when he'd realized it, that was even more terrifying than baring his heart to her. It was even worse than boarding a ship for a dashed sea voyage. If he survived, he would never let her go.

Stomach roiling at the very thought of what was to come, Freddie had called for his coach.

Now Freddie felt his stomach lurch again, and he made a valiant effort to keep the contentious organ inside his body. He was so green with sickness, he was even seeing green. Then he noticed that the green haziness before him was wearing boots. With effort, he looked from Sebastian's green pantaloons, past his cousin's orange waistcoat, to his smug face. "'My love is like a fever, longing for that which longer nurseth the disease.' Still feeling diseased, coz, or want something to eat? We've got greasy sausage or eel—"

Freddie practically flung himself back over the ship's rail. When he'd heaved up his liver, he growled at Sebastian, "What do you want?"

"We're ready to board the ship. If you have the strength to walk, that is. If not, perhaps we could play pirate and kidnap Charlotte?"

"No," Freddie moaned. "I have my legs under me now."

Those legs were wobbly and uncoordinated as a new colt's, but with sheer determination of will, he crossed to the ship carrying his wife. That dashed ship was larger and not rocking as much as Sebastian's yacht, so Freddie was able to survey the crowd gathered on deck. There were a few warmly dressed passengers and a gaggle of uniformed sailors. Everyone stared at him in wonder.

But Freddie only cared for one person. He scanned the faces turned toward him, the lines of rigging, the polished deck. There, rising above the uniformed sailors and the pale travelers, was Addy, and then his heart tumbled into his stomach. *She* was there, standing a bit behind Addy, hidden by one of the masts. But her hair gave her away. The copper locks were caught by the wind and streaming out behind her.

Freddie took a step forward, and the people standing on the deck moved aside so that his path to Charlotte was clear. Seeming to sense that she'd been discovered, Charlotte took a small step forward as well.

She wasn't hiding from him, and for that he was truly grateful. He didn't know if he could have survived a long search for her.

"What can we help you with, my lord?" the captain asked. Freddie tried to hone in on the man's voice, but he was unable to focus.

"I need passage on your ship," Freddie answered, swallowing another bout of nausea. "I'll pay my way."

"You'll be dead in two days. You've got the worst spell of seasickness I've ever seen."

"No matter," Freddie forced out. "I'm going to the col— America."

He'd kept his gaze on Charlotte, hoping the sight of her would settle his stomach, and he was ready for battle when she pushed through the crowds to stand before him.

"What are you doing?" she said, managing to sound both concerned and exasperated.

"Going with you."

Her jaw dropped. "You can't be serious."

Freddie looked about him. "Are you certain?"

"But—but why?" she stammered. "You won't like it in Charleston."

"I am not convinced. I know a lady who waxes poetic when she speaks of the place."

Charlotte shook her head in frustration. "But just because I like it doesn't mean you will. The fashions are always behind, and my set doesn't care half as much for all your silly social etiquette, and—and you just won't like it."

Freddie raised an eyebrow—or at least made a valiant effort to make any expression other than a grimace. "Will you be in Charleston?" He took a step forward—close enough to smell the scent of honeysuckle that always seemed to cling to her—and just for a moment, the dizziness and nausea subsided.

"Yes, I'll be there, but what has that to do with it?"

"I am willing to brave even the wilds of the colonies to be with you, Charlotte. If you're there, I'll love it."

Charlotte blinked, stared at him, and for the

first—and he suspected only—time, he had a moment's enjoyment on the seas.

She swallowed. "But you don't love me."

"You seem to know quite a bit about my feelings," he said, taking another step toward her, and catching her arm when she tried to scoot away. He drew her closer and spoke quietly. "But you don't know everything. Marry me, Charlotte. I want you to be my wife."

"But—but you don't mean it," she whispered. "You're only saying this because you feel obligated."

"Obligated?"

"Yes, because we—" She gestured feebly.

Freddie shook his head. "I shall have to get used to the strange way you colonists think. Do you really think me such a fool as to marry a woman I didn't love? I'm a gentleman, Charlotte, but even chivalry has its limits."

"Then you *do* love me?"

Freddie sighed, leaned down, and kissed her unfashionably freckled nose. "Of course I love you, you frustrating American. I've loved you from the moment I saw you. I loved you in that horrid black dress, and I loved you when you spit cabbage soup on my table, and I especially love when you take me inside you, arching your back so that I fill you to the hilt."

Charlotte stared at him, sherry eyes wide. Taking advantage of her speechlessness, he bent and kissed her lips. "Tell me you love me, Charlotte."

He looked into her face. For a long moment she said nothing, and his chest hurt so bad with the pent-up breath he was holding that he thought he might explode.

"I love you," she said finally, and the passengers surrounding them erupted into applause. "You know I do."

Freddie pulled her hard against him and caught her mouth again in a long kiss. "There is just one small matter, madam," he murmured when they parted. He kissed her neck and ran his hand through her wavy hair, leaning down to whisper in her ear, "I do hope you are more discreet than I."

"Discreet?" Charlotte frowned. "About what?"

"My feelings for you. You know that it's dreadfully unfashionable to be in love with one's wife."

Charlotte's eyes narrowed. "Yes. And?"

"I intend to be the most unfashionable man either of our countries has ever seen."

Charlotte raised an eyebrow and curled her arms about his neck. "Oh, but I'm not going with you to Charleston."

Freddie stared at her. Her eyes met his with no hint of mischief, and he had to grip a nearby rail to steady himself.

"You see, sir," Charlotte continued, "Your life is in England. Your family. Your friends. I could never ask you to give all that up because I know what it is to lose it."

Freddie swallowed. "What are you saying, Charlotte?"

"I'm saying that I want to be where you are. I want to stay in London with you." She smiled. "That is, if you'll have me."

Freddie pulled her against him. "I'll have you. I'll love you in any country you choose. America. England. I'll love you in any place and any language, more than words can say." He kissed her gently, speaking his love for her without saying a word.

Epilogue

Hampshire, 1814

"Lucia, you do not know how close I came to killing him. I still cannot believe he did it!"

Lucia had to lean on Charlotte for support as the laughter poured out of her. Charlotte sighed, then couldn't help but smile herself.

It was a beautiful day. The sun peeked out from behind wisps of clouds and a cool breeze swatted at the ribbons of Charlotte's bonnet. Lucia and she walked arm and arm through the manicured gardens of Grayson Park, Alex's country estate.

Charlotte loved the contrasting rugged and bucolic landscape of Hampshire, and she thought Grayson Park matched the countryside in its charm. The massive gray building was more than a hundred years old, having been built in the time of William and Mary. Charlotte had been stunned at her first view of Freddie's country home, Wyndham Oaks—the red brick and white columns were stately and, in Charlotte's mind, gave the house the appearance more of a castle than of a home—but Alex's estate was nothing short of imposing. It was still difficult for her to believe that people actually lived in such breathtaking structures.

Lucia and Charlotte paused at the steps leading to the north front. While Lucia caught her breath and stifled her last giggles, Charlotte turned and took in the waterfall gurgling behind her and the carefully cultivated flowers and shrubs as well as the wild section of the garden to the right. The two women had meandered about the garden for almost an hour and were now in sight of the house's conservatory, a room Alex and Lucia were presently remodeling.

Lucia straightened and took a deep breath. "I *would* have killed him, Charlotte. But as you have allowed the wicked man to survive, you most certainly will have to exact some retribution."

Charlotte nodded as she and Lucia resumed their walk up the garden steps, down the little gravel path, and into the dusty conservatory.

"We're traveling to Charleston in the spring. With his bouts of seasickness, I think that trip will be punishment enough. And if Freddie ever dares to even so much as think of placing another bet . . ."

Discarding their bonnets, the women strolled

through the conservatory doors and into a cool antechamber of the large house. From the adjoining drawing room, they heard laughter.

Exchanging a look, they opened the door and stepped into the light blue, brightly lit room. There, on the floor between two couches, were Alex and Freddie. Alex was making faces and waving his hands about his head, while Freddie babbled nonsensically.

Lucia glanced at Charlotte. "Our husbands have turned into fools."

Alex and Freddie froze and turned in unison to face their wives. They shared the same sheepish look.

"Oh, don't stop your playing on our account." Charlotte rounded the chair-back settee in front of her and knelt down next to Freddie, taking her newborn daughter, Alvanley Adele Dewhurst, into her arms. As she had told Lucia, she had been furious when she learned a wager over a horse race had decided her child's name. And Charlotte supposed she would rather suffer torture than admit to her husband that she was getting used to the name Alvanley, even liking it. Of course, the child's middle name came from her Addy, and Charlotte could not wait for Addy to meet her namesake in the spring.

Lucia swept Allegra Madeleine Scarston into her arms, and the little girl giggled with pleasure.

Alex and Freddie settled back on the couch opposite their wives and contentedly took in the domestic scene.

"I say, old boy, this fatherhood thing isn't half bad," Freddie crowed. Charlotte rolled her eyes.

"Charlotte did do all the work," Lucia said, sitting down in a light blue armchair and bouncing Allegra on her lap.

"Now wait just a moment, madam. I was with my wife the entire labor, and I've helped with everything," Freddie protested.

"Except with her name," Alex said.

Freddie glared at him. "Now see here," Freddie objected. "I explained all of that. What else was I to do? A gentleman—"

"—honors his bets," the three of them chorused in unison.

"Yes, we know," Charlotte said. "You've told us a hundred times."

Freddie continued his defense as a footman in blue livery delivered a letter to Alex. Alex glanced at it, rose, and handed it to Charlotte.

"It's from Addy," she said in surprise. "I know she said she was going to school, but I can't believe she's learned to write so quickly."

Freddie took the baby, and Charlotte read the note over twice. As she read it, her face blanched.

Freddie was immediately beside her. "Bad news, darling?"

Charlotte looked up into the worried faces of Alex, Lucia, and her beloved husband. From Freddie's arms, her daughter reached out a tiny hand a grasped a red curl of her hair. "You're not going to believe this."

"What now?" Alex inquired. "Has Alvanley bestowed his name on another of our illustrious peerage?"

"Selbourne," Freddie growled.

"Addy is getting married! She's fallen in love with her schoolmaster—a free black man in Boston, where she's living now. She wants to know when we'll be in America and if we'll attend the wedding."

"Absolutely not. Addy couldn't be bothered to attend our wedding."

Charlotte scowled at him. "That's because we married in Scotland, and she was in the middle of the Atlantic Ocean, on her way home, at the time."

"Excuses, all of it."

"This from the man who has a hundred excuses why he can't travel to America in a few months." She looked at Lucia. "Two days ago he said he'd forgotten that he'd invited Lydia and Westman to Wyndham Oaks. Of course, Lydia had no recollection of the invitation. Then yesterday he told me he thought he was allergic to Yankees."

"And what did you say?" Lucia asked.

"That I'm not a Yankee. I'm a Southerner." She smiled at Freddie and then her daughter, who smiled back. "I think the real problem is that Freddie fears he might end up liking America. And how gauche would that be?"

Freddie cradled his daughter in his arms and looked into her face, his emerald eyes dark and full of love. He leaned over and kissed Charlotte's cheek, whispering, "I'll be the most gauche man in Charleston if it means I'll be by your side."

She melted. "Keep that up and I might—*might*—forgive you for naming our child after a rotund dandy with a fondness for apricot tarts."

Freddie scowled. "One day you will laugh at this."

Charlotte raised a brow, but she knew he was right. She could imagine the two of them, white-haired and stoop-shouldered, smiling over all the years and all the memories. Smiling over his pride and her prejudice and their love.

Coming in March 2006 from Avon Books...
Four amazing love stories, by four outstanding authors!

Portrait of a Lover by Julianne MacLean

An Avon Romantic Treasure

She met a stranger on a train . . . and suddenly Annabelle Lawson was swept away by a passion she could not control. But Magnus Wallis is a scoundrel—a man who would seduce a young lady and then leave her to face the consequences. And when the two meet again, Annabelle is the lady scorned, while Magnus is determined to show her that he has reformed. And everyone knows there is no better lover than a reformed rake.

Running for Cover by Lynn Montana

An Avon Contemporary Romance

Cole Bannon is handsome, rugged—and perhaps unscrupulous . . . but Lexie Chandler needs this dangerous man. She's on a mission that threatens her life...and she's not about to let anything go wrong. Cole is her best bet when it comes to facing a small army and a tiger or two—but even if she makes it out alive, she faces a greater danger than mere gunfire: seduction by Cole himself!

A Study in Scandal by Robyn DeHart

An Avon Romance

Lady Amelia Watersfield is over twenty, very unwed...and longing for adventure. So when a priceless family heirloom is stolen, she is determined to retrieve it. And the help of the breathtakingly handsome inspector, Colin Brindley, is most certainly welcome! Not only is he sharp-witted and brave, but he's unleashed a wild desire in Amelia . . . a desire she has no intention of taming!

The Bewitching Twin by Donna Fletcher

An Avon Romance

Aliss is being held against her will—by Rogan, a strong, sexy Scotsman who insists she use her bewitching healing powers to save his people. He swears to return her home once her task is complete, but he doesn't want to let her go. And when it comes to being captured in a game of seduction, Aliss begins to wonder just *who* has captured *whom*!

Visit www.AuthorTracker.com for exclusive information on your favorite HarperCollins authors.

Available wherever books are sold or please call 1-800-331-3761 to order.

REL 0206

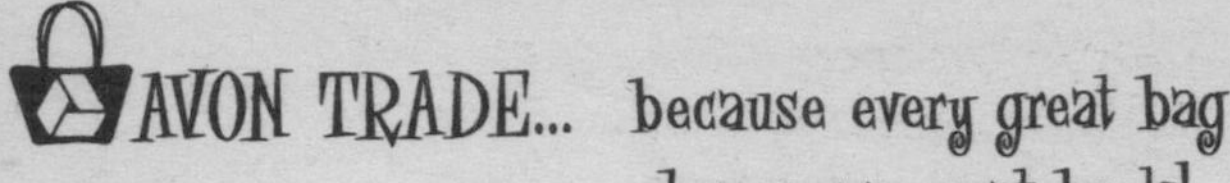

Paperback $12.95
($16.95 Can.)
ISBN 0-06-076272-1

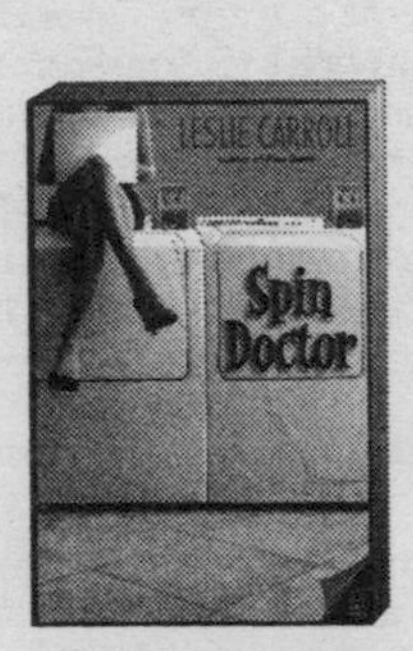

Paperback $12.95
($16.95 Can.)
ISBN 0-06-059613-9

Paperback $12.95
($16.95 Can.)
ISBN 0-06-078636-1

Paperback $12.95
($16.95 Can.)
ISBN 0-06-077875-X

Paperback $12.95
($16.95 Can.)
ISBN 0-06-075474-5

Paperback $12.95
($16.95 Can.)
ISBN 0-06-073444-2

Visit www.AuthorTracker.com for exclusive information on your favorite HarperCollins authors.

Available wherever books are sold, or call 1-800-331-3761 to order.

ATP 0206